MY STOLEN LIFE

A DARK HIGH SCHOOL ROMANCE

STEFFANIE HOLMES

Cover design: CJ Strange

ISBN: 978-0-9951342-3-2

❋ Created with Vellum

MY STOLEN LIFE

From the author of Kings of Miskatonic Prep, the Amazon top-20 internationally bestselling bully romance series, comes this new dark contemporary high school reverse harem.

Psst. I have a secret.

Are you ready?

I'm Mackenzie Malloy, and everyone thinks they know who
I am.

Five years ago, I disappeared.
No one has seen me or my family outside the walls of Malloy
Manor since.
But now I'm coming to reclaim my throne:
The Ice Queen of Stonehurst Prep is back.

Standing between me and my everything?
Three things can bring me down:
The sweet guy who wants answers from his former friend.

The rock god who wants to f*ck me.
The king who'll crush me before giving up his crown.

They think they can ruin me, wreck it all, but I won't let them.

I'm not the Mackenzie Eli used to know.
Hot boys and rock gods like Gabriel won't win me over.
And just like Noah, I'll kill to keep my crown.

I'm just a poor little rich girl with the stolen life.
I'm here to f*ck up three princes,
before they destroy me.

Grab a free copy *Cabinet of Curiosities* – a Steffanie Holmes
compendium of short stories and bonus scenes – when you sign
up for updates with the Steffanie Holmes newsletter.

*To all the essential workers
For your strength and bravery*

"She had always been fond of history, and here was history in the stones of the street and the atoms of the sunshine."

– Henry James (1843-1916)

PROLOGUE
MACKENZIE

I roll over in bed and slam against a wall.

Huh? Odd.

My bed isn't pushed against a wall. I must've twisted around in my sleep and hit the headboard. I do thrash around a lot, especially when I have bad dreams, and tonights was particularly gruesome. My mind stretches into the silence, searching for the tendrils of my nightmare. *I'm lying in bed and some dark shadow comes and lifts me up, pinning my arms so they hurt. He drags me downstairs to my mother, slumped in her favorite chair. At first, I think she passed out drunk after a night at the club, but then I see the dark pool expanding around her feet, staining the designer rug.*

I see the knife handle sticking out of her neck.

I see her glassy eyes rolled toward the ceiling.

I see the window behind her head, and my own reflection in the glass, my face streaked with blood, my eyes dark voids of pain and hatred.

But it's okay now. It was just a dream. It's—

OW.

I hit the headboard again. I reach down to rub my elbow, and my hand grazes a solid wall of satin. On my other side.

What the hell?

I open my eyes into a darkness that is oppressive and complete, the kind of darkness I'd never see inside my princess bedroom with its flimsy purple curtains letting in the glittering skyline of the city. The kind of darkness that folds in on me, pressing me against the hard, un-bedlike surface I lie on.

Now the panic hits.

I throw out my arms, kick with my legs. I hit walls. Walls all around me, lined with satin, dense with an immense weight pressing from all sides. Walls so close I can't sit up or bend my knees. I scream, and my scream bounces back at me, hollow and weak.

I'm in a coffin. I'm in a motherfucking coffin, and I'm *still alive.*

I scream and scream and scream. The sound fills my head and stabs at my brain. I know all I'm doing is using up my precious oxygen, but I can't make myself stop. In that scream I lose myself, and every memory of who I am dissolves into a puddle of terror.

When I do stop, finally, I gasp and pant, and I taste blood and stale air on my tongue. A cold fear seeps into my bones. Am I dying? My throat crawls with invisible bugs. Is this what it feels like to die?

I hunt around in my pockets, but I'm wearing purple pajamas, and the only thing inside is a bookmark Daddy gave me. I can't see it of course, but I know it has a quote from Julius Caesar on it. *Alea iacta est. The die is cast.*

Like fuck it is.

I think of Daddy, of everything he taught me – memories too dark to be obliterated by fear. Bile rises in my throat. I swallow, choke it back. Daddy always told me our world is forged in blood. I might be only thirteen, but I know who he is, what he's capable of. I've heard the whispers. I've seen the way people hurry to appease him whenever he enters a room. I've had the lessons from Antony in what to do if I find myself alone with one of Daddy's enemies.

Of course, they never taught me what to do if one of those enemies *buries me alive.*

I can't give up.

I claw at the satin on the lid. It tears under my fingers, and I pull out puffs of stuffing to reach the wood beneath. I claw at the surface, digging splinters under my nails. Cramps arc along my arm from the awkward angle. I know it's hopeless; I know I'll never be able to scratch my way through the wood. Even if I can, I *feel* the weight of several feet of dirt above me. I'd be crushed in moments. But I have to try.

I'm my father's daughter, and this is not how I die.

I claw and scratch and tear. I lose track of how much time passes in the tiny space. My ears buzz. My skin weeps with cold sweat.

A noise reaches my ears. A faint shifting. A scuffle. A scrape and thud above my head. Muffled and far away.

Someone piling the dirt in my grave.

Or maybe...

...maybe someone digging it out again.

Fuck, fuck, please.

"Help." My throat is hoarse from screaming. I bang the lid with my fists, not even feeling the splinters piercing my skin. "Help me!"

THUD. Something hits the lid. The coffin groans. My veins burn with fear and hope and terror.

The wood cracks. The lid is flung away. Dirt rains down on me, but I don't care. I suck in lungfuls of fresh, crisp air. A circle of light blinds me. I fling my body up, up into the unknown. Warm arms catch me, hold me close.

"I found you, Claws." Only Antony calls me by that nickname. Of course, it would be my cousin who saves me. Antony drags me over the lip of the grave, *my* grave, and we fall into crackling leaves and damp grass.

I sob into his shoulder. Antony rolls me over, his fingers pressing all over my body, checking if I'm hurt. He rests my back against cold stone. "I have to take care of this," he says. I watch through tear-filled eyes as he pushes the dirt back into the hole – into what was supposed to be my grave – and brushes dead leaves on top. When he's done, it's impossible to tell the ground's been disturbed at all.

I tremble all over. I can't make myself stop shaking. Antony comes back to me and wraps me in his arms. He staggers to his feet, holding me like I'm weightless. He's only just turned eighteen, but already he's built like a tank.

I let out a terrified sob. Antony glances over his shoulder, and there's panic in his eyes. "You've got to be quiet, Claws," he whispers. "They might be nearby. I'm going to get you out of here."

I can't speak. My voice is gone, left in the coffin with my screams. Antony hoists me up and darts into the shadows. He runs with ease, ducking between rows of crumbling gravestones and beneath bent and gnarled trees. Dimly, I recognize this place – the old Emerald Beach cemetery, on the edge of Beaumont Hills overlooking the bay, where the original families of Emerald Beach buried their dead.

Where someone tried to bury me.

Antony bursts from the trees onto a narrow road. His car is parked in the shadows. He opens the passenger door and settles me inside before diving behind the wheel and gunning the engine.

We tear off down the road. Antony rips around the deadly corners like he's on a racetrack. Steep cliffs and crumbling old mansions pass by in a blur.

"My parents..." I gasp out. "Where are my parents?"

"I'm sorry, Claws. I didn't get to them in time. I only found you."

I wait for this to sink in, for the fact I'm now an orphan to hit me in a rush of grief. But I'm numb. My body won't stop shaking, and I left my brain and my heart buried in the silence of that coffin.

"Who?" I ask, and I fancy I catch a hint of my dad's cold savagery in my voice. "Who did this?"

"I don't know yet, but if I had to guess, it was Brutus. I warned your dad that he was making alliances and building up to a challenge. I think he's just made his move."

I try to digest this information. Brutus – who was once my father's trusted friend, who'd eaten dinner at our house and played Chutes and Ladders with me – killed my parents and buried me alive. But it bounces off the edge of my skull and doesn't stick. The life I had before, my old life, it's gone, and as I twist and grasp for memories, all I grab is stale coffin air.

"What now?" I ask.

Antony tosses his phone into my lap. "Look at the headlines."

I read the news app he's got open, but the words and images blur together. "This... this doesn't make any sense..."

"They think you're dead, Claws," Antony says. "That means you have to *stay* dead until we're strong enough to move against him. Until then, you have to be a ghost. But don't worry, I'll protect you. I've got a plan. We'll hide you where they'll never think to look."

The thrumming bassline that rattles my bones and heats my veins with pure sex cuts off mid-riff, replaced by a tinny rendition of *Für Elise* blasting through the speakers.

Deedle-deedle-deedle-duh-dum-dum, duh-dum-dum...

The doorbell.

Shit.

I freeze mid-skank, one hand clutching my phone so tight my knuckles burn white, the other still gripping my ass like I'm a backup dancer in a Rhianna video. My eardrums shriek in protest at the piercing volume as the bell rings throughout the house's built-in speakers.

I listen hard. The jingle continues, and now it's accompanied by a loud thumping I can hear even though I'm miles from the front door.

Double shit.

It's been *months* since someone last approached the house. It's not an easy feat to achieve – you either have to scale the security gate with its iron spikes or clamber over the smooth limestone property wall in a Spider-Man feat of endurance. That is, unless you knew about my secret entrance, and no one does – only Antony.

The last time I had visitors, some drunk school kids managed to climb over the gate standing on each other's shoulders. They dared each other to run up to the door, ring the bell, and kick in the CCTV cameras while the rest hid in the garden and screeched like banshees.

I let them carry on with their games for a bit, but they were freaking out my cat, so I flicked the lights on and off and they ran screaming. One impaled himself on the gate spikes and ended up in the hospital. He gave a tearful interview in the tabloids about how he was attacked by the Malloy ghost.

Attacked by his own stupidity, more like. But I'm not calling in for a correction. It serves my purpose to have people believe I'm a ghost.

BANG BANG BANG.

Kids aren't knocking on my door at 10AM on a Tuesday morning.

No, this is the knock of someone who won't leave until they get answers.

I drop onto the rug of the media room and pull myself to the edge of the cathedral windows overlooking the sprawling front lawn. My all-black cat, Queen Boudica, leaps off her cushion and creeps along beside me, chest flattened on the ground and ears back. She thinks this is a game – we're working together to stalk our prey.

Perhaps there's truth to that.

At the window, I crane my neck to the side until I can see the figure standing on the porch, his dark uniform contrasted between the towering white columns. He looks completely out of place amongst the faux Grecian marble statuary and weird succulents in the garden – those stupid plants are taking over the place even though I never bother to water them.

Even from this distance, his uniform is unmistakable.

A police officer.

Triple shit.

Behind him, I can see the security gate swinging freely. The officer must have forced it somehow. I'll have to get Antony to come and repair it.

My fingers touch the glass as I study the officer – all square jaw and swaggering authority, one hand resting on his holster as he leans in to rap on the door again. In neighborhoods like this – a ritzy street of glittering mansions overlooking Emerald Beach from the top of Harrington Hills – police aren't feared. They keep the riffraff out.

But I'm not your ordinary Valley Girl – I have my reasons for staying hidden.

For now.

I trace the officer's outline on the glass, willing him to turn around and leave. Even though I haven't made a sound, the officer's head snaps up, his eyes landing on mine. I snap my head back from the window, my heart pounding.

It's too late. He's seen me.

"I know you're in there," he shouts. "Answer the door – it's the police."

His voice carries an unspoken threat. Queen Boudica tips her head at me and lifts a paw as if asking what I plan to do next. I debate my options. If I ignore him, he'll come back with reinforcements. But if I go down there, I might be able to bullshit my way out of whatever trouble I'm in. Antony does always say bullshit is my second name.

It's no problem. You can do this. You're Mackenzie Malloy.

I pull a Gucci hoodie over my workout gear and pad through the house. It takes me a good five minutes to navigate through the hallways to the grand staircase that leads down into the foyer. I pass gilded side-tables and weird blown glass art, all covered in layers of dust. Is it too much to hope that the cop will get sick of waiting and leave?

No such luck. I can see his shadow outlined through the frosted glass. He stands on the porch, arms folded, as I crack the door. The chain bites, and I give him the classic Mackenzie Malloy hair toss and withering stare.

"You've broken into private property," I bark at him – it's not a question. It's an accusation.

"Ma'am, I'm here to inform you that you're occupying this house illegally."

I toss my head so my golden blonde hair falls down my back, and I laugh. I laugh until my throat rasps, until the officer is squirming and looking unsure of himself. His fingers slip from his holster.

"This is a joke. Who's your superior?" I hold my phone up so he can see it as I tap the screen. "I'm going to report you for harassment. And for breaking my gate. You'll be paying for the repairs from your salary."

The officer's chin wobbles, and for a moment I think I've got him, but then he steps forward with a new determination. "I don't know what game you're playing, girl. This house has been empty for four years, yet neighbors have reported noises inside. Squatting in private property is illegal, and I'm under orders from the city to remove anyone caught on these premises." He shoots me a triumphant look. "Do you care to explain yourself?"

"Check your case law, officer. If I *were* a squatter, the owners of the property are required to send me a three-day written notice. But I'm hardly going to send one to myself." I lift my chin and meet his surly gaze with my own. "This is *my* home. I'm Mackenzie Malloy."

He staggers back, his hand flying to his chest as if I shot a dagger from my eyes that pierced his ribcage. It doesn't surprise me – my father always said my don't-fuck-with-me glare would topple kings. Glaring at people is my superpower.

"Miss Malloy, forgive me. No one has seen you for four years. Where are your parents?" He knows the stories. They all do. The rumors that flew around the world on the wings of the tabloids after my parents disappeared. After *I* disappeared. Rumors that the Malloy supplement company was involved in dark and nefarious deeds. That some rival had a hit out on us. That we returned as vengeful ghosts to haunt the hills of Emerald Beach.

The tabloids spin a web of lies so thick that even the truth gets trapped there occasionally.

"My parents are sequestered on our private Caribbean island. Mommy's last plastic surgery went wrong, and she vowed she wouldn't appear in public again until someone rebuilt her face. Her new surgeon uses this hormone from a rare species of Amazonian monkey, and it takes a long time to milk enough monkeys to fix the crater in Mommy's forehead." I shrug, the lie rolling easily off my tongue. "I'm looking after the property until they return."

"Your father is no longer the CEO of Malloy International. Doesn't that seem odd to you?"

I quirk an eyebrow at him. "It's illegal for a businessman to take a sabbatical now? Fine, I'll call our lawyers and they can come down here and explain to your supervisor that you broke our gate to harass me about my father's business decisions—"

He holds up his hands, unease flickering in his eyes. "That's not necessary, Ms. Malloy. If you show me some identification, I'll be on my way."

"Fine." I slam the door and march across the hall to where I left my ID in a bowl of glass apples that bore the mark of some fancy-ass Italian designer. My fingers seek the pendant around my neck – the gold locket hidden beneath my hoodie, thank fuck, because no way did I want that cop to see me wearing something so unfashionable. I tug at the heart charm on its thin gold chain, pressing my fingers against the familiar stamped surface and sucking in breaths until my heart stops racing.

This is it.

I knew the moment would come eventually. Luckily, Antony and I are ready.

Fuck, I hope we're ready.

I crack the door again. The cop holds out his hand for my ID, but I toss it at him. He has to stoop and pick it up, giving me ample opportunity to stare down my nose at him.

He frowns at my card, turning it over. "You're only just seventeen, Mackenzie. Why aren't you in school?"

I notice he uses my first name now. "I'm homeschooled. It's a free country. Shouldn't you be solving some actual crime?"

"Homeschool? A rich bitch like you? I don't think so." He notes something on his pad. "What institution? I'm going to check your enrollment."

"I'm not telling you anything without my lawyer."

"That line only works if you're suspected of committing a crime. We're just chatting."

"This feels like an interrogation to me." I fold my arms. "Don't make me call Daddy on the island to tell him about the trouble you caused just because some neighbors thought they heard a ghost. He's already going to be upset about the gate."

The cop sighs. He flips his pad shut and shoves it back into his pocket. "Very well, Mackenzie. I'll be checking up on you. You're still a minor, so if I can't see evidence that you're enrolled in school, I'll be sending around some CYF officers to talk to you."

Quadruple shit. I hunt around in my mind for something to tell him. I grasp for the memories tucked away into the corners of this impersonal home, the little touches that proved actual humans once inhabited it. My mind rests on the school prospectus in the drawer in the mahogany desk in the office. Students in sage-green uniforms, standing around under palm trees and grinning at the camera like smug bitches. "Stonehurst Prep. I'm about to start my senior year at Stonehurst Prep."

MACKENZIE

$\mathcal{I}$ smooth down the front of my sage skirt. Stonehurst Prep looms in front of me – rows of Corinthian columns jutting from a mock Classical facade, like serrated teeth protruding from the gaping jaw of a monster. Statues of languid gods and bare-breasted goddesses line the wide path leading to the entrance of the school. Students lounge in groups on the perfectly manicured lawn – the too-perfect brochure come to life.

On the outside, I might look like one of them – perfect hair, designer book bag, perfect smile.

Inside I'm a Visigoth storming into Rome to sack the shit out of the place.

I stride up the path, under the colonnade, and into the internal courtyard with its fountain depicting the rape of Leda by Zeus, disguised as a swan. Swans are dicks.

Whispers swirl around me. They start as a faint buzz – like a fly trapped in the room – but soon swell to a steady drone of gossip. I catch snatches of their conversation as I hunt for the main office.

"—can't believe that's Mackenzie Malloy. I thought her whole family disappeared without a trace—"

"—on a Caribbean island, and she's been living in that creepy mansion all by herself—"

"—I heard she's actually a vampire, and she's been sleeping in a coffin in the Malloy's basement all these years—"

This is a bad idea.

I spent the last week re-reading my diaries and searching through every object in my childhood bedroom. I needed to know I could pull this off with only snatches of memory from before the coffin, before my life became a living nightmare. What I read filled me with confidence – not a single birthday card from a friend or photo of me at a beach with another kid. Mackenzie Malloy had no childhood friends. I was a stone-cold bitch back then, and I'll be that same stone-cold bitch now. It's the only way to protect myself.

It's the only way for Antony and I to get what we need.

The office door looms ahead. The voices rise to a crescendo around me. After so many years fighting against the silence, all this noise is disorienting. I reach for the handle.

It's not too late to turn around and go home. You don't know for a fact what that officer might do if he doesn't see you enrolled in school. You can get Antony to put the shits up him. Problem solved.

Problem not solved.

My parents are still dead. I'm still a ghost. Brutus is still out there being a smug bastard, thinking he's won.

I turn the handle. My mind flies to my father's favorite quote from Julius Caesar – the words he spoke when he crossed the Rubicon and started a civil war.

Alea iacta est.

Let the die be cast.

Welcome to Stonehurst fucking Prep.

ELI

"—Track tryouts are next Thursday, so maybe we could meet after school and run through some drills? I know I have a weak finish in the 400m and—"

Noah runs his fingers through his perfect hair as he drones on about tryouts. We've been friends for so long – since our parents started holidaying together in Nantucket when we were four years old – that I know his tics. Noah touches his hair when he's nervous, and he's nervous as fuck about track.

I'm not gonna be the one to tell him, but Noah shouldn't even be going out for track. For as long as I've known him, Noah's sport has been swimming. He has a whole wall in his room covered in trophies from state swim meets. His older brother, Felix, was the track star. So three years ago Noah decides he has to be a track star, too, which means he's on my ass constantly to train with him. As if I don't have my own shit to deal with – being friends with perfectionist assholes like Noah Marlowe is hard fucking work.

I listen to Noah with half an ear as I toss my books into my locker. Around us, students yell and laugh as they catch up after summer break. I hear snatches of conversation about film sets and meditation retreats in Tulum and beaches in Majorca. Stonehurst is that kind of school.

A hand claps on my shoulder. "Did you see Melinda Perez's new nose?" A familiar British voice coos in my ear. "More's the pity, her glorious arse is smaller now."

"Gabe?" I whirl around. Standing before me, a leather jacket slung casually over his shoulder and the faint smell of weed clinging to his clothes, is Gabriel Fallen in all his glory. He looks like he just stepped off his tour bus, complete with his rumpled hair, eyes rimmed in dark shadows, and cheeky grin. "What are you doing here?"

"Causing all ladies' underthings within a mile radius to simultaneously combust." Gabriel breaks my gaze to flash his smile at two junior girls who are staring at him from across the hall. They break into giggles, because Gabriel Fallen has that effect on people. "I'm taking time off from the band to finish senior year."

"What happened to 'diplomas are for wankers who don't have groupies'?" I quote Gabriel's final words when he left at the beginning of summer for his European tour. My mockery of his British accent gets the hint of a smile from Noah.

"Please. I don't sound as posh as all that. All your lectures on 'rock music won't provide for your future' rubbed off on me, Hart." Gabriel shrugs, and there's a whole world inside that shrug. I know what happened. He might not have answered my texts, but he knows I know what happened. Everyone at Stonehurst has followed the headlines – DRUMMER OF OCTAVIA'S RUIN OVERDOSES IN HOTEL BATHROOM. As much as he's trying to pretend he's fine, the very fact Gabriel's back at Stonehurst and not holed up in a studio in Switzerland recording a chart-topping album of grief music suggests otherwise.

Yet another problem that will fall on my shoulders this year. I *almost* have it in me to smooth over Noah's intensity, but add in

Gabe's unpredictability, and I will not get a moment of peace. But still... senior year would not have been the same without Gabriel. I wrap my arms around him, patting his back, relieved that he's here and at least... *somewhat* sober.

"Oof, since when did you become the Incredible Hulk?" In true British tradition, Gabriel finds physical expressions of joy disconcerting. He gazes around the corridor as if looking for a line to join to restore his equilibrium, then grabs my books from my hands. He frowns at the cover of my AP Calculus textbook. "Just reading these titles gives me a splitting headache."

I grab my books from Gabe's hands. "You'd better be back here to focus on schoolwork, not party and drink yourself into a stupor like last year, because Noah and I refuse to tutor you."

That evil grin again. "I passed my SATs, didn't I?"

"You passed because you slept with the test assessor."

"I can't help it if my natural wit and charm had the poor woman so overcome that she—" Gabriel cut off, his eyes focusing on something behind me.

No, not something.

Someone.

The only thing that can cause Gabriel to lose focus like that is a chick. One with legs up to her eyeballs and, in his words, a shaggable arse.

If I'm honest, I could do with a shaggable arse in my own life. I wish I could be like Noah and Gabriel, who've both fucked their way through the student body at Stonehurst twice over. Nothing serious. Nothing complicated.

I'm not that guy, but sometimes I like to pretend I could be.

I turn around in time to see a blonde bombshell stride with purpose from the school office. Students leap out of the way as she stomps toward us in a pair of black spike-heeled non-regulation boots. Her lips are a bow of crimson. Her face stirs something inside me – a memory. A familiar sense of longing, of loss.

What draws me to her is the complete 'fuck-off' look in her eyes, like she's above everyone and everything.

I always fall hard for the impossible girls.

But maybe this can be different. She's new, which means she hasn't had a chance to fall head-over-heels for Gabriel's broken prince charm or Noah's bad boy intensity. But I'd have to work fast now Gabriel has his radar up.

"Do you know who she is?" I ask Gabriel. Even though he's been away from the city, he always knows the gossip.

"Mate, you been living under a rock? That's Mackenzie Malloy." Gabe licks his lips. "Crazy looks good on her."

My chemistry textbook clatters to the ground.

"Say that name again," I whisper. Behind me, Noah's breath comes out in ragged gasps.

"Mackenzie Malloy. You know, billionaire heiress to the Malloy nutritional supplement fortune, disappeared along with her parents four years ago, leaving that creepy house abandoned up on Harrington Hills. She's out of hiding and walking the hallowed halls of Stonehurst. Aren't we blessed?"

Mackenzie.

I didn't need Gabriel to tell me what happened. I know her story. I read the news articles and police reports a hundred times, trying to find some clue of where she went, of how we could be planning to escape to college together one minute and the next she's vanished. I can't count the number of nights I've watched her house, hoping to see a glimpse of her ghost.

And now here she is, strutting down the hall like she owns this school.

Mackenzie Malloy, flesh and blood.

Alive.

No wonder she seems so familiar.

It all comes rushing at me at once as I recognize her features – memories of the games we played with each other in stolen moments all those years ago. Both of us living our true childhoods in secret. I squat to pick up my book. I need a moment to collect myself.

A spike-heel slams into the cover, denting the pages.

I look up, and up, and up. A lump forms in my throat.

"You're standing in front of my locker." From atop legs as long and graceful as an ostrich, Mackenzie fixes me with this demolishing glare – like I'm a bug not even worthy of being stepped on.

I search those impossible ice eyes for some sign that she recognizes me, but she doesn't waver. Maybe she doesn't recognize me. The last time we saw each other was when we were thirteen years old. I've changed since then. And Mackenzie... phew. She was always pretty, but now with those legs and curves and that haughty twist of her lip – now she's *devastating*.

"Greetings, m'lady." Gabriel – who has no clue of the history he's stomping on – rests his palm on the locker behind Mackenzie and cocks his hand on his hip. He loves to play up his 'I'm a posh British rockstar, ask me about my friend Prince Harry' act. "Elias here is merely showing the proper deference to one such as yourself. If he continues to inconvenience you, just stand on him. He likes that."

Shut the fuck up, Gabriel.

Mackenzie brushes past Gabriel like he's nothing, which is so unheard of that Gabriel's mouth falls open. He could catch flies with that thing. As I clamber to my feet, I bite my lip to keep from bursting out laughing. Noah isn't as polite. He chortles – but it's a sound like a strangled cat. He has his own reasons for being unnerved by Mackenzie Malloy's sudden reappearance. I look over at him to see if I need to do damage control, but he's holding it together... so far.

I scramble out of Mackenzie's way just as she slams her locker door open, the sound ricocheting down the hall like a gunshot. The eyes of other students slide toward us – a sensation I'm used to. But this time, they're not staring with envy or longing. There's the scent of blood in the air.

"Mackenzie?" I try again. Her name sounds foreign on my lips. Out of place. A name from a fantasy novel – some dark fae queen too perfect and too dangerous to exist in the real world.

She buries her face in her locker, doesn't even look up.

"It's me." I lower my voice. "Elias Hart."

She jerks her head around to face me, whipping golden hair across my face. She smells the same – peaches and coconut, and underneath something wild and undefinable – and the scent threatens to undo me. She cocks an eyebrow at me. "You say your name like I'm supposed to recognize it."

I study her face as she drops her books on the shelf. On top is a battered leather volume – a book of Greek lyric poetry. It looks to be written in *actual* Greek. Where did Mackenzie go for four years that she developed a taste for ancient poetry?

"Elias Hart," I say. "I can walk you to class if you like. We can catch up on—"

"You're in my way, *Elias Hart*." She places a hand on my pec. The touch is so sudden, so unexpected, that I let out a weird noise, like a wheeze. *Smooth, Eli.*

In my defense, I did not expect Mackenzie Malloy to be touching me today.

She's painted her nails with a minty-colored polish that matches the cold of her eyes. Her fingers curl slightly, like claws. She shoves me. Hard. Caught off balance, I step back, crushing Noah's foot with my heel. Noah grabs me before I fall on my ass again.

There's a collective intake of breath – a reverse hurricane sucking the air from the corridor. I may be making an ass of myself, but I'm still Elias Hart. I'm not someone you fuck with if you want to survive at Stonehurst Prep.

"Fuck you, Mackenzie." Noah fixes her with his own signature glare – burning hot with a rage he'd never be able to control around her. Surely she remembers Noah. He'd sure as fuck never forgotten her.

Mackenzie regards him with a detached interest. I watch the anger take hold of Noah, squeezing him inside until he bursts. His arm flies out, and I throw up a hand to deflect him. But he's not trying to land a blow. Before I can stop him, he storms off toward homeroom. Great, now on top of everything else, I'll have to deal with sulky, moody Noah.

Mackenzie doesn't acknowledge his departure. She slams her locker door shut, spins on her heel, and strides off toward the Humanities block, her skirt hugging her thighs in a way that makes a hard lump form in my throat and something even harder strain my uniform pants.

Mackenzie Malloy.

After all these years, *how* is she back in my life?

And why is she pretending she doesn't know who I am?

MACKENZIE

Fuck. *Fuck.*

I knew it.

I knew this was a bad idea.

That guy at my locker, Elias Hart – the one with the too-perfect golden hair and the faint Southern drawl and the eyes that shine like the ocean. The one whose face seems oddly familiar, but I can't place the how or why.

He knows me. Somehow.

If he knows me, he can undo me.

I checked *everywhere*. No mention of an Elias in any of my diaries. No photographs of the boy with the sunset smile and fuck-me-slowly eyes hidden in my room. I'd remember that face – it's hard to forget, especially when he looked at me like I'm more than a morbid curiosity, like something precious he thought lost forever has suddenly appeared again.

What disturbs me the most is that some part of me recognizes him, too. Some part of me feels a connection to him that reaches back into the past, into *before*. And that's fucking terrifying.

And his friends... the angry one behind Elias, with the eyes like charcoal tears and the wavy hair that just begs to run my fingers through it. And that other dude with the labret piercing who looks uncannily like Gabriel Fallen, singer from Octavia's Ruin – only my favorite fucking band of all time. He even *sounds* like Gabriel – all sexy and British – but that's impossible because Gabriel's in Europe, writing a new album to honor the death of his drummer.

I shake it off as I walk into my assigned homeroom and slide into a seat near the back. I can't afford to get distracted by guys this year. It's tempting, because the whole sex thing is part of my stolen life, part of what I'm here to reclaim. But guys like them are also dangerous, in more ways than one. The only way I'm going to pull this off is to focus on getting through this year with my secrets intact. I can't afford to let some dude – or dudes – derail that.

Even if they...

I pull myself from my thoughts as the room fills up. Eyes flick to me, over me, exploring and delving, drawing conclusions from every tilt of my chin and fidget of my fingers. Heads lean together as students whisper about me. I roll my eyes and take out my phone, tapping on the screen as I pull up the contacts list. Who the fuck cares.

Let them stare.

I scroll through the contacts. The iPhone is pretty old – at least four years old, to be exact. It's got a case with a glittery pink heart on it, too young for me now, but I like it. The screen freezes, and I tap it on the edge of the desk. There are only twenty contacts, and I know them all by heart. I check anyway.

No Elias.

So who *is* the golden-haired god?

I glance through a curtain of hair as someone takes the empty seat beside me. *Great.* It's that Mr. British from the lockers. *He shouldn't put so much effort into looking like Gabriel Fallen;*

it's embarrassing. He drapes his arm over the back of his chair, angling his body toward me and doing a man-spread so epic poets should boast about it. The front of his uniform shirt is unbuttoned, revealing a torn Iron Maiden tank and beautiful black-and-grey ink underneath – thorny roses entwined around a Classical woman who reaches up with open fingers, releasing butterflies that flutter across his neck. *Pathetic. He's even copied Gabriel's ink.* Piercings dot his ears in blatant defiance of the school's uniform policy. His tongue plays with the bar threaded through his labret, and I notice he's also got a tongue stud that's identical to Gabriel Fallen's.

Ew, fanboy. I wonder if he went the full-hog and got Gabriel's dick piercing, too?

"Nice to see you back, Gabe." A girl with honey-blonde hair turns in her chair to bat her eyelids at him. Mr. British nods at her, but his gaze is on me as he flirts back at blondie. The intensity in his shale-grey eyes shocks me – the way he talks is all surface charm, but that look… it's like he's lifted up a corner of my skin and is peeking at my soul, and for all the blood and bruising, he likes what he sees.

Fuck.

He doesn't just look like Gabriel Fallen, he is Gabriel Fallen. My ears ring as the lyrics to my favorite songs filter through my head. How did I miss the fact that Gabriel Fallen goes to Stonehurst Prep?

Fuck me dead.

Thanks, universe – way to make my 'no boys' rule infinitely more difficult to follow.

It makes a sick sense – Stonehurst is the most prestigious school in the city. All the rich families send their kids here. Emerald Beach is built close enough to LA to be a hub for the entertainment industry. Many of the major studios have lots out the back of Beaumont Hills, not far from my place in Harrington

Hills. The school's brochure lists famous actors who've graced the halls, so I expected a ton of teen stars and social influencers.

I just never expected *him*.

"I think we got off on the wrong foot back at the lockers," Gabriel says to me, blondie forgotten. He blinks at me, and his eyelashes are so long they tangle together. I say nothing, because if I open my mouth I will throw up.

We're the only two people in the back row. Gabriel leans over my desk, using his index finger to turn my schedule toward him so he can read it. A rush of his scent hits me – this sultry, sugary, smoky fragrance that makes me think of torrid winter nights dancing around a wild bonfire. Not that I've ever danced around a fire like a pagan, but if Gabriel asked, I wouldn't refuse.

He studies my schedule, then studies me. His arm presses against mine. I'm coming apart under his gaze, my edges fraying, my secrets dancing on the tip of my tongue.

"I'm Gabriel. And you are?"

Gabriel fucking Fallen is touching my arm.

This is like the start of a bad teen movie. I marathoned a ton of the classics over the weekend – *Mean Girls, Easy A, Clueless, 10 Things I Hate About You, The Craft* (because you never know, witches could walk the halls of Stonehurst and I want to stay on their good side) – hoping they might somehow prepare me for my first day of high school. But nothing could prepare me for the electric jolt that fires through my veins at Gabriel's touch.

"Mackenzie Malloy," I manage to choke out. I fancy my voice sounds husky, mysterious. Not like I'm desperately trying to hold back bile. "Your friends seem to know me."

"Your reputation precedes you, Mackenzie, which is the way a reputation should be." Gabriel's smile manages to look both arrogant and mischievous. "I'm pleased I decided to come back to school this year after all."

I nod, because that's what you do when the singer who's

wept with pain from your speakers implies he wants to spend time with you.

"We have our first two classes together," he continues. His British accent makes every mundane word sound musical. "I'll walk you there – this place can seem a bit like Pan's Labyrinth."

"I don't need your help." I swipe my schedule back and shove it into my notebook. Too late, Gabriel notices the sticker on the inside of the cover. The latest Octavia's Ruin album art. Fuck. Now he's going to think I'm a band-junkie stalker.

"Nice taste in music." That arrogant smile tugs at his lip again, making the piercing wiggle. "I've heard their lead singer is a real wanker. Though he makes up for it by being a demon in the sack."

I turn my face away, willing the heat rushing through my veins to leave my cheeks the fuck alone. My heart hammers against my chest. It's like the universe is determined to mess with me. It knows how important this year is to our whole fucking plan, so it throws the one guy in front of me I might've wanted to get to know.

All those nights when the silence of the house gets too much for me, when the walls close in, dripping with memories I don't want to face, I turn on Octavia's Ruin and scream the lyrics into the empty rooms, attacking the silence with power chords. Questions swirl inside my head – all the things I'm dying to ask Gabriel about the meanings behind his lyrics, about the way his voice cracks on 'Requiem for a Rose' as if he can barely stand the pain any longer...

But I don't.

Every moment of homeroom is torture as I force myself to ignore Gabriel. The teacher reads announcements, and I don't hear a word. All my brain-space is taken up with the awareness that Gabriel's leg hovers next to mine and how fucking tempted

I am to drop my knee against his and feel that heat searing between us again.

Finally, the bell rings and I snatch up my bag and shove my way to the front of the room. The homeroom teacher calls my name, but I'm already out the door.

So much for my Visigoth pride. At this rate, by the end of the day I'll be a puddle of goo formally known as Mackenzie Malloy.

MACKENZIE

*I*n chemistry, we sit in groups of two along laboratory benches filled with equipment I don't recognize or understand. I slump down beside a brunette in the middle of the room. She opens her mouth to say something but I hit her with my classic Mackenzie Malloy death glare and she leans back, folding her arms and staring straight ahead. At least my superpower still works and I have a partner who won't distract me with sexy Britishness or a weird magnetic connection.

Gabriel saunters in last. His eyes meet mine and he stops by our table, flicking his head at the girl. Without a word, she gets up and walks to the back of the room, and Gabriel takes her empty seat.

Bastard.

"I guess we're partners," he says, flashing me that smile – the smile of a guy who isn't used to hearing no. I desperately want to be the one to fling that word at him and make it stick, but he's Gabriel fucking Fallen, and I'm only human. I settle for glaring at him, but all that does is make him stick his tongue out to wiggle that bar at me.

"You're cute when you're mad." He opens his textbook and

gestures to the glass tubey things in front of us. "I hope you're good at this stuff, partner. Because I'm terrible."

He isn't lying. As the teacher leads us through a simple experiment, Gabriel mixes the wrong chemicals and creates a putrid stench that clears the classroom for a good ten minutes. Then, he measures out 50mls instead of 5mls of hydrochloric acid. I grab his arm before he pours that into our beaker and singes off his perfect eyebrows. I deserve a medal for public service for that one. Not least because touching his skin is like sticking my hand in an electrical socket, but in a fun way.

I'm not any better at the work. Every brush of Gabriel's skin against mine sends my heart into freefall. By the end of the class we're the only ones who haven't completed the experiment, and I'm a puddle of fangirling mush on the floor.

"That would usually be an F on this module," Mr. Dallas frowns over our station. "But I know you're new, Mackenzie, and you might need some time to catch up. And Mr. Fallen, the faculty are aware that you're dealing with certain personal situations. So if you come after class one day this week and try again, I'll allow you to make up the grade."

Gabriel leans over and squeezes my hand. "Our first date. Should I bring the Champagne, or are you more of a beers behind the bike shed kind of girl?"

I race from class with Gabriel's laughter peeling behind me. I can't decide if he's amused by himself, or if he's laughing at my expense. No one else laughs at me. *Yet.* I'm too new, an unknown. Plus, there's the fact they all thought I was a ghost until I strutted in the door.

My next class is English, which I expect to be easy, but is anything but. *Isn't Shakespeare supposed to be in English?* I glare at the nonsense in my textbook while Gabriel's grey eyes dig holes in my back. A pair of girls in the front row with cheerleading jackets slung over their chairs keep turning around to look at me, then whispering to each other. As I fly out of class the moment the bell rings, I overhear a snatch of their conversation.

"...I heard she killed them and hid the bodies in the basement. Gabriel better watch out, or he'll be next—"

My next class is Physics, which might as well be Sanskrit for all I understand. A bell rings for lunch, and I'm swept along in the crowd. My stomach growls, but I hesitate in the doorway of the dining hall, taking it all in. Waiters in coat and tails sweep from the kitchen doors, carrying platters piled high with gourmet food, which they deliver to a magnificent buffet where students line up to serve themselves. Steak in some kind of red-wine reduction. Broccolini toasted with pine nuts. Mashed potatoes sculpted into tiny wedges, an entire table bulging under the weight of cakes and desserts. My mouth waters – this sure beats the fried crap I scarf down at the diner whenever I can catch a spare minute on my shifts. I grab a tray and pile it as high as I dare. If school lunches are like this every day, I won't need to worry about dinners. More money saved.

I palm a soda and turn toward the tables, and the flaw in my plan becomes apparent. All around me, students wave to their friends as they sit at their regular tables. Every face a stranger, every pair of eyes promising an interrogation.

My mind goes to all those teen movies I binged over the weekend. They always start the same way, with the new girl staring out at a sea of faces who all know each other but don't trust her. At the last minute, she's saved from loserdom by a hot guy or a quirky but lovable new BFF—

But this isn't a teen movie, and I don't need saving. I need to be left the fuck alone.

I spy an empty table in the far corner and make a beeline for it, dropping my book bag into the chair next to mine in an attempt to keep others out of it. I pull out my history book while I shovel food into my mouth. At least my afternoon classes will be more my scene – we have units on the Founding Fathers and Classical history and Tudor-Stewart England...

"Mackenzie Malloy, as I live and breathe."

I glance up as a guy shoves my book bag off the chair and slides in beside me. He's got the broad shoulders and cocky smile of a jock and the cold eyes of a serial killer. He looks vaguely familiar, but I don't care enough to enquire further, especially not when he leans close and I catch a whiff of alcohol on his breath.

"Not interested." I shovel another mouthful of food, hoping he gets the point.

He doesn't.

"I'm surprised you don't remember me." He takes the fork from my hand and tosses it at a nearby waiter, who nearly drops the stack of dirty plates he's carrying. My unwelcome table guest flashes me this smile that's all white teeth and menace. Behind him, I notice a couple of other jock-looking dudebros watching the scene with interest. "I'm Alec LeMarque. We went to junior prep together. You slammed my hand in a classroom door."

"You deserved it." I don't remember, of course, but it's a solid guess.

Alec LeMarque... that name sounds so familiar... I've seen it written somewhere recently... I sneak another look at him through the corner of my eye and realize he's one of the stars from a dorky teen movie I watched. He plays the obnoxious jock that gets his ass kicked by the geeks in the end. Justice at its finest.

"I believe that's what you told our teacher. But look at you, all grown up now. An ass like that, you don't belong in this corner all by yourself. Come join my friends." Alec pops a shoulder in the direction of a rowdy table at the end of the room – a prime spot in front of the French doors opening out into a sunny courtyard lined with palms. Gabriel Fallen sits at the end of the table, telling a story to three model-thin girls who are hanging on every word. He sees me and waves. Beside him are the other two guys from my locker this morning. The dark-haired one stirs his food around his plate, but the golden-god, Elias, stares at me with this intense look, like he's reading my secrets from my skin.

Nope. Not happening.

"Pass." I angle my chair away. Alec *still* doesn't take the hint. He places both hands on my shoulders and starts rubbing in circles. It's fucking gross. My skin crawls under his touch. It's the exact opposite of what happened with Gabriel. I flinch away as he leans in close to coo in my ear.

"You know, the hard-to-get act is old, Malloy. I'm king at this school, and my friends are like a royal court. You'd be well advised to take this offer before it's rescinded and you end up another one of the plebs. I know for a girl like you that's a fate worse than death."

He hisses the last word, the death. He wants me to *feel* it. His hot breath curdles my skin, and it takes me back to another night, another guy's hot breathing on my ear, another set of hands on me that I didn't ask for. Stale air. A satin-lined box I couldn't escape...

I'm done.

I don't even think.

I slam my fist into Alec LeMarque's nose.

I've been at Stonehurst Prep less than five hours and I'm already in the principal's office.

I stare at the wall behind Mrs. Foster's face as she drones on about responsibility and solving my problems without violence. It's weird – the adults in my life have never tried to dissuade me from violence before. Violence has always been part of my world.

Not at Stonehurst, it appears.

I rub my sore knuckles, feeling the satisfying jolt of pain from where my fist connected with the cartilage in Alec's nose. I wonder if he'll get a lecture about not sleazing onto girls who aren't interested. He got carried out of the cafeteria in an ambulance, screaming something to me about a lawsuit. Which I definitely need to ask Antony about, but it has to wait until Mrs. Foster's tirade is over.

I itch to touch the locket hidden under my collar, but I don't want to give Mrs. Foster a reason to prolong this torture.

"I know you've had it tough, Mackenzie." She steeples her fingers together, and there's this look on her face like she's trying to pretend she gives a fuck. "These past few years can't have been easy on you. What with your parents... But that's no excuse for antisocial behavior. If you need to talk about what you've been through, we have a guidance counselor available any time you need, and my door is always open if you want to talk."

The question hangs in the air between us, unasked and unanswered. She doesn't give a shit about getting me to talk about my feelings, she just wants the scoop like the rest of them. *What happened to your parents, Mackenzie? Why are you suddenly back at school? Where have you been the last four years?*

By the time she dismisses me with a month of detentions and an order to write a note of apology to Alec LeMarque, I've got one class left – Political Science.

The eyes follow me as I take the only available seat, near the windows. Only instead of curious, they're hostile. I hurt their leader, their king. I made a big ugly bloodstain on the pristine white tablecloth.

I don't belong.

My seat is next to the dark-haired hottie, the one with the eyes like coals fresh from a fire. The one who could be an MMA fighter for all his bulk and the danger rolling off him in waves, but he's too pressed and neat in his tailored uniform to last a round in the ring.

"Mackenzie." He rasps my name under his breath, quiet enough only I can hear. There's a finality to his tone, like a wizard speaking a curse.

(I also watched *Harry Potter* this weekend, just in case Stonehurst turned out to be a wizarding school. Can't deal with any surprises this year.)

I glare at Coal-Eyed Wizard. "What do you want?"

"You should have stayed hidden. You should never have come back."

His shoulders square, and the hatred in his eyes is so deep, so dark, that a shiver of fear runs down my spine.

"An eye for an eye, Mackenzie Malloy," he hisses, and my blood turns cold. "You took something special from me. I'll take everything from you."

That was a day.

I trudge through the small wood running between my house and the neighbors' perimeter wall to my secret entrance. I keep the front gates locked (and will continue to do so, now the police paid to replace the broken gate) to continue my ghost facade. The longer we can hold off on the press getting ahold of my story, the better. My house contains a ten-car garage on the first floor, with a car lift that can drop a vehicle into the basement where they exit down a concrete tunnel under the garden onto a private road at the rear of the property. The maintenance shed for the lift, the security gates, and the house's extensive electronics and networking has an external door to allow staff and repairmen to come and go. It's this door I unlock now and duck inside.

I hurry between the racks of switches and into the tunnel. It's pitch black inside, but I can find my way in my sleep so I don't bother with a light. The *clop-clop* of my heels echoes along the length, rising with the slope so it almost sounds as if I'm chasing myself. Mrs. Foster expects me to be in regulation shoes by the end of the week, but Mackenzie Malloy doesn't give a shit about the rules when an extra three inches of height are involved.

I clamber up the spiral staircase into the garage, cross between the rows of dusty vehicles, and reach for the door that connects the garage to the house. I kick off my heels with such force they hit the wall and leave a black scuff against the pristine white paint. My right big toe stings from the stiff leather pinching them all day. One must suffer for beauty.

Queen Boudica sits on the rug, her black fur gleaming from the shadows, her head cocked to the side as if she's been waiting there for me all day.

"Meow." She stomps one foot on the rug, demanding to know where I've been.

"Don't give me that shit. I've had a bad day." Too tired to drag myself upstairs to the media room or across the house to the ballroom, I flop into one of the uncomfortable chairs by the French doors that look out over the pool.

Big mistake. A black paw jabs me in the ribcage as Queen Boudica – sensing a lap has been created – climbs up and settles in. Cat gravity officially in effect. Now I can't move. And I have homework to do.

Homework. What the fuck? I thought rich people didn't have to do homework. Isn't that the point of being a rich asshole – you get to make the rules, and the rules never include algebra.

I stroke Queen Boudica's fur as I gaze out across the ruined pool. Sunlight gleams off the puddle of murky water in the deep end. Weeds choke the filter and dangle over the cracked tiles, snagging a deflated unicorn floatie.

I allow myself to imagine how inviting it would be tidied up and filled with clean, azure water, how good it would feel to dive in and let the water wash away the stench of today.

Maybe one day, if I can make it through this year, I'll be able to do what the fuck I want with the pool. And the whole house.

If I finish my homework.

But I don't move. I stare out at the pool and think about everything I have to lose. Sitting by these windows is a risk I don't normally indulge in, even with the tinted windows and the high perimeter wall. If someone sees me here, during the day, looking less like a ghost and more like a pissed-off brat, I'll bring a world of trouble down on my ass.

Antony said it was risky going to school, but it would be worth it in the end. I'm not so sure.

I'm crazy to think I could pull this off. I can't—

My phone buzzes. Only one person has this number who actually calls me. I press it to my ear.

"Tell me all about your first day, Claws," Antony purrs, using my childhood nickname. I can hear music and people talking in the background. He must be at his club. I wish I'm there, too, drowning my sorrows with cheap whisky and watching men beat each other bloody.

"It was shit. As predicted. Gabriel Fallen goes there. And I broke some teen actor's nose."

"I knew you wouldn't last one day at that stuck-up school." Antony laughs. I love his laugh – it's *so* him; uncontrolled, teetering on the edge of mania. People fear that laugh, because it usually precedes bloodshed. I find it comforting.

What that says about me I don't like to consider.

I tell Antony about Alec LeMarque's blood splattered across the table. "By the way, could he sue me for that?"

"A guy like him?" Antony snorted. "Fuck no. First of all, he believes you have the power of your father's fortune and connections behind you, and he's not gonna cross that. Second, if he goes after you he risks the press getting hold of the story. Little Alec won't want the world to know he got beat up by a girl. His revenge will be in private, away from prying eyes. You'd better sharpen those talons of yours, Claws. If he does come after you, call me. I can have someone over there—"

"I'll handle it." I decide not to tell Antony about Elias recognizing me or me recognizing him, or Coal-Eyes' threat. That look in Coal's eyes concerns me more than Alec, but I need more information before I get Antony involved.

"Fine, fine. I know not to mess with you, *Mackenzie Malloy*."

Just saying my name has Antony in a fit of giggles again. He must be drunk. Or high. Probably both. My older cousin loves a good time.

"By the way, thanks for fixing things with the school for me. And for the ID." I pat my pocket containing my new driver's license. "You saved my ass."

"It's an ass worth saving. But we're not through this yet, Claws. Our plan just got risky. The press will get wind of your return. Family members might reveal themselves, people we can't trust. Are you prepared for that?"

No. "Yes."

Antony sighs. "Claws..."

"What? We've come this far. It's only a matter of months. I can deal with anything for a few months if..."

...if it gets you out of that world. I don't say it, because I know Antony doesn't want to hear it. He hasn't agreed on our next step. But in nine months it won't matter what he says.

My phone beeps. A message. "That better not be a picture of your dick."

"Not me. Maybe it's Fallen's dick. You should try selling the pic on eBay. Maybe you'd get enough for it that we wouldn't need your crazy plan."

I peer at the screen. The name reads 'Jace' – one of the few contacts in the phone without a last name. I remember Jace leaving a ton of text messages a few years back, when my family first went AWOL. I never answered any of them, and he must've got the message because I haven't heard from him again. Until now.

"Why wouldn't you talk to me at school today? What happened to you?"

Great. This Jace goes to Stonehurst Prep, too. It's bad enough with Elias staring at me and Dark-Hair's threats, but now I've got another guy on my ass who knows me from before? I thought Mackenzie Malloy didn't have real friends. At least, that's what my report cards from eighth grade say.

I glance at the time and groan. "I gotta go. Work calls. It's my last night."

"Good. I never liked that you worked there. It was too risky, even with your disguise."

"I was never going to hide away in here and let you pay for everything," I roll my eyes. "Who knew state-of-the-art mansions have such insane property taxes?"

"Hopefully we won't have to worry about that for much longer. Be careful, Claws." The irony of Antony telling me to be careful when I just heard a guy's skull crack against the concrete behind him makes me smile. Antony and I are more alike than we first appear.

I toss the phone on the chair, push a protesting Queen Boudica off my lap, and pad down to my room. My real bedroom is on the second floor – a suite of rooms painted soft pink with a balcony overlooking the swimming pool. Sleeping in there is not an option – far too freaky with all the porcelain dolls lined up on shelves and closet filled with clothes too small for me – so I'd taken a guest room on the first floor. It's more my taste – dark jarrah wood floors, crimson linens, soft, modern lighting, and a bathroom lined with tiny black and silver tiles that looks like something Mötley Crüe would shoot up in.

I step under the rain shower, letting the water and fancy bath products sluice away my makeup. My armor removed, I pull on my uniform, tucking my hair into a bandana until not a single scrap of blonde shows through. I tilt the makeup mirror toward me and apply a completely different face – natural colors, dark eyebrows and lashes, a light pink lipstick that makes me look younger, more innocent.

When I stand back to admire myself in the mirror, Mackenzie Malloy has disappeared. In her place is Claudia Jones – waitress from the wrong side of the tracks. Claudia grabs her purse, gives Queen Boudica a scratch behind the ears, and walks down the hill to catch the bus to her final shift at her shitty job.

GABRIEL

"I just... can't believe... she's back," Eli puffs, drawing back his racket to serve. I brace myself, knowing this is going to be hell.

SMACK.

Eli's racket connects. I dive out of the way as the ball hurtles toward my face. My knee slams into the turf just as the ball smashes into the wall behind me, sending leaves and chips of tile flying everywhere.

"Bloody hell, mate." I stand up, wiping off my palms even though they aren't dirty. Eli's mother would never dare let a single speck of dirt blow onto her tennis court. My knee throbs, but at least I don't need it to play guitar.

Why does it matter? You're not playing anyway, a voice taunts me. My own voice. The voice that used to gift me with lyrics to break girl's hearts and open their legs, but now spends its days making me as miserable as possible.

"Watch the face, okay?" I glare at Eli. "I'm shooting with *Rolling Stone* next week."

"Fuck *Rolling Stone.*" Eli wipes sweat off his brow. "Can we take five, bro? I need a drink."

You need ten drinks, mate. But before I can reply, Eli stomps off the court. He heads over to where Noah lounges under a palm with his face buried in one of his AP History books.

"Scotch," Eli barks. Noah doesn't glance up.

"Make mine a double."

Eli grabs a bottle from the outdoor bar and slams down three glasses. He sloshes top-shelf Scotch all over the table, managing to get some of it into the crystal. Noah grabs a glass and knocks it back in one hit, not even looking up from his book. Eli takes his and stands on the edge of the garden bed, twitching with agitation. This is fucking weird. Eli is usually the calm one. Nothing can ruffle his Tennessee feathers.

I glance between them. "If you two insist on being miserable sods, I'll go home, shall I?"

Neither of them responds.

"We should be celebrating. It's senior year – nothing but one endless party. Or are you two threatened by my presence? I understand completely – there will be less hot women to go around now that I'm back."

The glass weighs a hundred pounds. I raise it to my lips, but I don't drink.

"Why are you back?" Eli fixes me with that stare of his, what I like to call his 'Sherlock-Holmes-Orgasm' face when I feel like pissing him off. Eli loves to figure things out, solve problems. He always wants to be the one to find a solution, which is a super-annoying trait in a friend when you're trying to hold your secrets close. "Aren't you supposed to be making a new record?"

"I *can* write music *and* go to school *and* continue to be the same lovable rogue who makes your lives worth living." I slump into a lawn chair, dangling the glass from my fingers. "It's called multitasking."

"Multitasking is a myth perpetuated by productivity gurus,"

Noah mutters without looking up. He makes a note in the margin of his book. "And you're a bastard."

What is going on here? "As much as I adore indulging in my favorite topic of conversation – myself – I want to know who shoved giant sticks up both your arses, and why they didn't call to let me in on the fun."

Nothing. Noah's shoulders tense, and Eli shifts his weight between his feet, glancing back at the tennis court like he wishes he succeeded in decapitating me.

I take a guess. "This is about the new girl, the Ice Queen?"

Eli stiffens, and I know I'm right.

Mmmmm. Mackenzie Malloy. Just thinking about those crimson lips, that haughty pout, the way she peers down that perky nose and makes lesser mortals quiver like jelly...

She's tempting. She's *dangerous*. I see myself reflected in those cold eyes. Behind that shell of ice, Mackenzie Malloy is bleeding on the inside. When her pain and my pain crash together, the world better watch out.

But I can't say that to these two, because you don't, do you? You can't talk to your mates about the dark things in the corner of your mind, about the wounds that cut where no one sees, about how nothing you do to yourself can ever hurt enough to make up for the pain you caused someone else. So instead I say what they expect me to say. "I bet the new girl is hot as fuck in the sack, as long as she doesn't give my dick frostbite."

"Don't talk about her like that," Eli snaps, then clamps his hand over his mouth.

With a snarl, Noah hurls his glass at Eli's head.

Eli ducks just in time, and the crystal hits the palm tree, shards raining down into the garden.

"What crawled up your ass and died?" Noah's usually a mess when he stresses about school, which is pointless because he'll probably be valedictorian unless Eli swipes the crown. But this is worse than I've ever seen him. "It's not as if you're lining up for a go. Or are you? And you're pissed I got in first. All's fair in love and war, and if it's any consolation, she seems immune to my many charms—"

Noah slams his book shut. He flashes me a murderous look and storms toward the house. While Eli watches him, I tip my Scotch into a planter box.

"Fuck, Gabe." Eli glares at me.

"What?" I pull a platter of cheese across the table and start loading up a cracker. Whenever we show up at Eli's house, his maid Maria throws food and drinks at us like she's afraid we're being starved. Maria was Eli's nanny, and she stayed around to look after the house when his dad went away. She still dotes on him like he's her own son – just as well, because Eli's mother's too busy with her yoga instructor to remember Eli exists. And Eli's dad… the less said about that sanctimonious wanker, the better.

"How can you be so dense?" Eli looks at me like I've sprouted tentacles. His Southern accent appears on the edges of his words. That only happens when he's upset. He assumes I don't notice shit like that, but I haven't made a career putting emotion to music by not noticing shit. "You can't talk to him like that. The new girl is Mackenzie Malloy. *Malloy.*"

Oh.

Shit.

"As in the Malloy's Supplements Malloys?" I ask, as if there could be any other Malloys that would elicit such a reaction from Noah.

Eli nods. "And you just told Noah all the ways you want to fuck her."

"All the ways I want to *shag* her. You Yanks have no sense of poetry." I lift an eyebrow. "But you're right. I'm an insensitive prick. I should've made the connection. Blame the distraction of

Mackenzie's glorious arse. I'll apologize to him. Later. When he's had a chance to cool off."

"That's good." Eli's looking out in the distance, and I know it's not Noah that's bothering him.

"What's up with you? Did the Ice Queen freeze your dick, too?"

"If I tell you something, do you swear you'll keep it to yourself?"

"Of course."

Eli grabs the bottle and pours himself another Scotch. I notice his hand shake, but I assume that's because the booze reminds him too much of his father. He leans back in the lounger and closes his eyes.

"We used to be friends."

"You and Ice Queen?" *Curious.*

Eli nods. He drains his glass. "We've been in the same classes since I can remember. One day at school, some kid made fun of my accent. Mackenzie stole the class snake and hid it on his chair. When he sat down, it bit him on the ass. We were friends ever since. But her parents and my dad had this stupid rivalry. Some kind of business deal that went sour when Dad first came to the city. I brought her over for dinner one night, and you'd have thought I proposed marrying a streetlamp the way they reacted. Our parents forbid us from being friends, so we hung out in secret."

"Noah doesn't know?"

Eli shook his head. "We didn't want to risk trusting anyone in case it got back to our parents, and then when it all happened with Noah's brother and her family disappeared, I *couldn't* tell him. You didn't know him then, but he barely held it together."

I grin. "Considering what a picture of mental fortitude he is now, I'll take your word for it."

"Anyway, I've been looking for her ever since she disappeared. I even hired a private detective last year, but he couldn't tell me anything. I'd given up hope of ever seeing her again. But today, she walks into school and looks at me like I'm scum. I tried texting on her old number, and I can see she read my message, but she hasn't replied. I can't understand it. Mackenzie and her parents have been missing for four years – what has to happen to a person to turn her into a stranger?"

I want to say that people are turning into strangers in front of you, every single day, and you don't notice until they've swallowed every pill in your stash and died in your arms in a rancid hotel bathroom. I want to say that sometimes you're closer to random people on the public bus than you are to the people you profess to love. (Not that I've ever ridden a public bus. Like a commoner. No thanks.)

I want to swipe the bottle from Eli's hand and toss the whole thing back, to feel the burn of whisky in my throat and the sweet oblivion that alcohol brings, the void of nothingness where I can live with myself until the hangover comes.

But that's fucking morose, and Eli already looks like he's fronting a 90s emo band, so I keep my mouth shut.

Eli stares at the sky. Notes dance around in my head – snatches of a song that might, in the hands of someone who hadn't completely bollocksed up his life, become something sorrowful and beautiful. But the notes are snatched away like a firefly snuffed out, and I'm left with only the darkness in my own head.

NOAH

Fuck you, Gabriel.

I bury my foot in the floor and yank the wheel, throwing the car around the corner at an irresponsible speed. The wind whips my hair across my face, and my chest squeezes tight. Red welts dance in front of my eyes, but I don't lift my foot from the accelerator until I see our house up ahead.

The wind does nothing to ease the heat of my rage. My fingers grip the steering wheel so hard they're numb. I wish I was numb.

I slide the Lambo into the garage beside Dad's Aston Martin and click the button to lower the doors. A breeze blows in from outside, fluttering the edge of the white cover that hides my brother's car. Dad gave him the keys to a Bugatti Veyron Vivere when he got his acceptance letter to Harvard – the dream car to go with Felix's full-ride athletic scholarship.

Now, the Veyron sits in the shadows, hidden beneath a shroud. Not unlike my brother.

I fling off my books and gym bag. They hit the wall with a *THUMP* and drop into a messy pile on the tiles – out of place, out of order. Like me. I don't stop to pick it up. Who cares? Some maid will be along to arrange my things in the neat little rows my father demands.

My shoes squeak on the tiles as I wander through the hallways, peering into the rooms, half-desperate to see another person, half-dreading what would happen when I do. The grandfather clock ticks in the foyer – the sound ricocheting like a gunshot through the silent rooms. When Felix was around, he made this house fun – we stood on either side of the grand staircase and tossed a football to each other and wrestled on the furniture until we broke expensive things and Mom yelled. But Felix's easy smile would always get us off the hook in the end.

Without that smile, this house is a Pharaoh's tomb – a shrine to a dead king. Everything and everyone inside made of shards of precious gems. Pretty to look at but broken, and liable to make you bleed.

I find my stepmother Grace in her drawing-room (she likes to call it that, says it makes her feel like the heroine in a gothic romance novel). She's curled up in a puddle of mink blankets on the window seat, one of her romance novels clutched between her fingers. Around her, the buttercup yellow walls and pastel-pink furniture pulse in my vision. Today, even this cheery room has a sinister quality.

Grace reminds me so much of my mother, with her dark curls falling over her soft features in a curtain. It makes sense that she does, since she's my mother's younger sister. My dad married her only two years after Mom died. I might've been angry about that, like I'm angry about most things, but having Grace around is one of the only things that keeps me sane. Sometimes she smiles my mother's smile at me, with the dimple in her left cheek, and the pain in my chest twists – a knife cutting deeper. I'd worry about it slicing out my heart, but I have no heart left.

I hover in the doorway, watching Grace read. I battle with

the words I need to say. She senses my presence, looks up from her book. The smile that tugs at her dusk-pink lips is the only genuine thing in this house. "Noah, you're home."

I shrug off my backpack and slide in beside her, wrapping her into my arms. She's so small, so fragile. It feels like she might shatter into pieces at any moment. In reality, Grace is the one holding things together – she pulls Dad's rage and my darkness into herself, and gives back only light. But even her light gets lost in the void where my heart used to be.

Sometimes, I forget that Grace lost everything too.

"How was school?" she asks.

"Fine. Track trials are next Thursday. I'm going to work with Eli on my 400m every day after school."

"You don't have to make track, Noah." She squeezes me extra hard. "You could go back to swimming—"

"No." The word comes out harsh, final. I'll never get back in the water again. Not after it took my mother.

"—or something different? As long as you have something on your college application. It doesn't have to be track—"

"I enjoy track. Well, not the 400m," I try to smile, but I'm pretty sure it comes out as a grimace. I haven't smiled in so long I don't think the muscles work any longer. "Don't worry about me. I'm fine."

"It's my job to worry about you. Tell me something happy." She peers up at me with my mother's eyes. "Are there any girls after you?"

Mackenzie's face flickers in my mind. I stiffen.

I swallow. "Is Dad home?"

She nods. "I saw him head into the reception room."

Of course. The grand sitting room where Dad receives foreign dignitaries and state officials, where he introduced Felix to all the important people who were going to help him succeed. Dad's never far from that room now. Sometimes, when I sneak down to his study in the night to steal his alcohol, I see him sitting on the sofa in his boxers, staring up at the portrait, mourning his shattered dreams.

I know I have to tell him. I don't want to; fuck, I'd rather stick my hand on a hot stove than tell him. But if I don't, he'll find out anyway, and then he'll be pissed at me for not telling him.

I slink away from Grace. I can't bear to feel her warmth with Mackenzie's face in my head. "I need to talk to him."

"Don't upset him. It hasn't been a good day."

I stiffen, my hand on the door. *It hasn't been a good day.* I know what that means.

I'm worse than useless. I can't help Grace. I can't save my father from himself. Grief takes many shapes – Grace's grief follows her like a friendly ghost, touching her hands with kindness. Mine is a noose around my neck and a red mist that shrouds my vision before I throw a punch.

Dad's grief has transformed him into a monster.

I drag my feet as I approach the reception room. My fingers curl around the doorframe. Dad stands beside the fire, a whisky glass in his fingers. He grips it so hard his knuckles are white. He doesn't look up when I enter.

I stand behind the sofa, gripping the carved back so I don't fall over under the weight of Felix's presence. My brother's portrait hangs over the fireplace – he's practically life-sized, painted in photographic detail with a dramatic sky behind him. I can practically hear the crowd roaring as his results are announced – not only did that famous throw qualify him for the Olympic team, but he broke a national record.

The painter had every detail right – except for the eyes. Felix's eyes were always warm, kind, shimmering with light, like dipping your feet into the emerald water at the beach on a hot summer's day. But the Felix in the portrait has Dad's eyes – cold, stormy, demanding.

"Dad." The word catches in my throat. He makes no movement, no sign he registers I'm here.

I cough, swallow, try again. "Dad, Mackenzie Malloy is back at school."

There. It's out.

I can't take it back now.

Dad's shoulders stiffen.

He turns to me, but he can't meet my gaze. He stares past me, doesn't see me.

His coldness breaks something inside me. The red mist falls over my eyes. I need *answers*. "Did you know about this? Did you hear anything? What about her parents? She didn't say—"

"Don't go anywhere near her," he rasps. The sound is a snake, coiling through the silent house, wrapping around my chest and squeezing the void until the sides collapse in.

"What?"

"You stay away from Mackenzie Malloy."

For the first time in months, in years, he tilts that aristocratic chin of his to meet my eyes. Cold green orbs study me, his one remaining son, and I catch the glimmer of a secret burning away the edges, eating my father from within.

He turns away, but it's too late. I've seen.

It's not rage in burning at the edges of his eyes.

It's not hatred that tenses every muscle in his body, that tears the glass from his fingers and hurls it into the fire.

It's *fear*.

MACKENZIE

*A*lec LeMarque wastes no time in exacting his revenge.

When I walk into Stonehurst Prep the next morning, all eyes turn toward me. Conversations stop. My footsteps echo along the hallway. It's worse than yesterday – the stares, the whispers, the judgment.

I square my shoulders and toss my hair. I spent an hour in the bathroom with a YouTube makeup tutorial, and I know I look *fierce*. My skirt hugs my hips, the hem just high enough that anyone looking can catch a glimpse of the garters holding up my thigh-high socks. I've got my spike-heeled boots because to hell with Mrs. Foster's write-up.

I am Alec LeMarque's wet dream, and he can't touch me.

I'm Mackenzie Malloy, and I've donned my armor, ready for battle.

I pretend their judgment means nothing. I pretend that I revel in their attention. I pretend I crave the eyeballs that crawl over my skin like ants seeking their next snack.

When I arrive at my locker, there's a photograph tacked to the grating. It's my face Photoshopped onto a porn star taking it in the ass from a fat guy in a bondage suit. I have to hand it to whoever created it – they did an impressive Photoshop job. As I tear the photograph down, snickers erupt along the hall.

Behind the photograph, someone scrawled 'Mackenzie is a ghost slut' in blood-red paint. I scratch the edge with my nail. Yeah, that's not coming off.

Fine. Whatever. If this is the worst they've got, I'll be their ghost slut. They think this is going to chink my armor. They have no fucking idea what I've seen, what I've *done*.

All I need to do is graduate. I'm here for that high school diploma and nothing else. I can get it with graffiti on my locker.

I can do that with Alec LeMarque's dagger in my back.

I touch my fingers to my chest, over where my locket hangs beneath my shirt.

I'm Mackenzie Malloy, the richest, most badass bitch of you all, and I can do *anything*.

I toss the photograph in the trash and open my locker. The hinges squeak, and the sniggers grow louder. I turn my back to the corridor. I'm not afraid of who's lurking behind me. I've already met the people who hunt in the shadows, and they're on *my* side of this war.

As I pick up my books for first and second period, my fingers brush the knife Antony gave me. I leave it where it is, tucked behind my makeup case. I don't need it.

Yet.

"Mackenzie." My name sounds like the dull thud of a bullet striking flesh. I brace myself for trouble as I turn my head just enough to see who calls me.

Elias. He's pushing his way through the students, shoving aside heiresses and child actors like they're trash (which they are). His handsome face is tight with concern, that stone jaw clenched, that too-pretty mouth turned down.

A dark twisted part of me – the part that isn't head bitch Mackenzie Malloy, but a lonely girl who's lived in a silent house for too long – aches to run to Eli, to have those muscled arms wrap around me and hold me close, to feel those pretty lips brush mine, to know what it feels like to be safe. That's what Eli looks like to me – someone steady and sure. And it's not just because of that faint familiarity of him – Eli seems like a person who always has to fix things, to avenge wrongs, to put the world back in order again.

But that safety would be a lie.

The only way to be truly safe is to keep guys like Eli away from me.

I slam my locker shut, ignoring Eli's shouts. I stalk down the hall, following the snickers toward the grand staircase. I turn to follow the stream of students ascending, and that's when I see him – Alec LeMarque leans against his locker on the end of the row, surrounded by guys who look like Beverly Hills 90210 castoffs. He catches my eye, and a dark smile twists across his face, creasing the edge of the dressing covering his nose.

I toss my hair. I want him to know how little I've thought about what I did to him.

My heel lands on the first step. Alec strides toward me. I move faster, but not fast enough. He throws his arm out, cutting me off. His fingers curl around my wrist – his skin cold and slimy. It feels like he's crawling over me, inside me. That touch stirs a memory – the glint of a knife in the shadows, dark blood splattered across my reflection, splinters digging under my nails.

Blood rushes to my head, pounding against my temples. Alec leans close, his breath hot on my face. I straddle two worlds – the memory of screaming into the dark, the need to be strong in the light – and when I glare back at Alec, I'm not sure if I'm seeing him, or another, more dangerous enemy.

"You broke my nose, bitch." If he's trying to sound tough, he fails. His voice is comically nasal from the damage I did.

"Is it bitch or slut? If you're going to be so unoriginal with your insults, at least make up your mind." I keep my eyes fixed on his. "And you broke your own nose. Don't touch a woman without her permission."

I stare down at his fingers, still curled around my wrist. I itch to break them all. It will only take a moment, and Alec would be on the ground in front of all his friends, howling in pain. But then I'd be back in the principal's office, and I am not going to get kicked out of Stonehurst Prep on my second day because of Alec LeMarque.

So I remain still, neutral, ready to strike if Alec decides to make a monumental mistake. I can see the indecision in his eyes – the desire to make me pay versus the social capital he'd lose if he hits me in front of a crowd of spectators. He doesn't know what to make of this girl who should desire him, who should fall over backward to give him whatever he wants.

"I don't need *permission*," he hisses. "I own this school. I'll make your life a living hell, and don't you forget it."

The urge to laugh bubbles up inside me, but I stamp it down. This pampered ass playing at the bad boy wouldn't know hell if it stole his fancy car. *I* know hell. After what I've been through, I'm pretty certain I could run the place. But laughing in Alec's face right now will only bring down trouble, and I've had enough of that to last two lifetimes.

"Let go of her."

Alec stiffens. I don't have to turn around to know who spoke those words.

Eli.

I don't drop my gaze from Alec, but I watch Eli out of the corner of my eye as he stands beside me, broad shoulders casual, that half-smile tugging at his mouth like this is no big deal to him. His arm brushes mine, and it's all I can do not to fling myself at him; that's how safe he feels.

Alec's eyes fall to Eli. Ribbons of tension coil between them.

This is new territory for me, this standoff. It's like dogs fighting over a juicy bone. I've never been anyone's bone before. The dark part of me – the same part that remembers the blood splattered on my reflection, the weight of earth pressing down on my tomb – likes it, but only if Eli wins.

"This isn't your business, Hart." Alec tries to smile, but it comes out more like a grimace. My skin buzzes with an electrical charge – a surge of power clashing as the two of them face off. Or maybe it's Eli's arm resting against mine. Maybe it's the hint of danger in his friendly eyes – that carefully constructed facade of gentility crumbling away to reveal the feral animal beneath.

Eli tilts his head to the side, his tone friendly, his words anything but. "You've got your hand on a woman who's not yours, and violence in your eyes. I consider that my business. Let go of her."

Alec's mouth twists up as he weighs his options. Two of his friends step forward, but from behind Eli, I notice a shadow move. Gabriel slouches up to my other side, peering down at Alec from over a pair of aviator sunglasses. With his leather jacket slung over his shoulder and the tattoos peeking out from his collar and cuffs, he looks tough as shit, but I doubt Gabriel would ever get into a fight and risk messing up his hair.

He doesn't need to. At Stonehurst, power doesn't come from your fists, and Gabriel has power Alec can't buy.

A murmur ripples through the hall. Everyone has noticed who stands on my side. Alec's two friends step back. Alec flings my arm down like he can't stand to touch my skin any longer. "Well, Ice Queen. I see you put out for Hart and Fallen. Perhaps it is ghost *slut* after all."

A snarl escapes my lips before I can stop it. Alec laughs as he turns back to his friends, but they slink off down the hall. There's a palpable release of tension in the air, and students turn back to their friend groups. A warm hand slides up my arm. Eli's dark eyes are full of concern. "He didn't hurt you?"

Gabriel throws his arm around me. "I think Alec was the one in danger from Mackintosh here."

It's on the tip of my tongue to thank them, but Mackenzie Malloy doesn't thank people who come to her rescue – they're doing a public service. So instead I fix Gabriel with my super-human glare. "Don't call me Mackintosh."

"Why not? It suits you. A macintosh is what we English gentlemen wear outside when Mother Nature decides to piss all over us. You're just like a mackintosh because you scare the rain away with your sunny disposition."

I can't help it. A laugh leaps out of me before I can stamp it down. Eli looks taken aback, while Gabe looks delighted. Behind them, Coal-Eyes lingers, glowering at me. I wonder how long he's been there, and if his presence has anything to do with Alec fucking off.

"You laughed." Gabriel squeezes me tighter. My whole body floods with warmth as the Alec incident flees my mind. "That means your nickname is official, *Mac*. That's the rules, right, Eli?"

Eli nods. He's studying me in that way of his, searching for answers to a question I don't understand. It's hella intimate and kinda sexy in this possessive, fucked-up way.

"That's a terrible nickname. I refuse to accept it." I fold my arms and glare at them both, but there's no fire behind it. I'm not supposed to be doing this, getting close to people. I'm not supposed to have nicknames. And yet, I can't bring myself to fling away Gabriel's arm. I'm only human. "Try again."

"No can do, Mac. Those are the nickname rules," Eli's smiling too, and it's this warm, bright smile that turns my insides out. I don't think anyone's ever smiled at me like that before. "You should be happy. The first nickname Gabriel ever gave me was God Almighty, because he thinks I sound like a TV preacher. I'm *so* grateful he spread that one to the track team in our freshman year and then left for tour before I could force him to undo the chaos he wrought."

Next to Gabriel's aristocratic voice, the twang of Eli's Southern roots is more pronounced. I get the sense that he tries to hide it behind an affected Californian accent. I never thought a guy like Eli Hart, who seems so popular and at ease with himself, would be self-conscious about anything.

At the mention of the tour, Gabriel stiffens. A dark shadow shrouds his eyes. I think of what I read in the news about the drummer from Octavia's Ruin, and realize that for all his silliness, Gabriel was still dealing with the aftermath of that horror. The darkness is gone in a moment, and the fun, flirty Gabriel is back. "I can't take all the blame for that one," Gabriel claps a hand on his friend's shoulder. "I might've planted the seed, but Noah was the one who yelled 'God Almighty' when you won that meet and spread the name to all the other schools."

They both glance over at Coal-Eyes. So, his name is Noah. It suits him, somehow. Gabriel's eyes flicker nervously back to Eli. There's a silent conversation going on between the three of them – a battle of wills over an outcome I cannot fathom.

Noah glares at his friends and, with a final fiery draft of hatred in my direction, he shoves past us and storms off.

"Don't mind him," Eli says, his eyes searching me again. "He thinks you're responsible..."

He trails off, his eyes flicking back to Noah. An awkward silence descends over the three of us.

"I have to go." I shrug Gabriel off. I can't stand to look into Eli's eyes any longer. This is too much, too weird. *Responsible for what?*

"See you in homeroom, *Mac*," Gabriel yells after me as I disappear into the bathroom.

"Mackenzie, wait," Eli says.

I don't wait.

I hide in a stall until the bell rings. In homeroom, students slide their desks away from me. I carry a bad smell around this school – I reek of trouble. I've only been here a day, and I have the blood of their king on my hands. Wisely, they choose to avoid me.

Well, most of them. Gabriel slumps into the seat beside me, and I catch a flash of his wicked smile before I angle my body away from him.

"You can't ignore me forever, Mac," he whispers in my ear. "It's better to give up now, because I have a black belt in annoying the shit out of people until they pay attention to me."

I stare at my books. Why does he have to be at this school?

Gabriel Fallen isn't supposed to be a person. He's an idea – a wonderful, discordant, calamitous *creation*. His music is the only thing that got me through the nights where the dark and loneliness clawed at me, leaving my skin torn in ribbons, my organs exposed. I'd turn on my headphones or the house speaker system and Gabriel's voice made me feel... seen. He made me feel *real* – like I could separate the pieces of myself from my stolen life.

He's not supposed to be a flirty guy with a touch that burns so good.

They say you shouldn't meet your idols because they always disappoint. But I can't imagine Gabriel Fallen ever disappointing anyone. Not with that wicked mouth and those long fingers. Not with the mind that forms such beautiful lyrics and those slate eyes that see more than they let on.

I try to focus on what Mr. Ross is droning on about – tickets for a senior class trip to Germany over the semester break available on the school app. It's not compulsory, but judging from the excited conversations around me, everyone will be going.

Not me – I'd be working for one of Antony's contacts that week, to try to make enough cash to pay the power bill for the rest of the year. Even though I drained the pool and turned off the circuit breakers in the wings I don't use, the house still costs an insane amount to run, especially because I need to keep at least some of the security features operating.

At lunch, I pile my plate with food and make a beeline for the outdoor area. Unfortunately, that means walking past Alec's table. Even that wouldn't be so bad – I can handle Alec – but it also means coming into range of Eli's savior complex and Noah's dagger eyes. That guy oozes hatred from every pore. If only I knew why all his rage is directed my way.

He believes I'm responsible... for what?

It doesn't matter. Eli and Noah are not my problem. All I'm here to do is graduate.

I'm Mackenzie Malloy, and I don't need anyone.

The more I repeat the mantra to myself, the less I believe it.

Now I see why the popular kids chose that particular table. Anyone wanting to eat in the quad has to walk past them. Two geeky-looking guys peel off the line in front of me and set off at a brisk pace, but Alec looks up at them like a hunter with prey in his sights, and at the last minute they veer off and take the unoccupied table in the corner. I see a girl in a wheelchair struggling to balance her tray on her knees while she wheels over the bump. Alec tosses a spitball at her head. It sticks in her hair. Her shoulders tighten. The wheels of her chair squeal as she surges forward, and she's free.

Lucky bitch.

I try to sneak out behind her, but no such luck. Alec slides off the end of the table and stands in front of me, leaning in close. "Where you going, Malloy?"

"To eat my lunch. Far away from you."

Noah stands up, his shoulders tense, his eyes charcoal tossed in flames – a dark void of hatred ringed in fire. No way do I want another confrontation with him. I can't see Gabriel anywhere, and Eli's down at the other end of the table. He stands up, too, but he's hemmed in by a group of girls. Besides, I don't need Eli to rescue me.

"Fine." I whirl around and stomp out of the dining hall, tray in my hands. A waiter yells that I'm not allowed to take food from the hall, but who the fuck cares? I stalk down the corridor to the bathroom, kick open the nearest toilet door, and lock it behind me. I flip the toilet seat down, balance the tray on my knees, and pick up my knife and fork with shaking hands.

I hide in that stall as other female students come and go, trying in vain to get the fire in Noah's eyes to stop scorching my veins. But it's no good – I'm intrigued by his ire. And by what Eli started to say, "He holds you responsible."

What am I responsible for?

I pull out my phone and do a quick search of the Stonehurst website and social media. He's not hard to spot – Noah Marlowe's statuesque features stand out from every image. He's president of the student council, captain of the debate society, and the center of attention at every party and social event. Noah Marlowe, son of Senator John Marlowe, a deep-pocket alumnus of the school. Now that I have Noah's last name, I Google him, just to see what comes up.

Most kids our age don't have much of an internet presence beyond social media pages. I'm the exception – at least, I thought I was. I'm surprised at the number of hits that come up for Noah. All of them news articles about a court case from four years ago.

I click on one and start to read:

–following the death of his son, Felix Marlowe, aged 18, Senator John Marlowe has sued Howard Malloy, billionaire CEO of the nutritional supplement company Malloy International, for negligence –

citing supplements supplied to his teenage son during an unregulated trial were responsible for his death. The case will be heard on Friday, with key testimony for the prosecution coming from 13-year-old Noah Marlowe, John Marlowe's surviving son.

I scroll down to another article from a few months later. My father won the case. The Marlowes claim of negligence couldn't be proved. The accompanying photograph shows Noah – younger, but just as dark and brooding and beautiful, exiting the courtroom with a beautiful raven-haired woman on his arm. His mother, Corrine, according to the captain. Another article, from two months after that. CORRINE MARLOWE DROWNS HERSELF IN FAMILY SWIMMING POOL.

My head spins. Fuck. So much death. So much pain. Everything I read I already knew – Noah spoke it through his eyes. I'd unwittingly enrolled myself at the same school as a guy who blames my family for the death of his brother *and* his mother. No wonder Noah hates me. I'd hate me.

Fuck, fuckedy, fucklestein.

I have to be careful. I have to stay out of his way – Noah Marlowe has already made it clear that he'd take great delight in ruining everything for me. I'm not going to give him the chance.

MACKENZIE

My alarm rings. Queen Boudica gives a 'mew' of disgust and snuggles against me. All I want to do is scoop her up in my arms and go back to sleep.

Groaning, I tear her off my face and dump her unceremoniously on the pillow. "I'm sorry. Blame Stonehurst – their stupid rules say cat gravity is not an acceptable excuse for tardiness."

Queen Boudica burrows her head back under the covers, turning her butt to me and holding her tail up. It's the cat version of giving me the finger. I grin as I pull on my uniform and start the process of painting on my armor. That cat couldn't be more perfect for me if she tried.

Even with my alarm set extra early, I struggle to get out the door on time. I don't really want to face Stonehurst Prep, but I have no choice.

As I'm jogging up the into school, Alec LeMarque steps out from behind a pillar, ruining my day before I'm even inside. He blocks the doorway with his bulk, leaning into my personal space in a way that instantly puts my back up.

"I think we got off on the wrong foot, Malloy." Alec's smile makes my blood freeze. He shoves his hands in the pocket of his letterman jacket, which the school jocks are allowed to wear instead of their blazer. "I'm having a few friends around to my place tonight – pretty casual. It'll be fun. You should be there."

"I'm busy." I try to step around him, but he shifts his weight to block my escape.

"I don't think you understand." He's still trying to be friendly, but beneath his facade simmers the full force of his humiliation. The dressing on his nose tugs up at the side. "It's not your fault. You've been in the Caribbean or fucking Siberia or whatever, so allow me to help you out. I'll throw a bitch a bone. In this school, this town, it's all about who you know. You used to be somebody, Mackenzie Malloy, but now you're just a freak ghost slut. I'm the guy you want on your side. Being my friend will give you all the connections you need to survive at Stonehurst. So, what do you say? Will I see you tonight?"

"She can't. She's hanging out with me."

A warm arm drapes over my shoulder. Gabriel Fallen faces off against Alec with his chin cocked and that aristocratic smirk on his lips – the one that carries all the power of the lord of the manor demanding loyalty from his serfs.

She's hanging with me.

"She your girl, Fallen?" Alec flashes him a smile that's all teeth and violence.

Gabriel shakes his head. His cheek presses against mine, and the touch feels so intimate it sends a shiver of desire through my veins. "Mackenzie Malloy is no one's girl."

I turn to Gabriel, pushing through my fangirling to flash him a wicked smile. "You took the words right out of my mouth, Fallen."

Gabriel turns back to Alec. "So, if we're done here, Mac and I have to get to homeroom."

I want to groan at that stupid nickname, but Gabriel shoves Alec aside and barges into Stonehurst, dragging me behind him.

Students gape at us, stepping aside to make room. From the way he smiles and preens, Gabriel's used to all eyes watching him, but I've lived alone in an empty house for four years, and it freaks me out.

"You don't have to save me," I hiss. My skin crawls as their eyes rake over me.

"Maybe I wasn't saving you. Maybe I wanted to have the pleasure of your company." Gabriel winks as he slides his arm from around me and leans against Eli's locker.

Fuck, the way he says 'the pleasure of your company' in that British accent of his... I need to rescue this situation. I'm in serious danger of falling hard for this guy, the exact guy who could end up destroying me. I open my locker and collect the books I need. "I'm not hanging out with you tonight."

"Sure you are," he grins. "We have our chemistry make-up."

Fuck. I completely forgot. An hour being stuck in the chemistry lab with Gabriel. I lean my head against my locker, allowing the cold metal to drop my body temperature. This is a bad bad bad idea. But no matter how many times I say that to myself, when I think about Gabriel's eyes fixed on mine with such interest and the feeling of his arm around me, I can't see how it can possibly be bad.

I'm in trouble.

I need a cold shower and—

My locker door slams into my face, knocking the sense back into me.

"Ow." I grab my throbbing nose with one hand and lean back to see who wants to die today. I find myself facing off against a girl who belongs on a magazine cover – deeply tanned skin, pouty lips, sleek black hair straight out of a shampoo commercial. She's flanked by a triangle of other girls – their faces caked in makeup, their hair perfectly styled. Some of them wear cheerleading jackets over their uniform blazers. But my focus is on their leader.

"Oops." She smirks, flicking her hair over her shoulder. Every strand falls perfectly in place, like it's too afraid to disobey her. "I didn't see you there. Melrose, was it?"

"Mackenzie."

"Oh, right. *Mackenzie*." She says my name like she's talking about a new type of bathroom cleaner. "Mackenzie Malloy. The girl who *used* to be somebody. Allow me to reintroduce myself, since you seem to have forgotten the way things work around here. I'm Cleo St. James. That's short for Cleopatra. As in, the Queen. It's an appropriate name, because I'm Queen of this school."

Jeez, what is it with these people and royalty? "That's... quite some introduction."

"I couldn't help but notice you draping yourself over Gabriel." She rolls her eyes. "You've been on a desert island or a mental asylum or whatever, so I don't know if you know this, but we don't appreciate it when crazy bitches break people's noses just for being friendly. You should apologize to Alec – your actions cost him an important audition."

Is this bitch serious? "I don't appreciate it when people try to intimidate me because I don't want to sleep with them, so Alec can shove my apology up his ass. Why has he sent you to bother me? Are you his secretary?"

Cleo's eyes narrow. "I thought we should get to know each other again, since you seem determined to make enemies of people who should have been your friends. Your father may have been a big shot, but he's old news now, and you're *nothing*. I will make your life a living hell, *Melrose*, unless you step in line. That includes staying away from Gabriel Fallen."

I slam my locker shut. "You choose my friends now? I'd have

thought you wouldn't have much spare time between plotting the downfall of Rome and bathing in your ass milk."

Behind me, Gabriel snorts, and I get a little flutter of excitement that I made Gabriel Fallen laugh.

"I'm telling you this out of the kindness of my heart." The smile Cleo gives me is anything but kind. "I know what you're feeling – Gabriel's pretty and famous and he makes you feel special. But you're not special – you're the ghost slut, and he's only after you because he wants to be the first to fuck the mysterious girl. He'll use you and spit you out and leave you a bloody mess, just like he's done with every girl in our year. Leave him for the woman who can handle him."

From the way her eyes raked over Gabriel, I knew she meant herself.

Gabriel gives a dark chuckle. "That's a rather revisionist view, Cleo. If I recall, you broke into my hotel room after junior prom, and when I politely declined, you *pushed me through the French doors* and cut yourself on the glass. I may be a man whore, but I don't do crazy."

One of Cleo's minions giggles, but a stern look from Cleo soon puts a stop to that. She turns back to me and addresses us both in a sickly sweet voice. "I'm talking to Melrose now, Gabe. But we should catch up later, *in private.* I want to hear all about your tour. Now that no-good druggie drummer is out of your life, maybe you'll have more time for your *real* friends."

Gabriel stiffens. My blood boils. If this girl is sinking her claws into Gabriel, she should at least bother to know something about him. I've read every press interview and seen hundreds of YouTube clips of Gabriel and Dylan playing and laughing and crying together. They'd been friends since they were in diapers. Gabriel has to be cut up about Dylan's death, and Cleo can't even figure that out?

I meet Cleo's glare with one of my own – a glare that would reduce a lesser mortal to a puddle of goo, but Cleo wouldn't be so easy to break. "Look, I don't know what you think you're achieving here. I'm not after your crown or your man. Gabriel can make his own decisions, although if he wants to avoid venereal disease, he should probably keep away from you. On account of the ass milk."

Gabriel is laughing so hard his whole body trembles, but no one else dares. There's an intake of breath from Cleo's minions and the surrounding students.

Cleo smirks. "You think you can walk back in here and own this school? I know you believe you're special because you disappeared for four years. You were probably in Tijuana getting your nose and boobs done." She gives this condescending nod to my chest. "You should go back. They're uneven, and no one wants you here. Go back to being a ghost slut, and stay away from Gabriel."

No one wants you here.

The words coil around my heart, squeezing the air from my lungs. *I'm unwanted.* That word brings up all kinds of pre-coffin shit I didn't want to think about right now. I don't know what I expected, showing up at Stonehurst during senior year, where everyone else knows each other, has this history, has this sense of the way things should be. I should have known I couldn't fade into the background.

But I came anyway, and as much as I tell myself it's to achieve what Antony and I need, I know that's not the whole truth. Deep down, I'm sick of being lonely. I'm sick of empty rooms and playing music at top volume to drown out the darkness and the voices in my head. I'm sick of staring at the fancy dining table that seats twenty or sprawling out on the monster sofa in the games room and wondering what it would be like to add a player two to a video game.

I want everything I can't have. The loneliness that is

crushing me also protects me. And I've gone and cracked that shit wide open. A single tear leaks out of the corner of my eye.

I blink the tear away, but it's too late. Cleo's seen my weakness, and she pounces. "Poor little ghost slut, crying because she can't handle it out here in the real world. Go back to the shadows where you belong. And leave Gabriel alone – he's *mine*."

Before I can formulate a scathing response, Cleo turns on her heel and trots away, ass swinging. The girls behind her all turn in unison, like this was a carefully choreographed act to impart maximum humiliation, and stomp after her.

I glance at Gabriel, blinking away the tear before he sees it. He shakes his head. "Cleo's rolled out the red carpet to welcome you, Mac."

"I'm not afraid of her."

"Really? I am." Gabriel shudders. "She may look like just another mean girl on a power trip, but Cleo St. James is batshit crazy, and not in a fun way. If you want me to stop bugging you, bring the heat off—"

"Hell no." I lace my arm in Gabriel's. He grins as we walk together in the direction of homeroom. "Cleopatra doesn't scare me."

But after our run-in with Cleo, Gabriel's subdued. He doesn't joke and flirt with me in homeroom or first period. He takes his books out and hunches over them, but I can see him doodling in the margins instead of working. I see too, that everyone around him whispers about him, watching him out of the corners of their eyes. I hear my name on their lips, as well as Dylan's.

I wonder if this is Gabriel's way of trying to take me out of the spotlight, or if it has something to do with what Cleo said about Dylan.

I can't pretend I know anything about what he's going through. I'd never found my best friend ODed in my hotel bathroom with a suicide note blaming me. Hell, I've never even had a best friend, unless I count Queen Boudica. But I do know a little bit about being infamous, about living your worst nightmares in the press for all to see.

Everyone in this school knows this horrible truth about Gabriel, and they know a completely different truth about me. They circle us both like sharks, waiting for us to tire, before they gobble up every broken piece of us that's left.

MACKENZIE

I debate skipping out on the chemistry make-up session, but I'm three days into class and already so behind that I know I'm in danger of flunking out if I don't put some work in. All I have to do is follow the written directions and write down what I observe. How hard can it be?

Next to impossible when faced with the glory that is Gabriel Fallen. As soon as I walk in the door to the lab, he's putting on a show for me. He has his lab coat on backward and his aviators on and he's spiked his shoulder-length hair so it sticks out at all angles. He holds up a test tube and announces in a trembling voice, "My greatest creation. It's aliiiiiiive."

"You're ridiculous." I roll my eyes as I slide my seat away from him. That scent of him swirls around me – the smoke and sugar of heathen debauchery. All the dark and tempting promises of his music drip from him, and I want to surrender to it. Instead, I pick up the worksheet containing the experiment we're supposed to complete and start measuring out the different chemicals.

"What are you talking about? This is my serious student face." Gabriel purses his lips. "I copied it from Eli."

"It needs some work." I stare down at the page in a vain attempt to keep myself from laughing. "It looks like someone's shoved a cantaloupe up your rectum."

"A cantaloupe?" Gabriel slides in beside me. "That's awfully specific. Do you have a lot of practice shoving spherical fruit into forbidden orifices?"

His arm brushes mine, and my skin crawls with heat. I look toward the windows – anywhere to avoid meeting Gabriel's eyes, because I don't trust myself around him right now – and see Eli and Noah walking across the quad, surrounded by their popular friends. Cleo hangs off Noah's arm, but his eyes are fixed on the classroom. On me and Gabriel. And he looks *murderous*.

"Your friend doesn't like me."

Gabriel looks up and sees his friends. He grins wickedly and flips Noah off. Noah frowns and returns the gesture, but I can tell from the tightness in his shoulders that this isn't friendly ribbing. Noah doesn't want Gabriel to hang out with me.

Cleo looks over and sees us. She shakes her head at me as if to say, 'what will I do with you?' Great. I'll pay for this later. Now Eli's looking, also great. He gives this friendly wave that makes my chest tight. The last time someone waved at me... I can't even remember. I whirl around to face the experiment again. No point wishing for what can't be.

"Noah's got a wicked hate on for you," Gabriel muses as he makes a table for our results on the back of the worksheet.

I grunt in reply. There's nothing else to say about it. If I were Noah, I'd hate me too. "Noah's your friend. You don't share his hate?"

There's a darkness in Gabriel's voice as he says, "I long ago gave up on letting other people dictate my life."

Gabriel's lyrics fill my head, the chorus to my favorite Octavia's Ruin song, 'Dance Macabre.'

You're the Senator and I'm the slave.

Watch me dance for your amusement.
We'll have a royal rave,
While Rome burns all around.

When Gabriel sings that song, there's a bite to his words, a bitterness that seeps into every note. Suddenly, I have to dig. I need to know if what I feel when I listen to his music is real, or if it's all an act he creates to sell records.

"So how come you're here?" Our mixture fizzes, but doesn't explode. I make a note on Gabriel's table. "Surely you'd rather be in the studio or on tour rather than at school. It's not like you need a high school diploma."

Gabriel's easy expression doesn't change, but there's a prickle in the air that wasn't there before. "I know you're a Ruins fan, Mac. You must have heard about Dylan."

"I did. It's terrible that he died. He was an amazing drummer, and I know he was your friend. But the band's still together, right? You'll find a new drummer and finish the album?"

Gabriel hums under his breath as he lights the Bunsen burner and rearranges the test tubes. "I haven't decided. That's why I'm here. Stonehurst is as good a place as any to figure out my next move, certainly better than enduring my parents back in England."

"The music press is talking like you're already hunkered down in a studio in Paris."

"Yes. Well, they don't know everything about me." Gabriel rests his chin in his hands and stares into the flame of the Bunsen burner. A shadow hoods his eyes. It's gone in an instant, but too late – I've seen it. I recognize it – the mirror image of a shadow that's haunted me ever since the night Antony dug me out of my own grave.

It's the shadow of regret and grief and misery so dark and so deep that it's impossible to see a way out.

I nod. "I can relate to that."

More than you can ever guess.

Gabriel flashes me that panty-melting smile, only this time it's tainted by the melancholy in his eyes. And I see him as he truly is – not Gabriel the rockstar, but Gabriel the human raging over the death of his friend – and I understand just how much of his wildness is a mask.

Something happened the night Dylan died, and whatever it was, Gabriel's here at Stonehurst trying to escape it.

MACKENZIE

I balance my lunch tray on my knees and struggle to open my mayonnaise packet. It's Monday of my second week at Stonehurst Prep, and I've got my routine down. I arrive at school just as the bell rings, avoid Eli, avoid Noah, peel pornographic stickers off my locker, nod hello to Gabriel in homeroom, go to class, stare blankly at the teachers as they blather on about stuff I don't understand, eat my lunch in the bathroom, repeat the blathering and blank staring, sneak through the wooded area at the rear of Malloy Manor to escape the attention of press encamped by the gate, curl up with Queen Boudica and stare blankly at homework, try not to think about Eli, Gabriel, and Noah. Rinse, repeat, blah, blah, blah.

When the stupid tab refuses to tear, I hold it in my teeth and yank. My elbow bumps the tray, sending my fork skittering across the tiles.

"Fuck." I may be the embodiment of pathetic right now, but no way am I eating with a fork that's fallen on the floor.

"Here."

I nearly jump out of my skin as a hand thrusts under the gap in the stall, holding a new, non-gross fork.

What the fuck?

"Shit." I capture my tray in both hands before it slides off my knees. The fork hangs there. The fingers gripping it are thin, elegant, tipped with black-and-white striped nail polish.

I exit my stall and thump my fist on the next door. "Open up."

There's a click, and a few moments later the door swings inward, revealing a girl holding a tray. She stands up as I lean against the door, and I find that even with my medium height, she only just reaches my shoulder. She's got chin-length hair dyed in streaks of blue and purple, all done in feathery layers, and emerald piercings through her pixie nose. I notice her white socks aren't the uniform standard, but instead covered with tiny green aliens.

Her eyes widen as she takes me in. She looks *exactly* like the kind of person I'd expect to be eating in the bathroom. Which also means she's fascinating to me.

"Um... hi, Mackenzie," she says in a breathless whisper. "I...I grabbed an extra fork by mistake."

"You know who I am?"

"Of course. You broke Alec's nose." Her eyes widen. "It was awesome."

I cock an eyebrow at her. "You're the only one in this school who thinks so."

"That's because Alec's..." she snaps her mouth shut, as though she was going to say something but changed her mind. "He's the son of Mark LeMarque, big-shot producer. Everyone who goes here wants to be in showbiz, so they'll suck up to him or Gabriel Fallen or Cleo St. James to claw their way to their big break. I heard Cleo flew to Paris over summer to tape a modeling reality TV show, but she got eliminated in the first round and she won't tell anyone what—" The bathroom door creaks, and the girl grabs me by the collar and yanks me into her stall, slamming the door behind her. Our food flies everywhere, splattering both our uniforms in red wine jus. The girl backs into the far corner, biting her lips as she balances her tray on top of the cistern, trying to appear as small as possible.

Outside, I hear voices. I recognize one as a girl I saw with Cleo when she accosted me in the corridor and another, unfamiliar voice.

"It's so annoying Mr. Ross made me do my make-up test over lunch," says Cleo's friend. "I'm *starving,* and the fascists who run this school closed the salad bar four minutes ago. It's practically child neglect."

Wow, I'm sure the actual horrors of fascism are equivalent to not getting your daily dose of kale. I bite back a retort that whips across my tongue.

"Don't worry, Daphne, you just missed the usual. Alec's planning the first party of the year, Eli wants us all to volunteer to plant trees in the Emerald Beach nature reserve, Noah grunted into his coffee. Oh," the second girl's voice drops. "You won't believe what I overheard at the lockers. Cleo asked Gabriel over to her place this weekend. and he told her he's hanging out with *Mackenzie Malloy* instead. I hope that girl knows what she's doing, because Cleo's ready to go nuclear on her ass."

What? Gabriel hadn't said to me about this supposed hangout. I assume he's just using me as an excuse to get out of Cleo's date, but I can't stop my chest constricting so tight I worry I'm having a heart attack. But it's just an attack of what-the-fuck-is-Gabriel-Fallen-playing-at, which is definitely more exciting.

"Personally, I think Cleo should stay away from Gabe," Daphne sounds worried. "You heard about what happened on his tour."

"No. I was in Nantucket all summer. Oh, that reminds me, I have to tell you what Chip and I got up to at the boathouse, but you were saying about Gabriel—"

"The drummer of Octavia's Ruin killed himself. Or, at least, that's the official story." Daphne lowers her voice. "I have a cousin who works in management for their opening band. He said Gabriel and Dylan had a massive screaming argument the day he died, and that Gabriel *threatened* to hurt him. Apparently, the police have their eye on him. They think he might've been responsible for his death."

"But he killed himself," the other girl points out, which is exactly my question. "That's not Gabe's fault."

"Suicides can be faked," says Daphne in a know-it-all voice.

What the actual fuck? That can't be true. Gabriel and Dylan were close. It takes a cold fucking person to murder their best friend and cover it up, and that's not Gabriel. It can't be.

But I think of the darkness in Gabriel's eyes, and I *wonder.*

I know better than anyone the depths of evil human beings are capable of.

I hear the water running, and the hand dryer blares, drowning out their voices. I lean against the door, trying to catch what they say about Gabriel. The door swings open, and their voices disappear down the hall. *Dammit.*

Behind me, the girl visibly relaxes. I'd almost forgotten she was there. I yank open the stall door and get my ass out of her space. "So, now we're both wearing each other's lunch, I should probably know your name."

"I'm Georgina, but everyone calls me George." She shoves the contents of her lunch tray – ceramic plate and cutlery and all – into the trash, and balls up a wad of toilet paper to dab at the stain on her collar. "When they bother to use my name. Usually, it's 'freak' or 'dyke'... Cleo has some imaginative names if you can't think of any."

"I think I'll stick with George. Why'd you hide when those two girls came in?"

George dips her head. "You probably don't want to be seen

talking to me. Especially not by Daphne and Brandy. It'll get back to Cleo."

"Why would I care what Cleo thinks?"

She rolls her eyes as if she's explaining something to a child. "Because you're Mackenzie Malloy, duh. You belong with the popular kids. You should be sitting at their table in the dining hall, braiding Cleo's hair or arm-wrestling Noah or whatever."

I stuck out my tongue and made a gagging noise. "No thanks. Those guys are dicks."

"Not Elias Hart," George says, her cheeks flushing with color. She gulps. "I just mean... I don't talk to him, obviously, but he seems nicer than the others."

"Mmmhmmm." I may be completely messed up and out-of-touch with the world, but I know a crush when I see it. I stare down at the stains on my shirt and for a moment, I'm not looking at jus but *blood* – my mother's blood splattered across my reflection. I shake my head and start dabbing. "So, George. Is this your usual lunch spot?"

She peels off her sweater and holds it under the tap. "I swear, when I offered you that fork, I had no idea you were, well, *you*."

"And if you did, you wouldn't have given me a fork?"

George bites her lip so hard I'm worried she'll draw blood. "I don't know. We went to lower prep together before, well... before you disappeared. You probably don't remember me. I looked quite different back then."

"You seem pretty memorable to me."

"You and Cleo sure thought so." A note of bitterness creeps into her voice.

I can read between the lines here – I did something shit to this girl. If I was friends with Cleo back then, that's not surprising. Fuck, I wish I'd known all this before I opened my mouth.

I sigh. "Look, you want to go eat somewhere that doesn't smell like urine?"

"With you?" George studies my face.

I glance around the empty bathroom. "I don't see anyone else offering."

I can see the torment in George's eyes as she weighs that Mackenzie Malloy was eating her lunch in a toilet stall against her past tormentor. Finally, she nods, although her shoulders are tense. "Sure. Let's go."

GEORGE and I stop by a vending machine to load up on snacks, then take our loot out to the bleachers, where the stoners hang out. She looks nervous as we climb up to the top corner and lay out our bounty. Out on the track is a lone runner – Noah. He's shirtless because the gods have to be kind to me sometimes. Sweat glistens on his naked skin, and I notice a single tattoo of a four-leaf clover, its leaves curling and crumpling at the edges, over his heart. His gym shorts pull across his muscled thighs, and my throat dries as I think about exactly what's inside those shorts. That boy is damn fine. Hatred looks good on him.

I rip open the wrapper on a no-gluten, no-sugar, no-taste dark-chocolate kelp bar (the school's snack choices suck), which I have no appetite for any longer. Why am I wasting precious brainpower thinking about a guy who loathes me, a guy so obviously and completely off-limits?

I tear my eyes from Noah and focus on George, who is nervously fiddling with the edge of a bag of dried mango slices and watching a group of guys gathered around an acoustic guitar a few rows over. "I thought these would be your kind of people." I nod at her hair.

She runs her hand through her rainbow hair. "Oh... I don't know. I've always been too scared to talk to guys like that. They'll think I'm a freak."

"I don't think you've looked at yourself in a mirror recently. You're putting out total hot freaky rocker chick vibes. That guy with the Metallica bandana down there is totally checking you out."

George glances down at the guys, then back at me, and I see a million questions burning in her eyes. "Who are you, and what have you done with the real Mackenzie Malloy?"

I smile. "I'm holding her hostage so I can steal her life, *obviously*. Gross, who thought kelp and chocolate go together?" I toss the bar down the bleachers. It bounces across the grass just as Noah steaks by and hits him in the chest, exploding crumbs of kelp all over him. He turns with a snarl and locks eyes with mine. Fuck, if looks could kill I'd be back in that coffin with Noah dancing on the lid.

George is giggling into her arm. "I can't believe you just hit Noah Marlowe. He doesn't look happy... are you going to eat that?"

For a moment I think she's talking about Noah, but then I see her eyeing up a cookie. I slide it over. "All yours."

"Thanks." George tears it open and takes a huge bite. She talks about school clubs and bands I've never heard of for the rest of the lunch hour. It's like I turned a faucet on inside her and unleashed a stream of word vomit. It should annoy the fuck out of me, but actually, it's nice, hearing something other than the shadows dancing around inside my head.

When the bell rings, startling her mid-sentence, George pushes her glasses up her nose and peers up at me. Something changes in her expression, her features falling one by one, like a house of cards crumbling. A minute ago she'd been glowing, tucking her hair behind her ears as she bobbed her head along with the guys' music. Now, she looks *terrified*.

Weird.

"I guess we should go in?" I stand up.

Her legs shake as she drags herself after me.

"I had fun. Let's do this again."

George nods. We descend the bleachers and start to cross the field, when suddenly her face goes pales and she runs off ahead of me. I call out, but she's already pushing her way through the crowds heading back inside. She's so short I lose sight of her in moments.

What's up with her? For the briefest moment, I thought I might have made a friend. But it seems that not even George the class freak wants to be seen with Mackenzie Malloy.

MACKENZIE

"In the week you've been at that school, you've managed to break a teen actor's nose, fall for the British rock god, get on the bad side of the head jock, discover some secret childhood friend you don't remember, piss off the head bitch *and* make friends with the school freak?" Antony's laugh bubbles up inside him. "So much for keeping a low profile."

I moan into the receiver. He's right, damn him. Being a student at Stonehurst is everything like one of those teen films I studied, and yet, all my studying didn't prepare me for shit. Every day I walk down that hall between throngs of friends laughing and hugging each other, every time Noah's eyes stare daggers into my back or Eli tries to talk to me or Gabriel flashes me that megawatt smile, I get this desperate churn in the pit of my stomach. I've lived alone for so long I had no idea how much I longed for friendship, for connection. I teased myself with daydreams of what I can never have. Cleo's words haunt me, running over and over in my head.

You don't belong.

No shit, Sherlock. It's senior year, the last year of high school, and I never got to have a normal life with friends and parties and drama. What I wouldn't give to worry about grades and apply to colleges and think about normal teenage things. I never had a first kiss, or got dressed up with my girlfriends for a school dance, or cheered from the stands at a school sports event. Instead, the only memories I take with me into adulthood are blood and loneliness and betrayal.

At least I'll have my fucking house.

Every brick. Every tile. Every triple-glazed window and gaudy column and faux Roman statue. It's mine, and I'd fight any asshole who stands in the way of making Malloy Manor my own.

Queen Boudica leaps onto my lap, batting at my phone. I'm lying on the chaise lounge in the ballroom – one of my favorite rooms in the house and one where the French doors face the back garden, so the press at the gate can't see inside. I pull one of her toys from between the cushions and toss it across the room. She skids on the marble floor, tiny black limbs flailing everywhere as she tries to beat the fuzzy mouse into submission.

"Gabriel keeps asking me to hang out with him," I tell Antony.

"So do it. Go 'hang out,' which you need to learn is teenager talk for 'fucking each other's brains out.' I won't stop you. I think you should have some fun, Claws. It's your senior year. You're almost all grown up—"

"Don't be a dick."

Antony chuckles. "I know, you've been grown up since you were born. All I'm saying is, if you want to jump up and down on that posh prick's cock, it's not going to screw up our plan. The world already knows Mackenzie Malloy is back. It might even work in our favor, give the press a new story to chew on."

I rub my temple. *What if it does, though?* There's so much at stake, and not just for me. This is Antony's life, too. Queen Boudica drops the mouse onto my chest, and I toss it for her again. As she claws her way around the bottom of the curtains, I notice a shape moving along the top of the garden wall. "Shit."

"What?"

"Some bastard paparazzi has climbed the wall." I can see him precariously perched on the narrow ledge, using wire clippers to cut away the barbed wire coiled around the top. Bastard. He's the first one of those slimy snails to try to climb the wall – so far the rest of them had settled for peering through the gates and snapping photographs of me as I entered school. Stonehurst employs a security team to keep them away from students, but they still hang around. This cheeky shit is trying to get the scoop on me, and for that, he will *pay*.

"I'll send someone to sort it out—"

"No. I'll take care of it. I have to go." I drop my phone on the sofa and back away from the windows. It's too late to turn out the ballroom lights – he's seen me lying around in booty shorts and my Octavia's Ruin shirt, tossing fuzzy mice for my cat. *Page ten, have I got a scoop for you.*

I won't have him out there, staring at me, polluting *my* house. I don't like being watched. It reminds me too much of... other things. Times in the past when eyes have followed me with ill intent. I'm not supposed to feel unsafe here. This is my house, my castle. How dare he sit on the parapets like he's earned the right to my presence?

My jaw clenching with determination, I storm up the staircase to the third floor. I hardly ever come up here – it houses the master suite and a strange turret thing with a hot tub and a small balcony and windows overlooking the hills and sprawling city below.

I turned the circuit breakers off in this section of the house years ago to save on power bills, so I creep across the room in the dark to the bar area, where crates of wine had been piled in the small walk-in. My parents – rich assholes that they were – kept barely any actual food in the house, but the four wine cellars (WTF) are stocked to last at least three apocalypses (what's the plural of apocalypse? Apocalyii? I guess there doesn't need to be a plural as there's only going to be one...)

Anyway... I stacked the bottles by the window months ago for... just this reason. I yank a couple of bottles out of a crate, fling open the window, and toss them at the pap.

"Fuck!"

He leaps off the wall just as one of the bottles smashes into the stone right where he'd been sitting. The second bottle flies wide, sailing over the wall and smashing on the other side. Great, now the guy's stuck on this side of the wall. He steps forward into the square of light cast from the ballroom windows, and I gasp as I recognize him.

It's Eli.

"I'm covered in sticky wine now," he shouts up at me.

In response, I lean out the window and flip him the finger.

"Mackenzie, I want to talk to you."

"We don't always get what we want." I hold up another bottle of wine. "If you don't get off my property in ten seconds, I'm shoving this one somewhere unpleasant. I'm counting. One."

"I don't think I can climb over the wall from this side," he points out, a little petulantly. "And if I open the front gate you're going to be swarming with reporters."

"Two. Hope you've lubed up your asshole."

Eli throws up his hands. "You run away from me at school, you ignore my texts. I didn't know what else to do."

"Three." *He's Jace.* That's the only explanation. Which means that for some reason, thirteen-year-old me didn't want anyone who might pick up my phone to know I was talking to Eli. I want to ask him about that, but I can't, and that pisses me off.

"I thought you were dead." His voice cracks on the words, and the pain on his face is open and raw. "All these years I've tried to find out what happened to you, but you just *vanished*. I couldn't even *grieve* for you because my fucking parents would figure it out. And then you just show up and act like you don't know me. Why, Mackenzie?"

No. no no no no no. This can't be true. Eli's talking like we used to be an item. But that was four years ago. Eli has girls falling all over him now. Why does he give a fuck about a girl he knew when he was thirteen? The way his face twists – he has feelings for me. Or, at least, for the old Mackenzie. For the Mackenzie who'd never been buried alive in her own coffin, who had her life stolen and her memories tainted forever.

I checked every last corner of my room. There was no mention of a guy, no loose ends I needed to tie up. I had to be sure of that or Antony and I never would have risked me attending Stonehurst. Yet somehow we missed both Noah *and* Eli.

I watch Eli's face twisting with pain, and it hits me.

I *know*.

I know why Eli seems familiar to me, even though there's no way I'd remember him from before.

The realization punches me in the gut, and I stagger back under the shock of it.

He's one of the faces I've seen peering through the gate, staring up at the windows of my old bedroom. He's been here several times over the years. I thought he was another thrill-seeking ghost-hunter. But he's not. He's been looking for *me*.

"Mackenzie?" Eli pleads. "I promise, I'll leave you alone if that's what you want. But can't you just tell me if you're okay?

Are you in danger? Is it your dad? Is that why you won't talk to me?"

I *want* to tell him everything. And it's that wanting that gives me pause. Because I don't know this guy, but he *feels* so familiar to me, so safe. I *want* to trust Eli, and that's dangerous.

"Go away." I slam the window shut, palming the bottle as I head back downstairs. I am going to need it.

MACKENZIE

I watch from the ballroom window as Eli pushes lawn furniture against the wall and clambers up. His shoulder muscles heave with the effort of pulling himself over, and he's not the only one hot and bothered by the end of it. I contemplate going out there and offering him a drink just as he disappears over the other side.

Instead, I chug the entire bottle of New Zealand's finest vintage while I tear my old room apart. I rip the heads off all the creepy dolls and poke around inside their stuffing. I stab at the wooden cupboards with the knife Antony gave me for my tenth birthday, looking for hidden compartments. Finally, I take the knife to the expensive mattress, tearing away strips of foam and sending springs flying in all directions.

Finally, I find it.

I'd hidden it well, shoved into the bunting on my headboard through a cut I hid behind a fold of fabric. No wonder I missed it during my last search. I wrap my hands around the tiny notebook and tug it free, holding it under the light as I inspect the cover.

It's pretty nondescript as far as notebooks go – the cover

decorated with watercolor flowers, a dent across the corner, and several pages crinkled from being constantly handled. I grasp it in shaking hands, knowing without knowing that I'm holding the key to unlocking the secrets of my life before, of memories that don't feel like they belong to me.

I crack the front page and begin to read:

Happy eighth birthday to me! Eli got me this diary. He slipped it into my bookbag when no one else was looking. His note says I should use it to tell the truth, because I never get to tell the truth any other time. I think it's dumb because no one will ever read this. I have to keep it secret or Daddy will be upset with me. But maybe Eli will read it. Maybe I'll say nice things about him here, just in case.

Mommy and Daddy gave me a new doll for my birthday. She has a porcelain face and beautiful long fingers and a dress with pink ribbons. They took me out to a fancy dinner at an Italian place on the boardwalk. I accidentally knocked over my glass, so Daddy refused to let me order a meal. I watched him and Mommy eat and drink and enjoy slices of pink birthday cake all to themselves.

The next entry starts with:

Some workers came to empty the pool and repair the tiles today. Mommy caught me talking to one of them. He was just asking me about my dolls, but Mommy made me sit on the bottom of the pool while she sprayed me with the hose. She made me stay down there until it was dark. My fingers are so cold I keep dropping the pen.

Fuck. That's dark.

I turn the page. With every word I read, a ball of bile forms in my stomach and rises into my mouth. What I describe in my childish scribble is pages and pages of neglect and torture. My father burning my elbows on the stovetop because I didn't keep them off the table during dinner. My mother forcing me to eat rotting, rancid meat in my sandwiches because she said my fancy school cost them so much money. And all of it recorded in my halting, eight-year-old hand, just lists of things that happened, like it's completely normal for parents to *burn your fucking elbows.*

I rub my elbows as I read this litany of horrors with a strange detachment. It doesn't feel real. *These things happened to someone else. Not me. Someone else.*

Daddy says I'm too soft, he says I need to be tough if I'm to survive in his world as his heir. He says for my own good I'm not allowed to sleep in my bed no more. All that Egyptian cotton and imported silk makes me soft. Last night I slept in my closet, but I didn't sleep much.

I'm several entries in before I spot Eli's name again.

Daddy's away on business, and Mommy went to see her doctor about a new face, so I snuck Eli in through the car lift. I haven't seen him in so long. We don't talk at school because it's too dangerous. If the teachers say something to our parents, we'll be in so much trouble. But today we hung out, and it was just like it always is. We went for a swim, and I wore my new purple bikini. Eli said I looked pretty. I liked hearing him say that.

Eli knows about the maintenance shed and car door. I don't like that. I don't like that at all.

I turn another page. Eli's name jumps out from every sentence. The two of us sneaking out our windows at night to have ice cream on the boardwalk, getting detentions just so we could sit together and pass notes, creating fake social media accounts to chat with each other and deleting all our messages. Secret friends. *Close* friends. And judging from the way I spoke about him, we'd been that way for a long time.

Fuck, fuck, fuck.

I curl up on my ruined bed and pore over the entries. It's filled with stories about Eli, years and years of them, starting from when I was eight and finishing the year the Malloys disappeared. I snuck him into Malloy Manor every chance I got, and we once told our parents we were going on a ski trip with the school and snuck out to his father's cattle ranch for the weekend. I never say *why* we had to hide our friendship (because duh, I obviously knew and eight-year-old me couldn't possibly predict my current situation), but I can tell from the way I'd pressed down hard on the pen that I was afraid of what would happen if we were caught.

And there's something else, too. Noah. His name comes up again and again later in the diary, when I'm eleven and twelve years old. He went to the same school as me and Eli, and they'd been friends forever. It doesn't sound like I hung out with Noah at all, but I talk about him constantly. How hot he is, how smart he is. Some entries are just Noah's name written over and over again, surrounded by hearts. On my twelfth birthday, I'd written:

It's my birthday. Eli's taking me somewhere special to celebrate. I asked him if he can invite Noah along, too. He got all weird about it, said Noah was busy even though I know he's not because his swim meets are on Thursdays. It sucks – Eli knows how much I like Noah. Why doesn't he want us to hang out?

I read over the very last entry. It's tough to make out the words because the page is torn and the ink is smudged from droplets I suspect are tears.

Today was horrible. It's the worst day of my life. Daddy came home from his trip early and found Eli and me in the pool. He grabbed Eli by the throat and dragged him out of the water. I cried and begged Daddy to stop. He threw Eli into the garden wall, and he just crumpled to the ground and didn't move. Daddy had his security team drag Eli away, and he made me scrub Eli's blood out of the stucco. I thought he was dead. I thought Daddy killed him.

Daddy told me never to go near Eli or his family again. He called them criminals. He said he'd ruin them and that would put a stop to my 'cavorting'.

I hate Daddy so much. I won't let him get away with this.

Tears roll down my cheeks. I can see I've pressed the pen so hard that I tore the paper. I read my anguish in every word.

Eli risked everything to be my friend. He risked his life to go swimming with me and to be there for me when no one else would. All these years of silence, and he's *still* willing to scale a wall to see me.

And I can't even remember his face.

The guard leers at me as I drive the Porsche up to the gates. "Greetings, Your Highness." His friend in the booth behind him laughs like it's Saturday Night Live.

"You're hilarious." I toss my paperwork and ID at him as his buddy walks around my car with a sniffer dog.

"Just you today, Your Highness?"

"Obviously." I am not in the mood for their shit. I hardly slept last night. I stared at the ceiling and thought about Mackenzie's face as she hurled those bottles at me. She *looks* like my secret friend, the Mackenzie who never cared about anyone or anything except me, but inside she's like a different person. What happened to her in the last four years to make her forget me so completely? What's left her with nothing but broken, violent rage in her eyes? I have to find out. I have to help her.

I want to be at school, where I might be able to talk to her. But I can't today. Duty calls.

The guard can't resist one final stunt, giving me a queen wave as he opens the gate and I drive to the visitor parking. At reception, I sign in and subject myself to the usual humiliating patdowns. Comedian Guard takes his time, makes sure to grab my ass as he searches me for contraband. Phone, keys, wallet, they all go in a tray to be collected when I leave – I surrender everything except the small leather pouch hanging off my belt. They all know what's inside.

I'm led into the booths. It reeks of piss, and I resist the urge to pinch my nose. I did that the first time I came here, back when I was still a kid, and the guards never let me forget it. I settle into the hard plastic chair.

I wait.

A few minutes later, the door on the other side of the glass swings open, and two guards escort my dad inside.

I try to make eye contact with him, but I can't do it. Even after four years, it hurts too much. I stare at a spot on the wall to the right of his ear. A dark stain, maybe blood? It was tough to tell in the dim light.

I'm made of glass. One word, one sound could shatter me.

He picks up the phone. "Son."

I try to say something, but the words catch in my throat. He looks worse than last time. There's a fresh cut across his hairline, and as he talks it opens, a dribble of blood running down his forehead. His eyes have sunken, and I think his nose has been broken again.

They don't like rich guys in jail.

Especially not my father, Walter Hart, founder of Memories of the Hart, Emerald Beach's celebrity funeral home. Anyone who was anyone wanted to be buried by my dad. For a while when I was seven or so, he even had his own reality TV show where cameras followed our family and filmed Dad creating these crazy themed funerals. Elvis and golf and Cinderella, complete with an enormous pumpkin-shaped hearse leading a procession down the boardwalk.

That was before the story broke. Before Walter Hart the affable Tennessee businessman who made grief fun was revealed to be giving people ground-up cement and animal remains instead of their cremated loved ones, and selling the bodies on the black market. Shortly after Noah's mother killed herself, an FBI investigation blew Dad's dirty laundry wide open, and it was my family's turn in the spotlight.

Dad's not having the best time in prison. Southern charm can only get you so far. Even murderers and rapists and drug dealers have grandmothers they cremated. Grandmothers whose body parts later showed up in laboratories and plastination exhibits when Memories of the Hart was investigated. The man sitting on the other side of the glass is the shell of my father – his skin doesn't fit properly, like all the bluster and bombast has been sucked out through his eyeballs.

"Hi, Dad." I force the words out. "I'm sorry it's been so long."

"That's my boy, always got something going on, got a scheme brewing. Just like your old man. How's that fancy school of yours?" He flashes me the white-toothed smile that used to grace billboards. Dad's so proud he got me into Stonehurst, even though with all his civil suits I can now only afford to stay there because of a scholarship.

I suck in a breath. *You can do this. Find the words.* "It's good, Dad. I've been made captain of the track team. We have our first state meet in a couple of weeks. And I'm beating Noah in History. He's pissed, but he's so distracted with Mackenzie that he—"

"Mackenzie?" My father's eyes narrow.

"Yeah." I swallow. I hadn't intended to mention her at all, but this place... it has a way of drawing secrets from me. "Mackenzie Malloy. She's... um... she's back at school."

"Well, I'll be damned. She's alive?" The word sticks in his throat. "Mackenzie Malloy? God love her."

"Yeah. It's kind of a wild story, actually. Her parents are still missing, but she just showed up at school one day, and—"

SLAM.

My father's fist pounds the glass. I leap back, my body reacting on instinct, even knowing he can't hurt me.

What the hell?

Walter Hart never lashes out in violence. With his tongue, he's inflicted wounds that will never heal. But even though he's an ex-football player built like a tank, he's never had to use his fists to get what he wanted when sheer force of personality was enough.

But Mackenzie's name has stirred something in him – the caged animal lurking behind his genial facade. I stare through the glass at the man that raised me, and I don't recognize him.

The guards leap forward and restrain him, but after a few stern words about behaving himself, they back off again. On my side, Comedian Guard cracks up laughing.

Dad picks up the phone again and glares at me through the glass. I think about the guard at the doorway, how easy it would be to turn around and leave without listening to what Dad's about to say.

After a moment, I pick up the receiver from where it clattered to the ground and press it to my ear.

"I apologize for my outburst, son." There's the old Dad again – friendly and agreeable and utterly in control. "You surprised me, is all. I never expected to hear that name again. I thought we severed your connection to that family a long time ago."

I don't like the way he says *severed*, with an almost gleeful relish. "It's just Mackenzie, Dad. Not her family. I don't think—"

"Listen to me, boy. I know what's best for you, and I can tell you that you don't want to be mixed up with anyone who has the surname Malloy, no matter how pretty their mouth looks around your cock."

That was so typical Dad. As much as he tries to smooth away the edge of his working-class upbringing, he always reveals himself in the end. It's why we moved to Emerald Beach – Dad's always been too big for his boots in Tennessee, and the flashy, wealth-obsessed culture of California called to him.

"Sure, Dad. I understand." I don't, but I remind myself he can't do shit outside these walls.

"How are your college applications?"

"Fine. I have interviews for early entrance to Stanford and Harvard starting in a couple of weeks." At the mention of the prestigious schools, a smile tugs at the corner of Dad's mouth. He's all about giving me the opportunities he never had. A real family man, except it's a crock of shit.

"That's my boy. You show them what the Harts are made of." There's that smile again – the megawatt grin he turned on whenever he was closing a sale. "I'm relying on you."

Don't fucking remind me.

"How's the appeal coming?" I dread the answer to that question.

"Sanderson's working on it." Sanderson is my parents' shady lawyer. His hourly rate is more than a downpayment on an apartment, and we've got nothing to show for it except a hefty mortgage on the house. Dad was caught red-handed, so we don't have a pot to piss in. "If he calls you, give him anything he asks for. Otherwise, I want you to focus on college. And stay away from the Malloy girl. I doubt she'll be around long."

"Sure, Dad. I—"

"Times up," the guard snaps. I glance at my watch. He's lying his ass off – I still have twenty minutes. But this is what the guards did – they were as much prisoners of this hellhole as the inmates, and they took their fun wherever they could get it. And they love to take out their frustration on the rich douchebag who got caught selling body parts and his asshole son who thinks he's above them.

"Wait, Elias—" but I slam the phone down and stand up to

leave. Dad presses his hand against the glass. Even through the bulletproof glass I can just make out his muttered words.

Don't disappoint me.

On the way out, I stop by the warden's office. He doesn't look up from his paperwork as I step inside and shut the door behind me. "I thought I could smell that fancy cologne stinking up the place."

I stand in front of his desk, feet apart, arms folded, looking down my nose at the little weasel while he takes in my rich-boy haircut, my clothes that cost more than a month's salary, my smooth hands that have never done a hard day's work. I hate doing this shit, throwing my weight and my money around, acting like the cocksucking entitled prats Dad's always railed against. "Someone's hurt my father again. I want him moved to a private cell."

"No can do, little man." His insult falls flat, and he knows it. His Adam's apple bobs up and down as he swallows. "I'm bursting at the seams here, and private cells are for inmates who are a danger to the prison community, not second-rate crooks like your old man."

I open the leather pouch and dump the contents on his desk. Two rolls of bills fall out. The warden cups his hand over them and slides them into his lap, cool as a cucumber.

"I'll see what I can do."

I wait until I'm back in my car before the weight of what I'd done falls on me. I crank the stereo loud, so loud it drowns out the screaming in my head.

I punch the steering wheel until my fingers bleed.

"*B*astard," I mutter into the phone.

"You like this guy," Antony chuckles.

"Cocksucker."

"I bet he has a motorcycle. And dark, brooding eyes. You're so predictable."

"Wanker."

Antony laughs. "That's a new one."

"I learned it from Gabriel. The British have such eloquent insults."

My veins hum with rage, and I long to wrap my fingers around Eli's neck and squeeze, or pull him to me and crush my lips against his. I can't decide which. All I know is that every word in that diary has been burned into my skull. My house, my refuge, my ticket from hell is tainted now, the walls dripping with blood. It's a gilded prison, a coffin lid nailed down tight over my parents' abuse. And if it wasn't for Eli, I would still be blissfully unaware of the horror in my past.

Eli wasn't in school today, so I couldn't talk to him about what I read in the diary. Which means Antony gets the brunt of my annoyance. Once he stops laughing, he says goodbye. He's got a big fight this weekend, so he needs to focus on training. Even though I'm desperate to talk to him, I let him go – he's done me a solid and sent one of his thugs to scare away the reporters at the gate, so for now, tonight at least, Malloy Manor is safe again.

I shove my phone into the pocket of my hoodie as I move through the kitchen, tearing the lid off a can of cat food and tipping it onto a gold-rimmed saucer for Queen Boudica. Queens deserve the best. She jumps up on the table and buries her face in the bowl.

When I first found Queen Boudica two years ago, she was a skinny, scrawny bag of bones living in the trash cans behind the diner. My boss, Lenny, said someone dumped a bag of kittens in the alley, and he called the animal shelter, but they didn't seem to care. When I went out to dump some empty bottles, her fierce yellow eyes surveyed me from the shadows. She was scrappy. A survivor.

Like me.

At the end of my shift, I crawled behind the dumpster, scraping up my bare arms on the bricks. I managed to cradle her in my apron. I expected her to fight me, but as soon as I held her in my arms she curled up and went to sleep. The bus driver gave me a dirty look as I hopped on with her, but he let me sit down. I stared down at the tiny body in my arms and swore I'd look after her.

When I got home I set her down on the marble floor of the foyer and she sat as regally as an Egyptian statue, peering down her nose at me as if she expected me to wait on her. I named her for the Queen of the Celts, who stood up against the might of the Roman Empire. Ever since, she's ruled this house and my heart. She's probably the only thing that's kept me sane.

I pull out a container of leftovers from the school dining hall and dig in. Across from me, Boudica abandons her bowl to sniff mine. I push her away. "Just remember, until you can master the opposable thumbs thing, you need me as much as I need you. So don't piss me off."

When we finish our dinner, I cradle Queen Boudica in my arms like a baby, carrying her into the study to choose a book and a bottle of wine. I carry the cat, wine, and book to the ballroom and curl up in the pile of cushions by the window while Queen Boudica climbs all over the cat jungle gym.

I try to focus on the story, but my mind swims with everything that's happened since that cop appeared on my doorstep. Noah and his coal eyes filled with hate. Gabriel's relentless flirting and cocky smile, Eli's intensity and unrelenting kindness.

Insect legs prickle the skin on the back of my neck. *I'm being watched.*

I look outside, my fingers reaching for my knife. I start as I notice a figure sitting on top of the wall.

Eli.

I should be freaking out that this guy's watching me like a creepy stalker, but now I've read the diary, I can't see Eli as a serial killer. He's a man out of time, a knight-in-shining-armor come to save the maiden in the castle. Too bad he doesn't realize the maiden transformed into a fire-breathing dragon.

Eli sees me looking at him through the window and waves. His smile makes my heart flip.

The words in the diary rush back to me. Eli, my secret friend, who would keep watching over me even when I was a bitch to him.

But we *all* have secrets. Even my house has secrets that I now wish I'd never uncovered. Which reminds me, I need ammunition. I need to not feel as though I'm the only vulnerable one. I drop my book and pull up my phone, searching for Eli's name. It doesn't take me long to find news reports covering his dad's trial – Walter Hart, self-made man, owner of a funeral *empire*, going down for selling corpses on the medical black market. Apparently, civil suits were still ongoing as relatives of his victims sought damages for being given bags of cement instead of their loved ones.

I freeze on a picture of Eli, looking damn fine in a pinstripe suit that hugs him in all the right places, one hand on the shoulders of a woman who'd had too much plastic surgery. His mother, I guess – they had the same golden hair, the same piercing blue eyes. Eli's other hand pushes on a reporter's chest, his fingers splayed, shoving the man away from his family. Protecting them.

Just like he protected me. Maybe he's still protecting me now.

The thought makes my chest tight. Because that girl Eli was protecting, that girl he thought I was – she doesn't exist. Not anymore. He thinks I'm someone I'm not, and nothing I do or say will make him see that. The dragon will always be Mackenzie to him.

I open the window and toss the book at Eli's head. He catches it in his hands. Damn athletes.

"Your father's in jail," I say.

Eli looks up at me, and I read his pain in those ocean-blue eyes. "I went to visit him today."

"Nice boy like you, I bet you got the full cavity-search treatment."

Eli winces. "You laugh, but it's a very real fear of mine. The guards don't like me much."

"That's odd." I tap the window. "You're the Stonehurst golden boy. I can't imagine anyone not liking you."

Eli stares down at the book in his hands. The silent night stretches between us, but it's a different silence than what I'm used to. This silence crackles with anticipation.

When Eli lifts his head again, his eyes shine with hope. That too-pretty mouth tugs into a smile so genuine and beautiful it makes my chest ache. "Does this mean you like me again?"

"If you're going to sit out there all night, you might as well have something to read." I nod at the book in his hands. "This is one of my favorites."

He stares at the book. "Since when have you liked reading?"

I shrug. "I'm not the girl you remember, Eli Hart."

"Nope." His eyes bore into mine as he clasps the book to his chest. "You're so much more."

MACKENZIE

Ms. Drysdale walks around the history classroom, slapping papers on top of desks. Students groan. My gaze flickers on Noah at the front of the class. He tucks his paper into his bag, but not before I catch the mark scrawled on the top of the page. A perfect score. Dude is crazy smart.

It should be illegal for guys that hot to also be smart. Give some of the brain juice to the rest of us, already.

My mind drifts back to my diary, to that crush I had on Noah all those years ago, before he hated me. And I can see why I fell hard for him, even as a thirteen-year-old. Brooding, clever, assholes were my type.

Ms. Drysdale stops in front of my desk. My stomach twists with a weird kind of half hope, half dread. I worked hard on this paper – an essay on a woman we admire from history. I chose Queen Boudica – the Celtic queen who led an uprising against the Romans in AD60, not the feline who clawed holes in my Alexandra McQueen trench coat.

Ms. Drysdale passes me a paper, facedown, and the expression on her face makes my heart sink.

"See me after class, Mackenzie."

So, no good, then. I don't understand. I know the material. My father spent his entire life talking about the history of Rome. He was *obsessed*, so much so that most of the stories stuck in my head post-coffin, even though nothing else did. What went wrong?

I shove my paper into my binder, but not before I catch a glimpse of the mark on top. F.

Who cares about some stupid test? I don't need this school.

But the truth is, I do need this school for a hell of a lot, and I have to stay here all year or everything I worked for and everything Antony sacrificed will be for nothing. So at the end of class. I slink up to Ms. Drysdale's desk. "You wanted to see me?"

"Mackenzie, I know you've had—" she pauses, biting her lip. Bad move on her part. She already sees me as the alpha in this scenario. "—a difficult home life. But Stonehurst is a highly competitive school. Students who don't perform will find they have no place here. And your paper... it's not up to the standard I expect from a student at your level, especially given your excellent work on the application essay."

The application essay I hired out to someone on the internet.

"So I'm behind." I shrug. "I'll catch up."

Maybe I need to hire my internet nerd again. But we didn't have a lot of money left after we paid the Stonehurst tuition, and Antony says it's too risky. If my nerd figures out who he's writing essays for, he could sell the story to the papers and I'm kicked out of Stonehurst, and that's not going to work for us.

"There's behind, and then there's not understanding the basics. Your essay is... well, it reads less like an essay and more as stream-of-consciousness beat poetry performed by drunken dock workers." Ms. Drysdale dares a smile that brightens her whole face. She's pretty behind that lank haircut and boxy blazer with the sleeves rolled up. "Honestly, it's as if you've skipped your entire high school education."

Her comments sting more than I like to admit. I know I'm flunking most classes, but I enjoy history. I *know* the material. And I like Ms. Drysdale. And as weird as it is for me to admit – I kind of want her to like me. To be impressed by me. I haven't had teachers in nearly five years. I don't know how to act around them.

A lump forms in my throat, and I know if I try to say something I might start to cry. So I just nod.

"We have a student mentoring program which I recommend you take advantage of. Noah Marlowe is the coordinator. I can set up a meeting with him if you like—"

Noah. Of course, it's him. "Don't bother. I can do it myself."

"Noah, a word." I plonk my ass down on the seat next to him.

Noah stiffens.

On the opposite side of the royal table, Gabriel leans forward. Eli, who'd been about to take the seat I now occupy, shoves his tray down next to Noah. I've gotten to their table early, while Alec is still in line. No way do I want him to overhear this.

"Fuck off," Noah growls.

"Look, I'm not some masochist who's thrilled at the idea of working with a guy who hates me. Ms. Drysdale said I've got to pull my grades up or I'll be out of school. That's not an option for me. You run the tutoring program, and I need a tutor. This is a business transaction, nothing more."

"What subjects?" Noah's hands form fists in his lap, but he doesn't make any move to hurt me the way he wishes. He just stares at my face, those dark eyes searching mine. I don't like the intensity of him. I resist the urge to slide away.

"All of them."

"I'll tutor you," Gabriel pipes up. "You know how good I am at chemistry. You're sodium fine, we could do it on the table periodically."

"Mackenzie, I can help with geology. You're obviously made of mica rock, with that perfect cleavage," another guy down the table pipes up, and they all snigger. All except Noah, who still has me fixed with his death glare.

"Careful, guys," Cleo smirks as she sets down her tray next to his. "You don't want her to fuck up your nose."

"Forget it." I stand up. "I knew this was a mistake."

Noah sighs.

"Fine."

"Fine, what?"

"Be in the library during study period today, and I'll figure out if I can even help you."

"You're an angel, you know that? A real saint." I blow him an air kiss as I stand up to leave, and I swear I see the steam coming out his ears.

NOAH and I share a study period. The library isn't far from the bathroom where I eat my lunch, so I arrive early and spread my books over a table in the corner to save it for us. Not that any other students would consider sitting with me.

I'm reading my battered copy of Caesar's *The Conquest of Gaul* when Noah drops into the chair opposite me. He runs fingers through his dark, wavy hair. At first glance, he's calm, but I sense just underneath a storm is brewing.

A dark thrill runs through my veins as he looks me over, and that darkness in his eyes flares to life. Underneath that prepschool facade, Noah Marlowe is dangerous. And Jupiter help me, but I do love the bad boys. It's in my blood.

"All the other tutors in the program are booked solid," he growls. "So I'm stuck with you. Don't waste my time, and don't try to be cute. I'm here to help you pass, and that's it."

"Deal." I lick my lower lip.

"Show me your last assignments. That'll give me an idea of what I'm working with."

I pull my history essay from my folder and hold it out to him. Noah stares at it, letting my hand hang outstretched between us. *He can't even bear to risk our hands touching.* I drop it on the table, and he slides it toward him with one finger, as if it's infected.

Noah holds the pages right at the edge, his eyes flicking across the text. That same nervous dance I felt when Ms. Drysdale handed back my paper starts up in my gut again. I want this guy to think I'm smart and clever and interesting, and that's profoundly fucked up given everything I know and my situation.

When he's done, Noah tosses the paper back to me. "This is shit."

"You're not a very good teacher. Aren't you supposed to be encouraging me to be all that I can be?" I flash him a fake candy cane smile.

"Why are you here?" he growls.

"Because I know that essay's shit. But I don't know why." I shrug. "Because I need to pass senior year."

"No, I mean, why are you here at Stonehurst? Did you come here deliberately to fuck with me? Destroying my family wasn't enough for you? Running away to hide for four years so you didn't have to face what you did?" Noah's words drip with venom. He slams his fists on the table. "You had to come to *my* school and fake being stupid just so I'm forced to tutor you."

"I'm not faking anything." A lie, but he doesn't need to know that.

Noah spits on my essay. The glob of saliva lands on the large F scrawled at the top, making the letter appear bulbous and wobbly. "That essay is so comically terrible it can *only* be fake. It reads like you've never written an essay in your life. But I've been at school with Mackenzie Malloy since I could walk. I know she's a cold, calculating, clever bitch. And *this*," he gestures to the papers, "is just another one of her attempts to manipulate me."

"That's not what's happening here." I long to tell him the truth, that I haven't been in school since I was thirteen, that I thought all the books I've read would help me muddle through this year, but now I see school isn't about knowing the information but presenting it in a certain way that's completely alien to me, and I'm freaking out that my inability to craft an essay is going to be my downfall in a horrible and bloody way.

"My brother is *dead*. My mother killed herself because of what your family did, and you still think all you have to do is bat your eyelashes and the world will fall down to worship you. That shit may work on Eli and Gabe, but not with me." Noah stands up. "I don't need this. We're done."

"You haven't tutored me!"

"If you flunk out, I'll be doing this school a favor." Noah's eyes blaze with triumph. "Goodbye, Mackenzie. Have fun failing. I hope this is the last time I have to endure your presence."

My days at Stonehurst Prep fade together into a torrent of misery. When I first sent in my faked transcripts and signed the enrollment forms, I prepared myself to be ignored. Years living alone in that house of secrets will do that to you. Hell, I built myself a mega-bitch Ice Queen persona to keep the peons away. But I knew now I couldn't fade into the background – the whispers, the leering looks from the guys, the notes left on my locker describing cruel sexual acts, the Photoshopped pornography tacked to every noticeboard and saved to every lockscreen is only the beginning. *Mackenzie Malloy is made of shadows and secrets. She doesn't fit. We have to destroy her.*

Alec LeMarque's eyes follow me everywhere, devouring my body in a way that makes me squirm. He's not finished with me yet.

But not even he is as terrifying as Noah – the dark-haired god whose hatred could carve out my heart and pound it to rubble. Loathing rolls off his body in waves, threatening to sweep me away. Hatred like that can be intoxicating – I know, because I already had a gallon of it surging through my bloodstream.

I've only seen George once since we ate our lunch together under the bleachers. She was heading down the hall toward the Art suite. I waved and called out to her, but either she didn't hear me or the wrathful gaze of Noah and Alec as they headed the other way silenced her. She slammed her locker and ran the other way.

That hurt more than I'll ever admit. I lost a friend before I even knew what one was.

I wish I was smart so at least the schoolwork could be a distraction, but my F in history is my top grade so far. I wish I had college applications and tests to focus on, so at least my days would have meaning. I struggle through the classes, barely understanding a word my teachers say. It's like they're speaking a foreign language. I've finally learned what's come of not setting foot inside a learning institution since I was thirteen. Some days, I debate taking Gabriel up on his offer to tutor me, even though I know he's barely a better student than I am.

There are only two bright spots in my days. Ms. Drysdale teaches history and political science. She's young – mid-twenties I think, and with her short, trendy haircut and band tee shirts peeking out from beneath mens' blazers with the sleeves rolled up, she has this punk rock pixie vibe that's refreshing in this stuck-up school. She looks like someone I'd want to be friends with, in another life, when I could choose my friends.

She has a way of making history come alive. I lean forward on my elbows and listen with rapt attention as she talks about the Founding Fathers, or the Tudor Kings, or the Spanish Inquisition. I find myself nodding along with the familiar stories I've read, and devouring the extra reading lists she gives us.

The other bright spot is homeroom and chemistry class with Gabriel. He doesn't seem to care that everyone else at this school hates me. He makes flirty conversation and fucks up every single assignment. But most importantly, he makes me laugh. I relish it, knowing that with him, at least, my laughter doesn't come at a price.

After class Gabriel always offers to walk me to my locker, but I know Eli will be there, waiting with his kind smile and intense eyes, and I can't deal with that remnant of the old Mackenzie, so I fake women's problems and hide in the bathroom.

Too late, I realize Gabriel's attention paints a target on my back.

Apart from shooting daggers at me with her eyes every time she sees Gabriel and me together, Cleo hasn't been actively targeting me. Instead, she keeps her nose in the air whenever she passes me in the halls, as if I'm beneath her notice. Her minions do her bidding instead, stealing my things and spreading rumors about me that make me feel unsafe when I pass guys in the hall.

I believe that's the best they've got, that rich bitches like Cleo are incapable of real cruelty.

I'm wrong.

I have gym last period on a Wednesday, which I surprise myself by enjoying. It might have something to do with sneaking glances at Eli in his tight-as-fuck shorts. Scratch that, it's definitely because of Eli's ass. But also it's fun to run around, kick a soccer ball and pretend it's Alec LeMarque's stupid head.

This week we divide into guys and girls for fitness drills – seeing how many push-ups, chin-ups, burpees, and other tortures we can do. I'm surprised that most girls – even the fit ones on the cheerleading team – give up after a few half-assed attempts. I'm the only girl who can do a proper pushup, and I hold a chin-up for longer than anyone else.

"Mackenzie Malloy." The gym teacher, Mrs. Anderson, waves me over after class. "You impressed me today. You'll be getting an A on this unit."

"Thanks." An A in fucking *gym*. I'll take it.

"Cheerleading tryouts are next week," she continues. "I expect you to be there."

"Cheerleading?" I can barely hold back the sneer. The old Mackenzie would've bounced around in a short skirt and high ponytails, turning somersaults like it was nothing. But cheerleading is for girls with normal lives, who have boyfriends on the football team and futures worth cheering for. I have none of those things. It's bad enough I have to go to school with Cleo – I don't intend to be afflicted with her presence on my own time.

"I saw you out there today – you're strong. We need someone to replace Candice as base since she broke her leg over the summer. Did you keep up your gymnastics training?"

"Gymnastics? No, I..." I remember all the trophies scattered around my old room. I must've been a gymnast before. "I haven't been keeping up officially, but a lot of it is dance moves, right? I definitely dance."

If twerking in my ballroom counts.

"Exactly – Cleo and Daphne are our flyers. They execute the more complex stunts." She looks me up and down. "I remember you from junior prep, and you always had a perfect sense of rhythm. And if you're interested in pulling up your grades – you just have to shake your booty and you get extra credit."

Extra credit. Those magic words. I toss my hair over my shoulder. "I'll think about it."

Cheerleading. Antony's going to laugh his ass off when I tell him, but I have to admit, I'm excited about tryouts. This is a normal thing normal teenage girls do. I want to be part of it.

Besides, if I end up on the team, Cleo's head will explode, and I want to be there to watch the carnage.

When Mrs. Anderson dismisses me, I'm the last girl to enter the changing rooms. Steam rises from the showers as Cleo and Daphne step out. I strip off and drop my uniform and towel onto the bench, then shove my way into a cubicle as the warning bell rings. Outside, I can hear Cleo and her minions giggling. "Bye, Mackenzie," Brandy yells as the gym door slams shut. Peels of laughter echo through the walls.

Since I'm already late and my last class is mathematics, which I don't understand anyway, I take my time under the water, shampooing my hair with the fancy organic products the school supplies. When I reek of lavender and lemongrass, I step out of the water and reach for my towel and clothes.

They're not there.

I left them in a pile on the bench in front of my locker. I know I did. Now they're gone.

From outside, a fresh wave of laughter rises.

Those skank-ass bitches stole my clothes.

My head spins. Water droplets roll off the ends of my hair and cascade across my back. I debate my options – I could change back into my gym clothes... except I put them in my backpack, inside my gym locker, and the locker key was on top of the pile of clothes they stole. I slam my fist into the metal.

Fuck. *Fuck.*

My feet slap against the non-slip mats and I pace along the stalls, pressing the heels of my hands into my eyes until I see squiggles.

You've dealt with worse than this.

You've lived through a hell those princesses can't even contemplate.

Get your shit together.

I scan every corner of the locker room for a possible solution – some discarded clothing or even a towel I can wrap around myself. My foot skims something. I bend down and pick it up – someone's discarded Sharpie. I pull off the cap and test it against my palm. It still works.

Hmmm.

Maybe it's time someone shows Cleo what happens when you mess with someone who has nothing to lose.

MACKENZIE

The snickers hit the moment I step outside.

Cleo and her crew are waiting for me, and they've roped several guys into hanging around, forming a gauntlet of shame along the corridor.

The laughter lasts for three steps. Three agonizing steps where I relive a world of agony. Where I remember another sound – my scream echoing back on me inside the coffin – and the horror it seared into my soul. Even though I hold my chin high, my insides burn with all the rage and terror of that night.

Three steps, and the laughter dies.

Three steps, and they read the words scrawled across my skin.

WHORE.

BITCH.

ICE QUEEN.

GHOST SLUT.

YOU DON'T OWN ME.

I AM NOT MY BODY.

And down my arms and across my chest, in huge, loopy

letters that circle my nipples between a lopsided doodle of a crown, the words:

I AM MACKENZIE MALLOY.

It is a total bitch to write legibly on yourself upside down, especially across my breasts, but I got the hang of it. Now my whole body is covered in graffiti – words of affirmation, words of rage. The words I've had to tell myself in the dark over and over and over again, until I believed them.

My words of war.

Cleo's perfect lips freeze in this O-shape, like one of those bobbing clowns at a fairground. Behind her, Daphne's hand flies to her mouth. At the end of the row, I can feel Alec LeMarque's eyes sweep over my body, and it's like something slimy sliding across my skin.

Noah stands beside Alec, his hands in his pockets. His eyes never leave mine, and although they still burn with that same seething hatred, there's a respect there, too.

Eli elbows Alec in the side as he shoves his way to the front of the crowd. He starts to shrug off his blazer. "Mackenzie, here. Take this. I'll—"

"What's going on here?" A voice cuts through the chaos. A hard lump forms in my throat as Ms. Drysdale pushes her way through the crowd. She takes one look at me and throws up her arms in front of me. "All of you, get to class."

No one moves. Eli stands there with both arms still trapped in his blazer.

"Go. You too, Mr. Hart. Or I'm hauling all your parents in here to explain why you're being suspended for sexual misconduct."

One by one they peel away. Cleo shoots me a triumphant smile as she loops her arm in Noah's. The two of them climb the stairs, their heads bend together in whispers. Eli looks like he wants to argue, and he's got his blazer off now and is holding it out.

"I said, go to class, Mr. Hart. I've got this under control."

Eli's eyes flick to mine, as if asking my permission. I nod. He backs away, his gaze not leaving mine until he's around the corner and out of sight.

Ms. Drysdale shrugs off her jacket and loops it over my shoulders. "What the hell do you think you're doing? Is this a joke?"

"No joke," I say, my face serious. "It's my political science project. How did I do?"

Her eyes bug out. "What?"

"You told us to explore propaganda and social justice movements. I've done that by using my body – a woman's body, which has long been exploited for political propaganda – as a tool to reclaim my own narrative." I skim my hands over my breasts, smudging the M of Mackenzie. "You have to admit, if the idea is to get people to pay attention, it *has* been remarkably effective."

Ms. Drysdale's mouth quirks up. "You've got some ovaries on you, Malloy. Tell you what, I'll give you a perfect grade if you go back into the changing rooms and put your uniform back on."

"I can't. My clothes were stolen."

She sighs as she yanks her coat closed across my chest. It's a dark maroon trench reaching to my knees, and I belt it at the waist to cover all my lady bits. It's an awesome coat – the kind of thing I might have worn in another life. Now that I'm covered up, she snaps her fingers. "Come with me."

I follow my history teacher into a cramped office at the back of the Humanities block. She gestures for me to sit as she roots around in a suitcase behind her desk. I stare at my feet, which I kick out in slow circles. My toe brushes the corner of a quilt tucked under her desk.

"This is cool." I hold up a corner of the quilt. It's covered with different-shaped helmets from history – the Corinthian helmet of the Greek hoplite, a Roman centurion's *galea*, a medieval great helm. It looks hand-stitched.

"Oh, that." Red flares in Ms. Drysdale's cheeks. "It gets cold in here. This patriarchal establishment wasn't built with a heating system because they believed frostbite would turn boys into men, and I'm not allowed a space heater because it's a fire hazard. Even with two layers of thermal stockings, I freeze my ass off in winter."

I nod, but I can't help but notice the pile of clothes in the suitcase in the corner, the takeout containers scattered across the desk, and the corner of a pillow behind the bookshelves. Ms. Drysdale is sleeping in her office.

I shouldn't give a shit, but it seems so ridiculous that I have this whole big house with twelve bedrooms and its own indoor bowling alley, while the only person in this entire shitty school who has actually been nice to me is sleeping in her office. I open my mouth to say something, but Ms. Drysdale dumps a load of clothes on my lap.

"Put those on and get out of here. You won't be allowed back into class without your uniform." She holds up a crumpled Mötley Crüe band tee. "I'll be expecting these back."

I finger the edge of the t-shirt, loving the distressed fabric. "I would, too. You have great clothes."

"Please," she scoffs. "You could trade my entire wardrobe for one of your designer handbags and still have money to spare. Don't try to butter me up to get yourself out of trouble for this ridiculous stunt. I'm concerned about you, Mackenzie. From the minute you walked into Stonehurst, you've been determined to paint a target on your back. And you never got a tutor as I suggested—"

"I tried. Noah refused to tutor me."

She sighs. "That's unlike him. I'll find you a tutor."

"That's okay, I'll—"

She didn't let me finish. "You clearly enjoy history, which is rare in a school like this. I stand at the front of class and look out at future leaders and influencers, and not one of them understands how important it is to look to the past. The triumphs and the mistakes. *Especially* the mistakes. You could do well here if you gained a better grasp of academic writing, and that's a skill you can learn with the right tutor. I'll help you, but you'd better not let me down."

She says it with a little tug of her mouth, to show she's half-joking. But I suddenly don't want to disappoint her. Ms. Drysdale points to the door. Her elbow hits a takeout container, batting it off the edge of her desk and into the trash. "Go home, Mackenzie."

I leave her office, wrapping her coat around me to ward off the chill as a light breeze blows off the ocean just down the road. I debate ducking into a bathroom to change into Ms. Drysdale's clothes, but her coat covers me fine and I really just want to go home. I hurry down the front steps of the school and check no one's looking before I hurry toward the bus stop. I check the schedule – twelve minutes before the next bus leaves for Harrington Hills. I pull up the collar of the coat and shrink against the shelter, hoping no one will—

"Well, well, well. Mackenzie Malloy waiting for the bus, looking like Holly GoLightly's sexy cousin."

I whirl around, my heart pounding. Gabriel Fallen steps out from behind a tree, a joint dangling from his fingers.

"I'm going home," I snarl.

"That's unlikely. Mackenzie Malloy doesn't ride the bus like a pleb." Gabriel pauses. "You should see the inside of my tour bus. Now *that's* a bus. I've got a king-size bed in back, silk sheets, a fully-equipped bar. This swing that you hook to the ceiling—"

I turn away so he can't see the blush creeping across my

cheeks. I've read wild stories in the tabloids about Gabriel and that swing. And the idea he might want me to be on it... "Maybe Mackenzie Malloy is trying to save the environment."

Gabriel chuckles. He reaches out and takes my hand, leading me back into the trees that line the parklike-grounds of Stonehurst. He holds out the joint for me. "I heard what happened in gym. Cleo's an evil wench, but you are something else. Want to hang out?"

"You're just asking me that because you know I'm naked under this coat."

Gabriel's eyebrow shoots up. "I didn't, actually. But now I'm *very* interested."

I glance down the street, at the bus rounding the corner toward my stop. There's not another bus for an hour.

Gabriel smiles. The barbell in his lip jiggles.

I take the joint. I'm only human. "What do you have in mind?"

MACKENZIE

As we cut across the park toward the beach, Gabriel
throws his arms around my shoulders, like it's a totally
normal thing to do. My chest tightens, and I find myself struggling for breath.

Gabriel Fallen has his arm around my shoulder.

Chill, bitch.

I don't remember a moment of the walk. Gabriel chats with
ease about things that are completely foreign to me – psycho
fans, stadiums packed with people screaming his name, sharing
a shower with four other guys on a cramped tour bus. He asks
me questions about myself, and I struggle to remember my
name, let alone keep my story straight. I'm relieved when he
turns off the pavement.

"We're here."

Here is a block of ultra-modern apartments overlooking a
private beach. The facades are painted a stark white with all
kinds of weird angles and invisible gutterings – the kind of
design architects go nuts for but would be a complete disaster to
maintain.

From his blazer pocket, Gabriel pulls out an electronic fob

on the end of a chain. He holds it up to a security box, and the metal gate swings open. We walk down winding sandstone steps to a grand front entrance. One entire wall is rough-hewn granite with a waterfall cascading over the top.

Gabriel nods to the waterfall. "I had that installed over the summer. It's too quiet here, even with the surf roaring. I'm so used to being on tour sometimes it's hard to sleep without noise."

Riiiight. He needed some noise, so instead of blasting some music he makes a waterfall down the side of his house. That's totally normal.

"This is yours?" I step into the open-plan kitchen, living, and dining space, taking in the vaulted ceiling with exposed beams and the industrial features. One entire wall is filled with a big-screen TV and state-of-the-art speakers – on the opposite wall, floor-to-ceiling bookshelves are crammed with books and vinyl records.

"Yup. I purchased it when our last album hit it big. I wanted somewhere I could come between tours so I don't ever have to go back to Fallen Castle."

"Your parents have a castle?" I knew Gabriel's family was wealthy, but that's a whole other level.

"Yup. Battlements, swords hanging everywhere, bitter and twisted Lord and Lady torturing the serfs in their dungeon – the works."

I know from his lyrics just how much Gabriel loathes his parents, but it's strange to experience it in person – the twist in his lip and spark of hate in his eyes when he speaks of them. "You're too fucking cool for words."

Gabriel gazes at me, an odd smile tugging at his lips. "Don't look so impressed, Mac. Everyone and their uncle has a castle in Britain. They practically give them away at the airport. I like it here much better." He leans in to lovingly kiss the central heating controls. "Trust me, endure one British winter in a drafty stone hall with no central heating and the romance of a castle wears off."

Intrigued, I pad across to the shelves, pulling out album sleeves at random, taking in the records. Progressive rock, indie, jazz, Scandinavian black metal... Gabriel's tastes were diverse and intriguing. Many of the records are signed or limited editions, still in their sleeves.

It's so odd being here, inside Gabriel's private space. It's not what I imagined. In rock magazines he's always photographed in the midst of chaos – smoking a joint in a recording studio surrounded by trails of guitar leads snaking across the floor, or slumped over some bar in Budapest, or on stage, his hair whirling in all directions as his fingers fly over guitar strings.

"The bathroom's through here if you want to wash that stuff off." Gabriel holds a door open for me, and heat burns in my cheeks as I remember I'm still naked underneath Ms. Drysdale's coat, my skin covered in scrawled words of power. I go into an enormous rain shower, scrubbing at the marker with fancy-smelling soap until the words fade a little. My mind conjures an image of Gabriel naked under this same shower, water cascading over his beautiful inked body, his long, dark hair plastered to his back. I blast the shower on cold, trying to drive out the need that heated my veins from the inside.

When I emerge wearing Ms. Drysdale's clothes, Gabriel takes my hand and gives me a tour, showing off the hot tub on the deck overlooking the ocean, the walk-in pantry stocked with weird British candy, and the guest bedroom he's converted into a studio space, stacked with guitars and recording equipment, the walls covered in tour posters and photographs I long to pore over. His bedroom is a mezzanine floor over the kitchen, open to the space below and the double-height windows overlooking the beach. Up here I can hear the trickle of the waterfall on the outside wall, and over it, the roar of the ocean outside.

I try not to look at Gabriel's bed or think about Gabriel in his bed. I fail. My feet root themselves to the spot at the top of the stairs, and I'm in desperate danger of melting into a puddle on his shiny wood floor.

I try to cover my discomfort with snark. "With all that water running outside, how do you not wet the bed every night?"

Gabriel's grin rends me. "Maybe I have better things to dream about than not reaching the bathroom on time."

I swallow, taking in the diffused light, the rumpled comforter in soft grey, the band tees strewn around the laundry chute. "I'm surprised you don't have an enormous round bed for your harem of groupies."

"A shagrificial altar?" Gabriel smiles. "Why, Malloy, how little you must think of me. You're the first girl I've ever brought here."

I snort, assuming he's lying. But Gabriel's face is easy, free of tension. I wonder, if he's being truthful, why he chose *me* to bring here, to step inside this private piece of him.

Gabriel flings open the balcony door. The roar of the surf rushes in, enveloping me. Gabriel sits on a recliner, crossing his boots on a small table. He lights up a joint. "I'm a rockstar. I've never had to look far for pussy and all the drama that goes along with it – I don't need that shit cluttering up my home."

Then why am I here? I ask inside my head as I lean back in a recliner and accept the joint from Gabriel. Smoke curls between us as we pass it back and forth in silence. He scrolls through his phone and selects a playlist. And a song comes over the built-in speakers – slow and sultry, mournful piano and two string instruments dueling for supremacy.

"This is my friend Dorien's band, Broken Muse." Gabriel flicks his tongue against the barbell in his labret. "He's this hyper-intense goth dude, but he knows how to party. You'd hate him."

"I hate most people." I let the music fill me. It's like nothing I've ever heard before. I never knew classical instruments could create a sound like that.

"But not me?" He cocks an eyebrow.

"You're tolerable."

"So Mac, do you ever feel like you're an imposter in your own life?"

I glare at him. "What happened to small talk?"

Gabriel shrugs. "People always talk bollocks around me. I got into music because I wanted to do something real, but instead I'm surrounded by fake people all the time. Go on, then. Do you ever feel like an imposter?"

So weed makes Gabriel pensive, then. I should have guessed, him being a sensitive, brooding rockstar and all. I nod, blowing a trail of smoke. "All the fucking time. What if I told you I'm not who you think I am?"

"I know you're not," Gabriel says, and I choke on the sweet smoke. But Gabriel's smiling. He wouldn't be smiling if he truly knew. "I know all your secrets, Mac. I know that beneath your Ice Queen facade beats the heart of an even colder Ice Queen."

I punch him in the arm. "You're a dick. And I'm not all ice. I've got layers."

"Like an onion?" he grins.

"More like a triple-chocolate-cherry layer cake."

He nods. "We should stop talking about food. You're making me hungry. But yeah, you wear a mask. We all do. I don't think you've taken yours off in a long time. I get that. The only time I ever took my mask off was when I played music, or when I was hanging with Dylan. But now—" Gabriel shrugs.

I notice his past tense. "You're not playing music anymore?"

"I can't. I haven't played since Dylan died. We're already late with the new album. Everyone's on my arse to finish writing the songs – the band, the manager, the label. But I *can't*. All my life, all I've had to do is *listen* and the songs appear, fully formed. It's as if they already exist, and all I have to do is pluck them out of the air. But now, when I listen all I hear is this deafening, apocalyptic silence."

And I wonder if that silence has something to do with the waterfall outside. And if Gabriel's silence is anything like the silence of being a ghost inside an empty house for four years. But I don't say that, because I don't want to talk about myself. I just want to fill my head with THC and listen to Gabriel talk forever. "Is it because of Dylan that you can't play?"

Gabriel takes another long toke. "Dylan's family works on our estate – we've been mates since we could crawl, raising hell everywhere we went. We spent so much time hanging out together, going hunting in our forest, that I didn't notice the things that divided us. Like, Dylan couldn't go to my posh school. As soon as he was old enough, he had to work on the estate. He and his family came on all our fancy holidays, but they were still expected to cook and serve and ferry us around. I never thought any of that mattered, because I'm a self-obsessed wanker. And then I read his suicide note. He spent his childhood watching my spoiled arse get everything I wanted, and then when my music – *our* music – took off, he was still in the background cleaning up after me, holding my hair while I threw up, dragging me away from bad situations. No wonder he hated me. I'm not surprised the music died with him."

I study Gabriel as he talks. His flirty, happy mask slides away, revealing the dark edges of his soul. His fingers tremble as he brings the joint to his mouth, and I long to rest my hand on his leg, to pull him into my arms, to kiss away the horror of what he saw in that hotel room.

"Right." He gives me this sad smile. "I've spilled my guts. Your turn. Why have you been a ghost all these years, Mackenzie Malloy?"

The words trip over my tongue, desperate to escape. For four years, Gabriel has been the moonlight shining through the bars of my prison window. He sings the stars and the blood and the rain. I'd give anything to give him back the stars to sing again, even reveal my darkest secrets.

Nope. Not happening.

I snap my mouth shut and glare at him. This is why I shouldn't be here, why getting close to people is dangerous. Especially sexy British rockstar type-people.

Gabriel leans forward, his face inches from mine. The raw beauty of his pain slips away as quickly as it appeared, tucked back in its heart-shaped box inside him. His sugary, smoky scent mingles with the pot in the air, making the warnings in my head float away as soon as they appear. Gabriel's flirty smile draws me deeper, and I sit on my hands to stop myself from reaching up and pulling him to me, taking that barbell between my teeth and tugging it until he begs for me—

"Come to a party with me on Saturday," he says in that cock-sure way. It's not a question. Gabriel Fallen isn't used to hearing no. "Normally, I'd say Stonehurst parties are bollocks, but I have a feeling with you on my arm, we'll fuck shit up."

"Whose party?" I can barely get the words out.

"Daphne Ballantyne. She's Noah's ex. He'll be pissed I invited you, which is even more reason why you should be there."

"I'm not sure I want to further incur the wrath of Noah, in addition to all the other enemies I made." I tear my gaze from his and rub my arm, where the words 'I AM MACKENZIE MALLOY' were still visible on my skin. I'd be scrubbing myself raw tonight to get the rest of it off before cheerleading trials.

Worth it.

"I'll protect you. I'm not Noah's bitch." Gabriel's face lights up with that wicked grin – the one that promised all sorts of delightful and filthy shenanigans. "I do what I want, and I want us to go to this party together."

"I'll go on one condition."

"Mmmm?" Gabriel tilts his head to the side. A lock of dark hair falls over his eye, and I think I might swoon.

"I'm not talking about where I've been the last four years. Don't ask. Don't ply me with alcohol or tell me sob stories about Dylan in an attempt to make me talk. Mention my past, and I'm gone. Got it?"

"Oh, phew." Gabriel pretends to wipe sweat off his brow. "And here I was thinking you wanted me to do something *taxing*, but ignoring deep-rooted emotional trauma to clear the path for superficial fun? That's my specialty. It would be an honor to have you as my never-talk-about-anything-serious-again date. Now, this is a costume party. You got any ideas?"

I rub my hands together. "Fallen, you and I are going to overthrow kings."

MACKENZIE

*R*ich people must go to a ton of fancy-dress parties, because my so-called mother has an entire bay of her extensive closet dedicated to glittering costumes. Not a single one of them contains enough fabric. I try on several different options before settling on a gold gladiator costume with a skirt so short an anime schoolgirl would raise her eyebrows.

I surprise myself by how annoyed I am at its lack of historical accuracy. I'm a gladiator, and I don't even have a weapon. At least I could do something about that. I hunt through a closet behind the sauna filled with unused sports gear until I find a small fishing net. I pull the end of the handle off and hide my knife inside.

Outside, in the groundskeepers shed, I find an old gardening pitchfork. I wipe off the dust and spiders and spray-paint it and the net gold to match my outfit. It's still not historically accurate, but when I add gold spike-heeled sandals that lace up my thighs, I know I look fierce.

Plus, if anyone says shit to me, I'll stab 'em through with my trident.

I sneak out through the maintenance shed and wait on the corner of Santa Casilda Drive for Gabriel to pick me up in his Jaguar Mark I. Such an obnoxious Brit. He's dressed as Julius Caesar in a purple-edged toga, with stems of laurel twisted through his hair. Tattoos encircle every inch of his exposed skin, and I swallow a lump of desire as I take him in.

Gabriel's eyes rake over my body as I slide into the seat next to him, propping my trident and net between my legs. "What's the net for?"

"I'm a *retiarius*. It's a type of Roman gladiator who fought in the ring using a trident and net."

"I thought you were trying for a sexy Poseidon or something. Fishing ain't hot."

I raise an eyebrow at him. "It is when I do it."

Gabriel tosses his head back and laughs. When he pulls his chin in again, he looks kind of shocked, like he hasn't laughed in so long he's forgotten what it felt like. He pulls me close, his arm around me, his fingers dancing ghosts along my bare arm.

"Well, sexy Poseidon, are you ready to cast that net?"

I nod. Gabriel's eyes linger on mine, his face close, some internal battle raging inside him. My breath hitches. Is he going to... but he draws back and, with a cheeky grin, guns the engine.

Gabriel drives exactly the way I expect – like speed limits don't apply to him, like he's forgotten which side of the road Americans drive on. We pull up at an impressive mansion on Beaumont Hill – spread over three levels with floor-to-ceiling windows looking out across the emerald water. Bodies crowd the downstairs rooms and spill out onto the balconies and gardens. There are more people here than go to our school, I'm sure of it.

Inside, it's wall to wall people. I recognize classmates but also faces from magazines – Instagram influencers, teen movie stars, reality TV hosts. The party spills out through sliding glass panels around an infinity pool with views over a sprawling tropical garden.

I grip Gabriel's arm as he leads me up a wide, floating staircase made of exposed steel to the second floor. Here, the entire wall of the house is glass that retracts into the wall. At one end of the balcony, a DJ spins hard house music while on the other, two bartenders shake cocktails. For a seventeen-year-old's party.

This is insanity.

I'll take two.

We stand in line for the bar. I have no idea what to order, but there seem to be only two options – a pink thing or a blood-red thing. Gabriel makes small talk with the bartender while he mixes us two pink things in highball glasses. Gabriel has this ease about him, finding conversation with anyone he comes across. I wonder again why he's decided to fixate on me.

I don't belong here.

On the surface, I appear to fit in – my golden gladiator costume looks like it came from the same store as the sexy devil in the corner or the slutty Tardis dancing with a masked Dr. Who. I even see a blonde in the corner striking a pose with a minor film star, her naked body painted gold, a crusader's sword gripped between her fingers. An Academy Award. *Gag me with a rusty fishhook.*

I feel naked, too, like they can all read my past on my skin. The things I've survived etched into my flesh, setting me apart, marking me as other. They're all far too comfortable, too sure of their future. Tomorrow they'll wake up hungover and they will still own the world. For me, every day is a tightrope walk without a safety net, and one wrong move could see my neck snap.

Gabriel hands me a drink. I sip it gingerly. It tastes like a unicorn farted into a case of top-shelf gin.

Gabriel links my arm in his and yells over the music, "Let's find Eli."

We walk a circuit of the room. Eyes flicker over me, their judgments burrowing into my skin. Gabriel tries to talk to some guy from school, but the music's too loud. The bass vibrates the bones right out of my body, or maybe that's the warmth of Gabriel's touch turning me to jelly.

Eli's nowhere to be seen, but we do find Noah hidden in a dark corner with Cleo draped over his lap, her lipstick smeared across his sharp cheekbones. She's dressed as Cleopatra, of course, with a gold lamé dress and a collar of glittering diamonds. Cleo must've decided Noah was a worthy new target. They both glare at us, but of course Gabriel ignores them and drags me over.

"Don't you two look cozy together," he yells.

"Get lost, Gabe." Noah pulls Cleo onto his lap. She wraps her arms around him and presses her lips to his. Their kiss is hot, searing. His fingers drift up her spine to tangle in her hair. I wish for a cold shower or the floor to open up and swallow me.

Noah's eyes never leave mine. He's kissing another woman, and all he can do is burn his hate into my retinas. A shiver runs down my spine – the kind of shiver that grows an ache between my legs.

As we walk away, Noah's eyes follow me across the room. I know better than anyone how hate can heat the blood, can stoke a fire of longing no amount of soft touches or kind words will ever quench. Does he feel it too? The all-consuming fire that draws us together? Is that why Noah looks at me as if he's burrowing into my soul? Is that why he can't forget me?

We head downstairs. A group of guys pass a crack pipe around. They offer it to Gabriel, but he declines. The music rattles in my chest, my bones, my brain. We move out to the pool. There's space to breathe out here, small groups scattered around talking, couples lying in the grass or pressed up against the walls, lips, hands pawing. I go to sit on one of the loungers, but it's occupied by a girl in an angel costume being fucked by two guys in devil horns. I jerk away.

Gabriel laughs, pulling me close. "You act as though you've never been to parties like this before."

"Sure I have," I shout back. "I just think this one's lame. Where's the petting zoo?"

"Nice try, but nope, I definitely don't think you've been around, because I'd have remembered that glorious arse." Gabriel's eyes are heavy-lidded, dangerous – just the way I like him. "Where have you been hiding away, Mackenzie Malloy?"

I wag my finger at him. "Nope. We have an agreement. You can't ask me about my past."

"Mmmm." Gabriel's lips graze my neck. "Fair enough. I can think of much better things to be doing than talking."

He kisses me. It happens so fast that all the things I expected to stress about during the moment of my first kiss don't even register. There's a flicker where my heart plunges into my throat, and then Gabriel's lips are warm and sweet on mine. The pressure has me sinking into his body, like he's melting my limbs into liquid and I'll slip through his fingers and end up a puddle on the floor.

I'm kissing Gabriel Fallen.

I'm kissing the mouth that sings the stars.

Gabriel's lips are hot velvet. He presses and parts and cajoles, and my mouth is falling open, and I'm falling into him. And then his tongue is in my mouth, tasting and touching, that stud a bite of ice against the heat of him. I want him to devour me from the inside out.

Gabriel pulls back, not a jerk, but slow and languid, his eyes sweeping over me, taking in the reaction in my body – the tremble in my hands, the heat pooling in my cheeks and in... other places. His eyes cloak with darkness, and the corner of his mouth twists up into his signature smirk.

Then he plants both hands on my shoulders and pushes me into the pool.

The cold water hits me like a freight train, forcing the air from my lungs. Icicles puncture my skin, piercing my organs. My net flies out of my hand, and I flail under the water, twisting my body to avoid impaling myself on my trident.

I struggle, gulp in water. I break the surface, gasping.

Gabriel dives in beside me, dog-paddling toward me. He smiles. "That was brilliant."

"What did you do that for?" I shriek. And in a moment, Gabriel has undone it all, the way being with him undoes me. He's peeled off the makeup and the fancy haircut and the designer costume, and laid me bare for the whole party to see. And they see, and they point, and they laugh, and they remind me with every peal of laughter that I'm not one of them. Anger seethes through me, irrational but justified.

Gabriel reaches me and tries to embrace me. "You looked like you need cooling off."

There's that smirk again. I know he's playing with me, keeping his promise to not get too deep. I raise my hand and slap it off his face.

"Fuck you, Gabriel." I swim to the side, trying to push myself out of the pool. The dress clings to my body, weighing me down. I slip back into the water.

Cleo stands over me as I try to shove myself out again. She grinds her stiletto into my hand. I scream and fall back, spluttering as my head goes under.

"Cleo, you bitch." Gabriel splashes her. Cleo shrieks and leaps back, but she's giggling. Any attention is good attention.

My lips still tingle from Gabriel's kiss, but the burn of humiliation in my cheeks overpowers it. Gabriel sends another wave of water over the side of the pool, but Cleo's too far back now and all he manages to do is drench the waiter who's offering drinks. He doesn't even apologize.

"Mackenzie, wait." Gabriel dog-paddles toward me. Behind him, the waves of laughter cascade over my head. It stings worse than the freezing water.

"Leave me alone." I dive away from him, ducking between entwined couples. I swim to the steps at the other end, kicking a guy in the chest as he tries to grab me. He leers up at me, his eyes bloodshot from some cocktail of drugs.

It's too much.

I see red.

The red of rage, the red of losing control.

The red of blood staining my reflection.

I run toward the house, the laughter following me. The logical part of me knows on some level they're not laughing at me. They don't know me. But logic can't force its way through the blood—

SMACK.

I slam into something hard.

The impact sends me sprawling across the patio. A fresh wave of laughter ripples through the crowd. My head swims. At first, I think someone has closed the glass doors on me, trapping me outside. But then I focus on the shape looming over me.

Noah, his eyes blazing, his hands curled into fists at his sides. "Get out," he hisses. "You don't belong here."

You don't belong here.

"I was invited," I snap back. It takes all my self-preservation to keep the sob from my voice.

Someone's behind me. Warm hands lift me under my shoulders, hauling me to my feet. It doesn't feel comforting with Noah bearing down on me. It makes me feel weak.

I'm not weak.

"Fuck, Mackenzie, I'm so sorry." Gabriel's silky voice caresses my ear. A note of distress creeps into his words. But it's an act. I know it's a fucking act. Gabriel pulls pain out his ass on stage every night, and we all believe it's real.

I believed it was real.

I shrug Gabriel off me. I realize too late that one of my heels broke in the fall. I pitch forward. I throw out my hands and steady myself on the only thing that will break my fall – Noah. I grab his shoulders, my wet body pressing against him. I feel the warmth of his skin through my sodden outfit.

His entire body stiffens under my touch, and I imagine even his heart shriveling in his chest. This close, I catch a whiff of Noah's deep, inky scent – shadowed and strange and tinged with salt and jasmine. Noah's breath hisses out between clenched teeth, and something hard presses against my thigh.

An erection.

He's hard.

I think I've imagined it, but no. I freeze in place, and his cock grazes my naked thigh, giving a little jerk like a nod of approval. Noah's hard as a rod.

For me.

"No one wants you at school, at our parties." Noah's lips press against my earlobe. His hatred stains my skin. "Not after what you did."

"I was thirteen when your brother died," I whisper back, my lips grazing his ear in return. I enjoy the way his body squirms. "I had such a crush on you. It's on every page of my diary, your name and mine circled in broken hearts."

On impulse, I reach down and cup him through his pants. I know people must see this, but I don't care – this moment is for Noah and me alone. This is our battle of wills.

Noah's body tenses, coiling in on itself like a snake eating its own tail. A strangled cry escapes his lips.

I am Mackenzie Malloy, and I can make even my enemies hard for me.

I rub his cock through his pants, and he squirms in this delicious way.

"Fuck you, Mackenzie," Noah rasps. He doesn't move, even as his cock jerks in my hand. "Stay away from me, or you'll wish you'd never been born."

And something about pressing my body against him, feeling every plane and curve of his muscled frame while I'm dripping wet in a ruined costume, breaks me. I know he's seen behind my mask, into the bruises that stain my soul. And I want to bruise him, too.

My fist grips his cock, holding him against me. I lift my knee and drive it hard into his balls.

NOAH

*F*uck.

Fuck.

MACKENZIE

I walk home, shivering, in bare feet.

Noah bellows a string of curses that follow me all the way to Malloy Manor. I revel in the feel of his body crumpling against me as he doubled over. The sight of his beautiful eyes bugged out and his face twisted in pain will comfort me on dark nights.

I spend the rest of the weekend playing with Queen Boudica in the ballroom of my blood-stained house. Gabriel calls me twice, but I don't answer. I can't face him. I put on my favorite Octavia's Ruin album and blast it at top volume. I listen to him sing the stars and the rain, and I let a single tear fall into Queen Boudica's fur.

I think about Noah, and about his cock grinding against me even as he spat words of hatred in my ear. And I think that even if there was a sliver of a chance we might burn up in each other's hatred, it's gone now.

The dread of school on Monday sits heavy on my skin. I consider staying home, but I know I can't avoid them forever, and I can't risk truancy officers coming here to look for me.

My phone pings. Even though I don't have social media, I

have alerts set up on my name. Hundreds of photographs of my wet, bedraggled ass flood my feed, making it outside of the Stonehurst circle to celebrity gossip sites. The comments scroll past. *Bitch. Skank. She looks like trailer trash. Did you see her with Noah? She threw herself at him even though he hates her. How desperate can you get?*

I hate them.

They're right.

I hate myself.

I press my palms into my eyes. Why did I ever think this plan would work? I should have known I couldn't fit into their world anymore. I'm too messed up. Too broken.

THE ALARM on my phone rings on Monday morning. Queen Boudica stretches out her paw, touching my cheek. "Mew?" She begs me to stay in bed, to keep her warm with my body. It's the only thing I can do right.

"I'm sorry, girl." A single tear rolls down my cheek – the third tear I've shed in as many weeks. It's disgusting. I give in to this one indulgence and allow it to fall, splashing against my chest and rolling off the end of my nipple. I wipe my eyes before the next tear can fall, pressing my fists into my sockets, pushing the pain back inside, where it belongs.

I lower my hands. My gaze catches my reflection in the mirror over my dressing table. Mackenzie Malloy stares back at me, her jaw set with determination. Haughty defiance burns in her eyes.

Bring it on, bitches.

My mask in place, my armor protecting me, I climb out of bed and prepare to face Stonehurst Prep.

SCHOOL IS JUST as horrible as I expect it to be.

But I get through it. Minute by minute, hour by hour. I stare straight ahead in class, trying to tune out the whispers, the laughter, the disgusting sexual advances lobbed at me. My locker is plastered with printed photographs from the night – me, kissing Gabriel beside the pool, struggling with him in the water like a siren possessed. Me, pressed up against Noah, my hand in his crotch, my face buried in his hair.

Gabriel. Fuck. I can't even look him in the eye. He kissed me, and I...

The double standard grinds my gears. Noah was the one hard for me. He started this shit, and yet he holds court like a king while I bear the brunt of their cruelty.

Classes crawl along at a snail's pace, but at least under the eyes of the teachers, I have some safety. I debate skipping lunch altogether, but I know my absence will be noted. I know Noah will count it as his victory.

Something hits my hair while I'm waiting in line for lunch. I keep my eyes fixed ahead, raising my hand to touch something slimy dripping down my hair. Out of the corner of my eye, Eli gets up from the royal table and strides toward me.

I can't deal with him today. I step out of the line and circle back toward the door. I slam my elbow into a weedy-looking guy loitering beside the condiment stand. When he turns in surprise, I grab his tray out of his hands and make a run for it.

"Hey, that's my lunch, you crazy bitch."

The laughter swirls around me like a tornado. I don't stop, don't look. No one touches me or accosts me. I run until I reach the bathroom, and I slam the stall door shut and lean against it, the tray wobbling in my shaking hands.

I've just about got my racing heart back to normal when the

bathroom door swings open, and a clan of hyenas enters, cackling and baying for blood. They crowd around my stall, beating their fists against the walls. The lock rattles.

Faces pop over the top of the stall. "That's her," Cleo sneers. "I told you she eats in here. What a loser."

Something hits my cheek. Wet, wadded up toilet paper. The cackling rises an octave. It pounds in my ears, and for the first time since I woke up to find myself trapped in a coffin, I *long* for silence.

I swipe at Cleo's face with my nails, but she's too fast. I'm trapped. "Grab the bins," she says.

Fuck no.

I throw my hands up to cover my head as a cascade of waste and filth topple over the sides of the stall. Wadded toilet paper, used sanitary pads and pill packets bounce off and pile up around me. Their fists drum a relentless beat as they empty the contents of the bins over the stall, over my head.

MACKENZIE

I wait in the stall, numb, surrounded by stinking trash, until the bell rings, until they leave, their laughter echoing down the hall. I wait until I'm sure I'm alone.

Alone.

I wrap my fist in one of the fluffy towels, smash one of the high windows in the bathroom, and crawl outside. The freshmen have gym class, so the playing fields are filled with students. I duck behind the trees as I make my way to the front gate. I don't want them to see.

I can't face the bus, so I walk up to Harrington Hills. The sun beats down on me, mingling sweat with my already disgusting scent. People cross the street to avoid me. Every stomp of my shoes against the pavement drives home the undeniable truth.

I don't belong here.

The walk takes over an hour, but finally, I see the tower of the manor's third story peeking between the tops of the jacaranda trees, the breeze blowing up from the ocean making the purple blooms dance in fairy-tale reverie. I duck into the wooded area and head for the door of the maintenance shed, digging in my pocket for the key. I know as soon as my hand rests on the door that something's wrong.

I locked the door when I left this morning.

I *always* lock the door.

Yet it swings open at my touch, revealing the rows of machinery that operate the car lift and other features of the house.

Shit.

I contemplate backing out and calling Antony. But he'll be at the club, preparing his fighters for the match tonight. He needs to focus. Plus, I don't want him to see me like this. I reek. I need a shower.

Righteous anger bubbles inside me. This is *my* home. On today of all days, the violation of my personal space is too much to take. I pull Antony's knife from my shoe and flick it open.

I slip off my shoes, padding forward silently on my stockinged feet. My eyes dart into the corners of the machine room as I step inside. The fans drop the temperature, and goose-bumps rise on my skin.

No one in here.

I reach the other side and nudge the door into the tunnel. It swings open. I duck inside, pressing my back against the concrete wall. Adrenaline pounds through my veins as I creep along the tunnel to the car lift. My fingers grip the balustrade, and I haul myself up the spiral stairs into the garage.

In the gloom, the rows of cars appear menacing – like ranks of Roman soldiers advancing on an outnumbered foe. I pick my steps cautiously, peering behind each car, checking around for signs of an intruder. My body coils with tension, ready to strike.

I reach the other side of the garage. Nothing. Where are they? *Who* are they?

The door into the house is ajar. I know I closed that, too – I don't want Queen Boudica playing in the machinery. A fresh wave of rage and panic assaults me as I hear a faint, pained 'mew' from the other side.

Queen Boudica is in there.

I bolt forward, my caution forgotten. I fling open the garage door. The garage opens into a wide hallway. On one side is a commercial kitchen where a personal chef would once have cooked for our family. On the other side, the chef's living quarters and a laundry worthy of a Victorian poorhouse. I breeze past these rooms, following my kitty's cries.

I turn the corner and gasp.

Queen Boudica lies in the middle of the floor, the marble around her smeared with blood. She lifts her head, those fierce yellow eyes swimming with pain, and gives me a pitiful 'mew.'

The sound breaks my heart.

Behind her, scrawled across the wall of the central atrium in wobbly letters, are the words:

GO AWAY

MACKENZIE

Cold, righteous anger embraces me. I rush across the room and scoop Queen Boudica into my arms, clutching her to my chest and feeling the racing patter of her heart. Blood dribbles from a slash across her abdomen – a knife cut, cruel and deliberate.

GO AWAY

The rage engulfs me, like falling through ice. I am frozen blood and bone. I am made of ice and vengeance. I am what this disgusting act has made me.

GO AWAY

I know who did this.

Alec. Alec, who swore he'd get me for his nose, for rejecting him. Alec, who wasn't at school today, lording it over me with his buddy Noah. He could have waited for me to leave the house through the maintenance shed. The door is heavy and set on counterweights, so it swings closed on its own time. I'm always in a hurry so I usually leave it to shut on its own. He probably hid in the bushes and waited until I left for school, then snuck inside and hurt Queen Boudica. But how did he know about the maintenance shed? I'm careful to cover my movements, not even the paparazzi have discovered it yet—

This isn't all Alec. I remember the face peering at me from the top of the security fence. *Eli.* He's friends with Noah and Alec.

He told them about the gate.

The words in my old diary flash in front of my eyes, and I'm so angry I black out for a moment. Eli's supposed to protect me. He—

Something crashes over my head.

My heart leaps into my throat.

He's still here.

He's inside my *house.*

When I recover enough of my faculties to think clearly, I cradle Queen Boudica against me and crawl down the hallway, keeping each movement as silent as possible until I reach my father's study.

SMASH.

I jump at the sound of something breaking. It comes from upstairs. I think of all my things scattered around the ballroom. *If they've destroyed my shit, I'm going to fuck them up.*

I'm tempted – oh so tempted – to creep upstairs and drive my knife into Alec's kidneys while his back is turned. My fingers tighten on the blade, and I imagine the satisfaction of feeling it sink into his flesh. I make the motion of twisting it inside him, mincing his organs to mush. But I won't leave Queen Boudica. I don't know how many people are upstairs or what they intend to do to us, and I won't put her in more danger. Right now, I need to get those bastards out of my house.

I crawl into the study, find the release for the panic room, and tuck us both inside. As the door swings shut behind me, I mash the buttons to bring up the CCTV. I've disabled several cameras to save money, but I still had five trained on different areas of the house. I flick through the feeds, and I see him – a figure in dark pants and a green hoodie climbing out an upstairs window.

He's alone.

The figure leaps from the ledge. I suck in a breath, hoping he'll break his leg on the flagstones. No such luck – he lands with remarkable grace in a soft garden bed, narrowly missing a towering cacti because the gods want to spit in my face today.

He's on his feet in a flash, running for the wall, right where Eli stacked the lawn furniture. He bounces on one of the chairs, grabs the top of the wall, and vaults over like he's in the fucking Olympics or some shit. He tucks his chin down, obscuring his face in the shadow of the sage-green hood, but as he sails across the wall I get a good look at his hoodie.

Only it's not a hoodie.

It's a Stonehurst Prep letterman jacket.

Alec LeMarque's jacket.

I clutch Queen Boudica to my chest as I press the phone to my ear. It goes straight to voicemail. "I need you," I whisper. "Alec LeMarque was in my house. Get Galen over here, *now*."

ANTONY'S BOYS swarm the manor, searching from top to bottom in case Alec left an accomplice behind. On the first floor landing, they find a table upturned, the porcelain vase smashed across the tiles. That was the sound that startled me. My room – my old room – is also a mess, more of a mess than I'd left it after I found the diary. My porcelain dolls had been thrown against the walls until their heads shattered. But the ballroom and my new bedroom remain untouched, thank fuck.

They don't find any intruders. We have no way of knowing what Alec might've seen.

I know this is bad, but it's a background concern to me right now. I'm covered in sticky mess from Cleo's stunt, my shirt stained with Queen Boudica's blood. I pace across the kitchen while Antony's doctor – the infamous Dr. Galen – lays Queen Boudica on the table and expertly stitches her wound. She stares up at him with those saucer eyes swimming in pain, her fur matted, her breathing labored.

The words flash across my vision. Words written in the blood of my best friend. GO AWAY GO AWAY GO AWAY GO AWAY GO AWAY.

My fist connects with the kitchen wall.

"Easy, tiger." Antony doesn't look up. He's on his phone, no doubt rescheduling the practice session.

"He cut my cat," I hiss. "I'm going to cut off his *balls*."

"All done. She's a tough girl." Dr. Galen kisses the top of Queen Boudica's head. She nuzzles in his arms, groggy from the drugs. "She'll be tearing up the joint again in no time."

"She's going to be fine?"

"The wound looked nasty, but it was superficial. Her attacker managed to miss all her major organs. She'll be groggy for a few days, and I'd keep her away from other cats." He strokes her head, and I notice several rows of claw marks across his hand. "She's much more accommodating than my usual patients."

Considering Dr. Galen is usually digging bullets out of crooks or repairing nasty wounds for cage fighters, I take his word for it.

I take Queen Boudica from him. She stares up at me with wide, pain-soaked eyes, her claws digging into my shirt. I'm never, ever letting her out of my sight again.

Dr. Galen washes his hands in the sink and exits with a nod to Antony. My cousin leans against the cabinets and fixes me with that look of his, the one that says he'll follow me into the fires of hell to fuck shit up with me, and he'll laugh the whole way. "What are we dealing with here?"

"Alec LeMarque," I growl. My fingers curl into claws. "He's been gunning for revenge over his precious nose. That prick Eli must've told him how to get into the house – I found out from the diary that I used to sneak him in through there. Eli's the only person who could possibly know about the maintenance shed – the paps haven't been anywhere near that side of the house. He's the only one I saw on the CCTV, but I don't know what he's seen or how much he knows."

"Shit." Antony cracks his knuckles. "Just say the word, Claws, and I'll make sure he never speaks again."

If he'd offered a month ago, I would have shut him down. I needed to deal with my own shit. Antony's solutions tended to be more... permanent. But that's before they invaded my space and fucked with my precious Queen Boudica.

This is *war*.

"I want them all to pay." A slow grin spreads across my lips as I savor the anticipation of vengeance. "And Alec LeMarque gets a personal visit."

MACKENZIE

*I*t feels like old times, Antony and I hanging out together. At least, it feels like the old times should've been, because after the coffin I really couldn't be sure of anything. After a few hours, Queen Boudica is back to her usual self, and I show Antony how she loves to chase bottle caps and fuzzy mice toys around the ballroom. He laughs as he watches her skitter across the floor, skidding on the shiny surface as she pounces on her prey.

I call the school and feign a stomach bug, tell them I won't be in for the rest of the week. I'm told I'll have to produce a doctor's note if I'm out for more than a day, but after everything I've done, forging a signature from some doctor isn't going to weigh on my conscience.

I miss cheerleading trials. I can't bring myself to care.

Both Gabriel and Eli text me several times, but I delete their messages unread. Every time I think about them, the memory of Queen Boudica lying on the blood-stained tiles makes me burn with anger so bright it blinds me.

"Don't you have to go back to the club? What about the fight?" I ask on the second day, holding Queen Boudica while

Antony stands over the stove, cooking his famous chicken stew. My mouth waters at the delicious smells wafting through the house.

"Tiberius will manage it for me." Tiberius is Antony's top fighter – and he's terrifying. He has this feral look in his eyes like he'll snap at any moment, and I am totally on board with that. "I'm here as long as you need me, Claws."

I slide into a seat and dump a can of meat into a bowl for Queen Boudica. She eats with two paws on the table, from her own chair, like a member of the fucking family. Because she is. "Do we have to wait until next week for revenge? I don't want to take your best guys out of the running."

"After tonight, my guys are yours." Antony flips pancakes into a stack and sets it down in front of me. I slather it with butter and maple syrup and dive in. "Write me a list. We'll hit them all at once, so they're in no doubt who's behind it."

I raise an eyebrow. "You got enough people for that?"

"For you, Claws, I'm calling in my troops."

Queen Boudica's body rumbles with happy purrs as she licks her plate clean. I pull up the Notepad app on my phone and start typing names. Alec, for invading my home and hurting my cat. Noah, because it was probably his idea. I kicked him in the balls so hard he'd be swallowing. No way did he not have anything to do with this.

Eli, for telling them about my secret entrance. Cleo, because she's a bitch and I hate her guts. I add all of their dumb jock friends and Cleo's minions. Gabriel... I pause over his name, feeling a tiny stab of guilt as I add it to my list. *This is for shoving me into the pool, for taking my first kiss and turning it into something ugly.* I push the phone toward Antony.

"That will do. For now."

Antony whistles under his breath as he reads the names. "Remind me never to get on your bad side."

APPALLED at the bare state of my cupboards, Antony sends his boys out for groceries. I notice him handing off a stack of cash to a fighter named Horace. For the first time in far too long, I study Antony with an objective eye, trying to see past my protective cousin filter into what's going on with him.

The first thing I notice is that my cousin's clothes are designer, and his suit hugs his cut body like he's been poured into it. The second thing I notice is the outline of a pistol strapped across his chest.

I think back to our conversation after the cop came to the house, when I was panicking over what I'd said. Antony was the one who urged me to enroll at Stonehurst for real. "We're in a position where this could work to our advantage," he'd said, and he used his connections to make it happen. And I wonder now, too late, just what my cousin had been doing to get himself *so* connected.

Antony and I may have been family, but we aren't immune to keeping secrets from each other.

"You sure you still want to be a lawyer?" I tug on his sleeve. "You're doing pretty well for yourself as the owner of an underground fight club."

Almost too well, I want to say, but I don't. I want Antony to tell me.

"The club is a means to an end," he replies, his voice easy. "I treat my fighters well. They're loyal to me, which gives me immunity. Brutus is too chicken shit to get through them to me, so I'm untouchable for now. That means you are, too."

Brutus. At the sound of his name, my blood runs cold. The echo starts in my ears – my screams bouncing back on me from inside the coffin.

I hadn't thought about him for so long. *Too long.* It's easy to forget in this glittering palace of lies and secrets that Brutus is still breathing air when my parents were—

No.

To think of him now will be to give over to the rage. And I'm not ready. Antony and I... we have a plan. We're playing the long-game, and we are so, so close to winning.

I have to keep a clear head, because there are other assholes much closer to home who deserve all my attention.

Queen Boudica will have her revenge.

WE HAVE HOURS BEFORE SHOWTIME, and Antony doesn't want me too agitated. We curl up in the movie room. I set the popcorn machine running, and Antony spreads out a feast of junk food. We watch a stream of horror films. Blood flows down the screen, limbs fly everywhere, and Antony giggles. I laugh, too. We're both sick in the head, probably because of all the horror we lived through for real.

That's Antony and me in a nutshell, laughing as the world drowns in blood.

Antony gets a message on his phone. He grabs my hand. "Let's go."

Reluctantly, I hand Queen Boudica off to Horace, who's guarding the house while we're out. As Boudica wraps herself around his thick neck, Horace's features soften into something like awe. He strokes her with his giant hands, and Boudica closes her eyes in blissful repose.

"You give 'em hell for both of us, Claws," Horace growls.

I nod. We exit the garage and climb into Antony's car. The windows are tinted and made of bulletproof glass, and I can barely see outside as we leave the tunnel and roll toward our destination.

We park down a side street, underneath overgrown oleander bushes that will help hide the car from the view of the mansion beyond. We walk toward the house, through the open gates, and down the drive like we own the place. I expect Antony to slide open a window, but he walks right up to the front door and kicks it open. His boys have cleared our way.

This inside of the house is a brilliant, glaring white. Every surface is either white or glass or gold, except for two bright pink heart-shaped chairs facing out a set of French doors to a heart-shaped pool beyond. Greek revival columns stretch through the central atrium, holding up a large circular skylight. As we move up the staircase, lights inside the columns flash through a series of garish colors, illuminating our path.

"What a delicate and understated interior design," I smirk. Antony cracks a smile. He holds his fingers to his lips as we emerge on the upstairs landing.

From deeper in the house, there's a sound like wet flesh slapping flesh, and a strangled cry. I follow Antony beneath more garish columns. Tiberius steps out of a room. Antony's top fighter is an ugly mofo with half his face caved-in. "He's all yours." Tiberius grins at me, the smile all the more sinister because it never touches the ruined half of his face.

I follow Antony into the suite. The windows are thrust open, leading out to a Juliet-style balcony overlooking the house's internal courtyard and that ridiculous pool. The breeze flutters the flames on a fire glowering in the hearth – the orange flames a spark of color in the strange room. Beneath a white canopy bed with the same blinking purple lights as the columns, Alec is tied spread eagle. He looks bad already – his face and naked chest a mess of purple bruises from Tiberius' attention. Blood runs from a cut above his eye.

When Alec sees me, his eyes widen. He thrashes wildly, but

the chains around his wrists and ankles hold him firmly in place.

"I heated this up for you." Tiberius passes me an object. The handle is already warm against my fingers.

I moved toward the bed. *I'm going to enjoy this.* "Hello, Alec."

"What the fuck are you doing here, slut?" He tries to sound indignant. He fails.

I hold my hand behind my back, and I don't think he can see my gift for him. I don't answer him. Instead, I slide off my shoes. With my free hand I slowly, slowly hitch up the hem of my skirt. It's split down the leg and the split slides further up my thigh, exposing more flesh. Alec's eyes watch my movements, and there's a sickening hunger in him that makes me so happy because he thinks he knows what's coming and I still have my beautiful gift to unveil.

I rest my knees on the bed, pressing my fingers into the sheets. "That's what you say I am, isn't it? A slut who wants to sleep with anyone and everyone, even people who were cruel to her. *Especially* them."

Alec's eyes lap up my flesh as I swing my leg over, straddling him. I expect touching him like this to make me feel sick, but instead, a rush of power heats my veins. Mmmmm, yes. I've forgotten how fun it is to be the master – or mistress – of your own destiny. To take what you want and to dish out the very best kind of justice.

"Hate sex is the best, isn't it?" I grind down on his crotch. He groans, and I can feel him going hard.

"If you wanted to ride my cock, you didn't need this charade —" Alec's words cut off as I whip my hand from behind my back and he sees the instrument I'm holding.

An iron.

A brand.

Hot from the fire.

Alec's eyes bug out of his head in a pleasing way. I climb up his body, crawling over his skin, holding the iron close to him so he can feel the heat begging to meet his flesh.

"I don't want to do this, but you leave me no choice." I press my hand on his cheek, shoving his head back against the pillows. "You think you're fucking untouchable because of your wealth and your fame. You and every other fucker at Stonehurst Prep. It's time you learned who you're dealing with. No one hurts my friend and gets away with it."

"What the fuck are you doing, you crazy bitch? Get that thing away from me! Help, help—"

I tut. "Pathetic boy. No one's going to hear you. Now hold still, unless you want me to accidentally get this in your eye."

Alec bellows as the brand touches his forehead, but that only makes me press it harder. He thrashes against his bonds, but I clamp my thighs tight and hold on. I imagine it's like riding a mechanical bull. His bellow turns into a scream and his scream into high-pitched cries, a cascade of gibberish sounds seared with agony as the brand leaves its mark. There's a smell like roast pork, like a home-cooked holiday meal with all the trimmings.

When it's done, I crawl off the bed to snap a couple of photographs of my handiwork and upload them to the school's Facebook group.

Burned into Alec's flesh is two letters – MM.

My initials.

My mark of triumph.

Alec's body is streaked with sweat, and he's murmuring under his breath. His eyes barely register me.

"This is so you never forget your place. Stay away from me and mine, Alec, or I'll cut your dick off."

Antony takes my hand and leads me from the room. Alec's

sobs follow us as we move back through the garish house. I savor each one like it's the finest square of Belgium chocolate.

On the front step, Antony leans in and kisses my cheek. "Any time you need me, little sister."

And then he's gone, disappearing into the night, back to the shadows where he belongs. He has other work to do tonight.

I think about the long walk back to Harrington Hills under the moonlight, with the sound of Alec's scream echoing in my ears – the sweetest music I'd heard in a long time. But I'm not ready to go home yet.

I have one last visit to make.

ELI

I trudge up the stairs to my room, peeling off my sticky workout gear and tossing it in the vague direction of the laundry chute. Noah made me stay behind for three hours after track practice finished to train with him. My own damn fault for assuming he'd let up once he made the team – he's freaking out more than usual because our first meet is coming up and he knows he's the weakest link.

When Noah says "I'm going to train night and day," he means that shit *literally*. We only quit tonight because the groundskeeper came out to turn off the lights on the field. The locker rooms were locked up for the night, so I had to drive home in my sweaty clothes and peel my ass off the leather seat of my Porsche.

Noah's obsession with being a track star will kill me. Or him. Or I'd kill him. One way or another, someone will pay for the hell he's put my body through.

I tiptoe past my mother's suite. I can hear her simpering on the phone with one of her boyfriends, but I don't want to risk an encounter. As I round the corner of the hallway, I notice the door to my room is shut. Weird. I never shut it. After my parents found out about me and Mackenzie all those years ago, they made sure I never kept any secrets from them again.

So why is it shut now?

There's a chemical scent in the air that sets my teeth on edge. It reminds me of being at the funeral home in Tennessee, back when Dad had a more hands-on role in the business, back before we had the big house and TV cameras everywhere and the shitty defense lawyer to pay.

Mom must've shut the door. Probably Gizmo was annoying her.

I hope she hasn't peed on my bed. I'm too tired for this shit. My shoulders ache in protest as I reach down and turn the handle.

The door flies open. Rough hands grab me and yank me inside, slamming my body against the wall.

What the fuck?

My muscles scream as I lash out at the intruder. But the guy holding me is a tank, and my fists glance off him. I try to get a grip on his ape-like neck, but he twists my arm behind me, leaning into it enough that I know he'll snap it in two if he feels like it.

"This is a message from Mackenzie Malloy," he rasps in my ears. "Don't fuck with her again, or I'll do my painting with your blood."

Before I can react, the figure slams my head into the wall and drops me. Pain erupts across my skull. I sink to the floor, my vision blurring. Out of the corner of my eye, I watch the blobby shape of him running for my open window.

I crawl across the floor toward him, but my head is made of cotton, leaking out my ears. He leaps over the side of the balcony. By the time I crawl to the balustrade and pull myself up, he's escaped through the garden. But there *is* a figure down there, standing under the floodlights surrounding the pool. Strands of golden hair circle her face like a halo.

Mackenzie.

This is the first time she's ever come to me, and I don't understand. Is it about the party? I arrived late because Dad's incompetent lawyer needed some papers copied. When I got there, Noah had already stormed off and Gabriel was wasted on some concoction of alcohol and pills, so I had to get him home. Then she hadn't been to school and she wouldn't answer my texts, and now she's here, at my house, with some thug?

Mackenzie lifts her chin, her head tilted to the side, watching me. "Did you like your present?"

"You mean my new boyfriend?" My voice cracks as fresh pain blooms across my skull. "Oh, sure. He's lovely. We had a tea party."

"Tiberius wasn't your present. You'd better turn on the light, Eli."

Panic hits me. *What's she done?*

I slam my fist against the light switch, bathing my room in light. The walls – usually a calming blue and covered in sports posters and college flags – are now decorated with red paint. It drips down the walls onto my bed and furniture, and over the decapitated head of Mr. Buttons, the stuffed bear I've kept on my nightstand ever since Mackenzie gave him to me for my eighth birthday. Under my bed, two wide saucer eyes stare at me from the darkness – my cat Gizmo trembling in terror.

Nausea gathers in my stomach as the red paint coalesces into words. The same sentence repeated over and over.

YOU WERE SUPPOSED TO PROTECT ME.

Fuck.

"SHE'S A FUCKING PSYCHO!" Noah screams down the phone.

My heart rate rockets up again. Gizmo whimpers as my fingers tighten in her fur. I've done nothing but hold her and stroke her and feed her treats for the last hour, but she's still terrified.

I'm pretty rattled myself. That guy broke into our house without a trace – Mom didn't even notice. I can't believe Mackenzie would do this and yet... Noah had a visit from a masked stranger, too. "This guy broke into my room and wrote all over my walls in red paint. Grace found it, and she freaked out. The police are swarming all over the house."

Poor Grace. "What did they write?"

"'This cat has claws'!" Noah yells. "What's she talking about? What cat?"

I pull my phone from my ear as Noah screams curse words, and scroll through my messages. It's already blowing up. Callum, Daphne, Cleo, Brandy... everyone's had a visit from one of Mackenzie's shadowy men.

"Alec's in the hospital," Noah says. "She burned her initials into his forehead."

"Fuck me dead." That's dark. But also... I can't say I felt sorry for Alec.

Why did Mackenzie do this? Because of the party? Because of the things that had been happening at school? It's a little crazy and yet... Mackenzie was always a law unto herself.

I open a drawer in my desk and rummage around until I find what I'm looking for. It's a strip of Polaroids we took in a photo-booth at Disneyland when we were... eleven, I think? I remember the day well. Mackenzie came to school late and ready for a fight. She sat at the back of class and refused to participate. She called the teacher a bitch to her face, then said, 'what are you going to do about it?' because she knew she was untouchable. A girl offered Mackenzie a cupcake, and Mackenzie pushed her into a trash can.

I saw Mackenzie closing in on George, who sat by herself on the edge of the playground. I knew this pattern of hers – Mackenzie's father did something awful, so she came to school and lorded it over the other kids to feel good about herself. I couldn't bear that stormy look in her eyes, and I didn't want to watch what she had planned for George – all I wanted was to see her smile. So for the first time ever, I skipped school. We took a bus down to Anaheim and spent the day at Disneyland. It was one of the best days of my entire life. We didn't have to pretend – we could be completely ourselves.

I hold up the photo strip to the light – the pair of us crowded inside the booth, dressed in sparkly Mickey Mouse ears and feather boas we got from a junk store. I'm wearing aviator sunglasses and trying to look staunch while Mackenzie pokes her tongue out at the camera. That day I peeled back the Ice Queen and the real Mackenzie shone through like the sun.

I run my fingers over her smiling face. I wonder if that smile still lurks somewhere inside Mackenzie, somewhere beneath this cold, calculating monster.

How does Mackenzie command the loyalty of a gang of thugs who can break into more than ten Emerald Beach mansions in the same night?

She burned her initials into Alec's forehead... that's fucked up.

Someone broke her. Someone snuffed out Mackenzie's sunshine so completely she's a stranger to me now. And I have a feeling I know exactly who it was.

Mackenzie's right. I *was* supposed to protect her, and I didn't. I couldn't. I was only thirteen. But I'm not thirteen any longer, and no matter what it takes, I will make sure she knows that I still see the sunshine inside her.

I pick up the phone again just as Noah winds up his tirade. A chill ripples down my spine at the venom in his voice. Vowing to protect Mackenzie may mean going up against my best friend, and I can't do that. Not after everything he's been through. But I had to.

"Mackenzie Malloy is going to pay," Noah hisses. And I wish, more than anything I've ever wished for, that I could save him from himself. "I'm going to kill her for this."

MACKENZIE

School the next day is... interesting. When I step into the corridor, students fall over themselves to get away from me. The fear rolls off them in waves, and it's intoxicating.

They wanted to know where Mackenzie Malloy has been all these years.

They wanted answers.

I can't be held responsible if they couldn't handle the truth.

I should have started with this power move, I think as I reach my locker and shove my books into my bag. A note flutters out. I unfold the paper and read the neat handwriting.

"Watch out for Noah," it reads. I glance up. Eli's down the opposite end of the corridor, in a circle of jocks. He looks up, his eyes meeting mine, and I feel that now-familiar zip of lightning through my veins, like I'm plugged into a power socket. I think of the last time our eyes met, across his pool as he took in my surprise. I needed him to see me there, to know I don't need his protection.

That's what the note is really about. Eli nods at the paper in my hand. He's trying to get in my good books again, to remind me he's looking out for me.

Message received.

I roll it the note into a ball and shove it into my mouth, chewing it with gusto.

I don't need you to protect me anymore, Eli Hart.

Something that might have been sadness flickers in Eli's ocean eyes. It's gone in a moment, replaced with that too-pretty smile. He wears his mask as I wear mine.

Eli turns back to his friends. I spit out the note into a trash can and get to class. Gabriel sits next to me and asks how I managed to cover his double-height windows in an enormous drawing of a dick when I'm so short. I smile enigmatically and ignore him for the rest of the day.

Stares and whispers follow me everywhere, but no one says a thing to my face. Alec isn't at school – he's probably still recovering from surgery – and Cleo doesn't offer more than a few violent glares. At lunch, I take my tray and walk past the royal table. No one stops me or yells anything, but there's an audible release of tension when I leave the dining hall and enter the outdoor courtyard.

George sits in the corner, earbuds dangling from her eyes. I make a beeline for her, but she quickly dumps her tray and races back inside. I sink down into the spot she left, feeling her warmth against the seat, wishing I hadn't been such a bitch in my old life so things could be different.

The entire school is afraid of me. I'm powerful. I'm *untouchable*. And in this noisy place surrounded by others, I've never been more alone.

MRS. ANDERSON IS SO keen to have me on the cheerleading team she invites me to try out at Friday's before-school practice, since I missed last week's official tryouts. Just the thought of walking into that gym filled with Cleo and her snakes makes my skin break out, but if I don't go, all Antony's work will be for nothing. They need to believe I'm not afraid of them.

I'm *not* afraid of them.

It's still dark outside when I arrive at school. I change into a cheerleading skirt and a racer-back tank top in the bathroom so I don't have to go into the girl's locker room. As I cross the campus, I see George running toward me, waving her arms. I don't want to be late, so I call out to her that I'll find her after tryouts, and enter the gym from the side door.

As soon as I step inside, the lights flicker out.

Someone grabs me from behind, slamming me into the bleachers. I kick out behind me, feel the satisfying crunch of my heel grinding against soft, dangly bits. My assailant drops me, but then someone else grabs my hair, yanking my head back so hard I feel something in my neck crunch.

The room spins as limbs and faces fly at me from all directions. Cleo rakes her fingers down my face. Someone else punches me in the gut, driving the air from my lungs. I kick and thrash and scream and howl. My fists connect with flesh, but there are too many of them. They pin my arms, kick my legs out from under me. There's nothing to break my fall as they slam me into the hard gym floor.

"Why are you doing this?" a voice screams, but the sound is far away. "You're hurting her!"

Watch out for Noah.

The words on Eli's note swirl in my receding vision, before the darkness swallows me.

MACKENZIE

I come to as I'm being yanked and tossed between people. My eyes fly open, but it's no use; it's too dark wherever I am, and my vision's blurred.

Not the darkness. I'm never going back to the darkness again.

I kick and wriggle, but everything feels slow, as if I'm trying to move through molasses. A pounding headache starts in my temples and flares across my skull.

"Get the bag over her head."

No no no.

Rough hands grab me, hold me down. I kick, lash out with my fists, but I'm throwing marshmallows at semi trucks for all the damage I do. My knuckles glance off something sharp, and a guy grunts in pain. His hand drops from my shoulder but it's replaced by another. Panic rises in my stomach as the headache lashes against my skull.

They pull a canvas bag over my head and tie the handles loosely under my chin. It reeks of sweat and male cologne. The smell fills my nostrils, closes my throat. I'm drowning in the stink of this horror.

The panic has me in its grip now. I thrash my head, kick and jerk. I can't go out like this, blinded, struggling for breath. It's too much like before.

They drag me outside and drop me on something hard. I land on my side and kick out my legs only to hit a hard surface. Metal. I smell gas and expensive leather seats. My cheek brushes rough carpet. I'm in the trunk of someone's car.

All around me, male voices leer and guffaw, calling me every hateful name under the sun, every word men have invented throughout history to throw at women who threaten them. The words hit my skin like arrows, piercing my soul, taking my power.

They tie my hands and the trunk slams down on top of me, sealing me inside. I slam my feet into the lid of my tomb, but it's sealed tight. I can't claw my way out of here.

Antony's not coming to rescue me.

The engine roars to life. I can hear them through the trunk, laughing and joking. Someone turns the music up. There's a speaker in here, and the bass pounds through me like a fist beating my ass from the inside.

My screams bounce back at me, hollow and useless. I fight the rising panic. *This is not the same. It's not a coffin.*

Yet.

I go still and quiet. There's no point wasting my energy screaming while the car's moving. I try to count the turns we make but it becomes too difficult. Instead, I pull my knees to my chest. As soon as the trunk opens I'll kick the first guy in the face; maybe I'll be able to fight my way out. Or at least, if I die tonight, someone's pretty face is going with me.

We drive for what seems like hours, until my head is screaming, until the darkness is all I know. And in the darkness I forget who I am now. I am back in the coffin, buried in six feet of dirt and the sins of my family.

The screams come again, rising wild and inhuman from

inside me. I don't hear any partying from the car any longer, just the tearing echo of my own terror.

I'm going to die tonight, and it's almost a relief because I know I won't be afraid any longer.

Somehow, I push through my fear, and I find something else on the other side. An anger so cold and final it's beyond wild rage – it's something calculated, focused. I take all the fear bottled up inside me, all the dark thoughts I've screamed into empty rooms, and I focus on staying awake, staying alert, keeping my mind clear and ready. Because if I die, these fuckers will get away with it. No one will look for me. Not even Antony. He can't take the risk, and even if someone finds my body, these assholes will get their rich mommies and daddies to pay off the police.

Mackenzie Malloy won't stand for that.

I think of Antony, and how hard he's worked to lift himself out of the mess our family left behind for him. I think of how close we are to our dream, and I've fucked it all up because I let Alec LeMarque get under my skin.

I think of Queen Boudica, waiting at the door for me to come home, pawing at the glass in desperate hunger when she realized I'm not.

I fumble in my pocket for my phone, hitting the buttons I hope will call Antony.

I slide my knife from my sock. I manoeuvr it between my bonds and saw at the rope.

The car jerks to a stop, slamming my head into the wall. I'm too far into the abyss to even feel the impact.

Doors slam. Voices talk and laugh, like this is a fucking trip to the seaside. I hear the trunk unlock and a beam of harsh light blinds me.

The first thing that strikes me is the heat. It bears down on me like another attacker, holding me down with fingers of fire. I can't see in the blinding light. I kick out with my legs, but I know I'm slow, useless. I snap the ropes on my wrists and swing with the blade. I feel contact, hear a male voice swear. Someone grabs my ankle and twists my leg against my chest, locking me in place. The knife is torn from my grip.

Hands grab me, drag me into the fire. Red welts sing across my vision. I discern that I'm outside, under the full fury of the Californian sun. I'm probably in the desert, judging by the orange haze blinding me.

My eyes start to adjust, and I make out shapes through the haze and the burning blue sky. Broad shoulders. Faces. One face in particular, leering down at me.

Alec LeMarque.

His forehead is covered with another dressing, and the skin around his eyes is tugged up, giving him this creepy clown expression. He curls his lips back into a smirk that would give small children nightmares. Hell, if I survive this I know I'll be punching that smirk in my dreams.

"Hello, Mackenzie Malloy." He leans in close, so I can smell the alcohol on his breath.

I hawk and spit at him. I'm so weak that my spittle runs down my own chin. My throat burns. How long has it been since I had a drink?

Alec's surrounded by his friends. They lean against two other cars – all the jock guys from school who sit at the royal table, all flashing that same sickening leer. Noah's there, at the back, his hands shoved into his pockets, the sunlight tinting his hair to flames of crimson and violet. Against the burning sky, his skin shines like alabaster – he's a statue, his expression unreadable, the only one not grinning.

I don't see Eli or Gabriel, and part of me wants to cry in relief.

"You're not such hot stuff now, are you?" Alec sneers. He

grips my shoulders, his nails digging into my skin. Two of his friends hold my arms, but they don't need to. I'm their prisoner. I'm not going anywhere. There's no escape. "You're a fucking psycho out-of-control ghost slut, you know that? Your thugs scared Noah's mother so badly she's in the hospital."

"Boo-hoo," I spit back. "You all should have thought of that before you hurt my friend."

"Your *friend* should know to stay out of our business. Clearly, whatever hole you've been in the last four years hasn't taught you any manners. We don't want twisted psycho bitches at our school, and it's time you were put in your place."

I don't understand how Queen Boudica could've possibly been in Alec's 'business,' but I can't find the bravado to mock him about it. It doesn't matter. We all know why we're here. I branded him, made him mine. He might have got the best plastic surgeon in Emerald Beach to repair the damage, but he can't erase the picture I shared. Everyone at Stonehurst knows that I owned him.

And now, he's brought me out here to return the favor.

"Bend her over the hood," Alec barks.

The two guys holding me slam me on the hood of Alec's sexy-as-fuck Shelby Cobra, forcing my hands wide and my neck down, searing my cheek against the hot metal. My phone flies from my pocket. I kick up my legs, but someone else grabs my ankles and pins them, too. A whole new kind of terror grips me as Alec grabs my ass, digging his nails into my flesh.

"You started this war, Malloy. You're only getting what you deserve. You're going to take each one of us until you know your place. You walked into Stonehurst like you owned the place. Today, I own you."

His hand slides down my hip, toying with the hem of my skirt, and I can't help it – a whimper escapes my mouth.

CRACK. Alec's hand slaps my ass, and the sound tumbles

across the barren desert, reminding me how fucking *alone* I am. He cackles like a comic strip witch, and the sound is glass shards under my skin.

"Fallen isn't wrong – you grew a damn fine ass, Malloy." Alec leans over the hood, his body covering mine, sealing. "I'm going to make it mine today. Would you like that? My big cock sliding in your ass? That's what you get you for messing with my face."

Alec's tongue slides across the back of my neck, wet and cold like a snake. I can already feel his poison slithering around inside me, poisoning me. I brace myself, searching my mind for a dark place to retreat into, far away from Alec's hot breath and his cock against my thigh and his gross fingers dragging my panties down down down—

He pulls back. I dare to hope he's had a come-to-Jesus moment. Hell, I'd settle for a come-to-Cthulhu moment if it meant he never touched me like that again.

"Noah!" Alec claps his hands. "You can do the honors."

Fuck no.

Please no.

Not Noah. Not those coal eyes and those cheekbones that could cut skin. I can't—

But nothing happens. I'm stuck, my skirt yanked up, my panties around my ankles. I twist my neck to watch them. Noah stares at a spot on the horizon, his shoulders rigid, his expression carved in stone.

"Noah? Bro, you listening?" Alec shoves Noah toward me. "Mackenzie Malloy on a platter. I did all this *for you*. This bitch broke into your house, she embarrassed you at Daphne's party. She *killed your brother*."

"I know that." Noah's jaw is so tight I could bounce a quarter off it.

"So?" Alec gestures to me. "She took something from you. Isn't it time you repaid the favor?"

Noah shakes his head. "This is fucked up, Alec. You said we were going to scare her, make sure she never came after our families again. But not like this. This isn't right."

"It's *justice*," Alec hisses. "This bitch branded my face. She deserves to be full of our cum."

"That's your idea of justice? Raping a girl?" Noah's gaze swivels to his friends, and the darkness in his eyes is unfathomable. "You're sick. All of you."

"Yeah, Alec," Mark pipes up from the back of the crowd. He has a hand to his cheek, blood seeping between his fingers. When he lowers it, I see the slash my knife made in his skin. "Come on, this is fucked."

"Dude, I've got an athletic scholarship to Stanford. No way am I putting that on the line for this bitch," adds Chad, dropping his hold on my wrist. Of course, the most important thing is the athletic scholarship, not the fact his friend is trying to get him to rape me. But I'd take it.

"Look at her. She's scared enough as it is." Noah shrugs. "You've had your revenge. Let's take her back."

Alec glares at his friends. "You fucking pussies. Fine, more for me."

And before I can cry out, he presses his body against mine again. His teeth dig into my ear. His cologne swirls around me – it's sickly sweet, like cotton candy. Bile rises in my throat.

"I'm going to enjoy this," he grunts, as he reaches down between us to undo his zipper and he's right there he's pressing against me I hate him I *hate* him he's—

—and then Alec disappears.

MACKENZIE

*I*t happens so fast I think I've imagined it. The heat and the terror have sent me outside my body, or I've gone to the void in my head to keep myself sane, and in the void I no longer feel Alec's snake coiling against my entrance.

But no, he's gone. He's no longer on top of me. *But how—*

I dare a glance behind me. Alec rolls in the sand ten feet from the other cars, his trousers around his ankles. He clutches his face. Blood covers his hands. Noah strides toward me. His arms go around my waist. He picks me up like I'm nothing and throws me over his shoulder.

"We're leaving," he barks at Alec. "Don't follow us."

Even though the jocks outnumber him, no one moves to stop Noah. Alec lets out a growl like a wild fucking beast, but all he can do kick a cloud of sand at us.

Noah nods once, then starts off across the desert.

He walks in silence. Each heavy tread of his boots jerks my body, but I don't ask to be put down. I'm not strong enough. The full horror of what nearly happened hits me in a shudder. Tears slide from my eyes, but the desert wind blasts them away. By the time we can no longer see the cars, my skin feels flayed alive by it.

The pain is good, cleansing. I want the desert to slough away my skin until there's no part of me left that Alec LeMarque has touched.

Noah's strong arms feel so good around me.

I hate him for rescuing me.

I hate myself.

I lose myself in the delirium of my humiliation. I don't know how long we walk, but Noah's breath comes out in shaking rasps. His steps become slow, shaky. His skin is slick with sweat by the time we reach civilization – and calling it civilization is a stretch. We arrive at a gas station on a crossroads, a few miles off the highway I can just make out winding through the desert beyond. Noah leaves me in a lawn chair and points at a payphone. "I'll be over there. I need to make a call."

I don't move or reply. I can't.

My fingers search for the locket around my neck, and when they find it still there, I slip it under the fabric of my top so Noah can't see it.

I stare out across the desert, at the scrabbly bushes and gnarled Joshua trees and Jurassic rock formations jutting from the earth like dinosaur teeth. I think about what happened, what *could* have happened. I close my eyes and see my blood-splattered reflection, feel a gnawing pain in my heart that will never heal.

Something plops down on the table in front of me. I cry out, tripping over myself as I struggle away.

"Didn't mean to startle you." Noah slides into the chair opposite me and holds out an object. A plastic spoon.

I peer through a curtain of blonde hair matted with dust and dirt and blood at the object on the table. It's a chocolate cake, five miles high – layers and layers of cake and cream and frosting and a mountain of fresh, glistening cherries on top. It looks like the kind of cake you'd see at a high-end wedding, not at a gas station in the middle of the fucking desert.

It's so fucking random and crazy that I burst out laughing.

Noah digs his own spoon into an equally ridiculously slice of key lime pie. "There's an entire cabinet of epic cakes inside. I remember you used to like cherry-flavored stuff."

"I did?" The words are out of my mouth before I can stop them.

"Sure." Noah gives me an odd look, those coal eyes studying me intently. "At school, whenever they had cherry pie for dessert you shoved everyone out of the way in the cafeteria line so you could get there first. You used to take three slices even though we were only allowed one. The rest of the class was too afraid of you to rat you out."

"I bet you did, though." I carve off the tip of the cake. It's so tall I can't get the entire thing on the fork.

"Nope. I was afraid of you, too."

Hmmm. I watch Noah as he carves off the tip of his pie and slides it between his lips. He no longer is the arrogant, aristocratic king. The desert has stripped him of his crown – his wavy hair rumpled and plastered to his scalp with sweat, his skin dry and patched with grazes, his eyes red and bloodshot. And yet, to me, he's never appeared more noble.

"Why are you being so nice to me?" I blurt out.

Noah turns away, hiding his face. "Eat your ridiculous cake."

"Answer me, Marlowe."

He sighs. "I'm not being nice. No matter how much I fucking hate you, I'm not going to rape you in the middle of the desert. What Alec tried to do was sick. End of."

I'm dying to ask him about the party the other night where his hard cock ground into my hip. But I can't deal with thinking about cock right now, so instead I carve off another corner of the cake with my fork and shove it into my mouth.

"Okay, this is amazing. You have to try it." I wave my spoon at him.

"I have my own."

"Not for long." I reach across and swipe a decent chunk off the side of his pie.

"What are you doing?"

"Enjoying the spoils of war." I grin as I shove the pie into my mouth. Something about the sugar and about being here with Noah and the relief at not being a corpse roasting under the desert sun turns me giddy.

Noah watches me out of the corner of his eye, and I notice that the fire on the edge of his coal-black irises has dimmed. The hatred that usually burns for me alone is now the warmth that dragged me from the desert. He swipes his cake away from me. "Are you high?"

"No, I'm hungry. And these cakes are amazing."

"See, I don't get it – you're not supposed to be impressed by cake. Especially not a cake purchased from a gas station. Every girl at our school is a hundred pounds of pure bitchy hummus, and you're supposed to be Queen of them all."

I poke my tongue out at him, showing him the half-chewed cake on the end of it. "Maybe I'm not like other girls. Also, when we get back, I'm trademarking 'bitchy hummus' – it would make a great health-food company name. Maybe it will supply snacks to Stonehurst vending machines."

Noah snorts. We finish our cakes in silence. Maybe I'm delirious from heat and trauma, but hatred doesn't seem to roll off his body any longer. Now it's more of a low-level annoyance that buzzes in the air around us like an annoying fly.

"I meant what I said at the party." I don't know why I say this.

"I used to crush on you hard. It must've been your superior cake-purchasing abilities."

Noah throws his head back and laughs. It's a real laugh, devoid of that hard edge. "Yeah, well... I had a crush on you, too."

"Don't lie. You acted like I didn't exist." I remember those weepy words in my diary, how Noah would avoid me at school and refuse to be in group projects or playground teams with me.

"Only because you were Eli's girl." Noah looks away again.

"I was thirteen. I was nobody's girl."

Noah shook his head. "You and Eli were written in the stars. That was obvious even to me, even when I wasn't supposed to know you guys were hanging out. Eli's my best friend, and when you disappeared, it nearly destroyed him. I hated you for that as much as for my brother."

"I can't imagine Eli destroyed by anything. He's so... steady."

Noah rolls his eyes, and for a moment, just a *moment,* I catch a glimmer of something like amusement in them before they return to their calm, dark state. "Oh yeah, Eli was *wretched*. He only spoke in sighs. For a whole year, he did no better than a B on any exam or test, which for Eli is like flunking out. He listened to that playlist you made him on constant repeat, and he even threw himself off his balcony like a character in a Shakespeare play."

"He did not throw himself off a balcony," I scoff.

"He did. He landed in his mother's prize rose bushes. Broke his arm in two places. He was pulling thorns out of his ass for weeks. The only thing that seemed to help him was getting his cat, Gizmo. And, weirdly, the FBI going after his Dad. Eli loves solving puzzles, and I think he figured if he couldn't figure out why you left him he could at least save his Dad's ass—"

An engine roars, drowning out the rest of Noah's words. A moment later, a Porsche rolls up in a cloud of dust. I cough, waving my hands to try and save my cake. The dust and sand settle, revealing the edges of the vehicle and driver at the wheel. Eli peers over the top of his glasses.

"Need a lift?" He cocks an eyebrow at me.

Dealing with Eli's intensity usually puts me off my lunch, but right now his car is a fucking chariot from heaven. I stand on shaky legs. Noah reaches out, his warm hand steadying me, and together we limp toward the Porsche.

"Careful." Eli's smirk crumples when he sees Noah holding me. In a flash, he vaults from the car and is on the other side of me, piling me into the passenger seat.

Noah climbs in back, sprawling out across the narrow seat, dangling his sand-coated boots over the side. "Possibly you should've put the top up before you went cruising in the desert."

"Shut up. Mac, are you okay?" Eli leans over the seat, his ocean eyes stormy, wide with concern.

I stare out at the gas station and the hostile landscape beyond. Now that I'm inside the car, everything that happened, that *nearly* happened, rushes at me in an avalanche of fear. A tremble starts in my feet and ripples through my whole body. I grip the edge of the seat and clench my teeth as I ride through the terror.

The reaction reminds me of the darkest night of my life, of getting into Antony's car after he dug me out of the dirt, of trembling on the seat while he told me what happened to my parents.

"Shit, she's not okay." Eli glares at Noah. "What the fuck did you do to her out there?"

"Nothing," Noah snaps back. "I put a stop to it. Get us out of here. She's having a trauma reaction. She'll feel better once we're back in the city."

Eli's face tightens. He reaches over me and pulls my belt across my lap. His fingers graze my skin, and I murmur something that might've been a protest, might've been a desire for more. "Mackenzie, do you want us to take you home? There's something at Gabe's you should really see."

I don't answer. The truth is, after what Alec did to Queen Boudica, home doesn't feel safe to me right now. But I don't have anywhere else to go. I don't have the words I need to ask.

"Let's take her to Gabe's," says Noah. He picks up Eli's phone from between the seats and chooses a new song. Pounding blast-beats and black metal assault my ears as Eli jerks the car away and speeds back down the highway. I lose myself in the bleakness of the music, imagining myself in a Norwegian forest, cold and surrounded by wolves and as far from the fucking desert as it's possible to get.

As we hit the outer suburbs of Emerald Beach, Eli switches the playlist to 90s grunge and indie music, and the boys sing along. I glance down at the phone and notice the playlist is called, simply, *Mackenzie*.

The playlist Noah mentioned – the one I gave Eli before I disappeared.

I watch Eli as he drives, one hand on the wheel, the other draped casually over the door. He nods his head to the music, and the breeze ripples through his blond hair, whipping loose strands around his face. He's wearing a grey t-shirt that hugs his muscles, and he looks every inch the fresh-faced, pretty-mouthed boy that every girl wants for a boyfriend.

He still has my playlist.

We merge onto the highway that hugs the beach, turning off to pass bars and shops and co-working spaces until we pull up at Gabriel's condo.

Gabriel opens the door wearing nothing but a pair of black jeans. My throat dries at the sight of his naked chest and those beautiful tattoos. All that skin begging to be touched. It's enough to make a girl forget she's just been assaulted.

I'm crazy. I'm totally screwed up.

"Hey, Mac. You look like shite. Gimmie a sec." Gabriel leaves the door open and pads up to his mezzanine bedroom. While Noah settles me on the couch and points out the faint outline of the giant dick still visible on Gabriel's windows, I hear Gabriel talking softly, and a girl's voice answering. My heart patters in my chest.

Of course, Gabriel has a girl here. I flattered myself when he said he never brought another girl to his condo. I thought it made me special, but it just makes me a gullible fool. *Even more reason why you should not trust these guys.*

A few moments later, Gabriel leans over the railing, his voice as sweet as triple-chocolate-cherry cake.

"Someone's here to see you."

He steps aside, and George stands in the stairwell, her face ashen, her arms covered in cuts and bruises, her cheeks smudged with tears.

That's not the face of someone who's just had sex with Gabriel Fallen.

"George, what happened?" I try to rise off the couch to go to her, but Noah shoves me down again.

"Mackenzie, I—" the words catch in George's throat. Fresh tears well in her eyes. 'I'm sorry. Alec and Cleo put around that no one should hang out with you, and I got scared. I should have—"

Her face crumples, and she buries her head in Gabriel's shoulder. He places an arm around her and glares at Noah. "Apparently, Alec saw the two of you hanging out at school, and with his expert powers of deduction concluded she's breaking his ridiculous rules. He won't come after me for hanging with you, but he feels good about attacking a girl."

"I had nothing to do with this." Noah's hands curl into fists.

"I wanted Mackenzie to suffer, but if I had any idea of what Alec was really planning, I—"

"What the fuck happened to George?" I yell. Eli winces.

"George works in a vintage store in Brawley where Cleo loves to shop. She overheard Cleo in the changing rooms with her friends last night talking about their nefarious scheme, so she went to school early to warn you. She couldn't catch you, so she went to the gym and saw them carrying you away. She went to find a teacher, but Cleo got to her first. While the guys took you to the car, Cleo and her snakes beat George up and locked her in the school basement. I only found her because I go down there sometimes to get blazed."

Realization hits me. In the desert, Alec wasn't talking about Queen Boudica, he was talking about *George*. Which is odd – he knows I came after him because of what he did to my cat, so why didn't he acknowledge it?

"Fuck." My head spins. "George, I'm so sorry. This shit is between me and Alec. Not you. You were never supposed to be involved. You were right to run away from me. I— I'm bad news."

Her eyes are wide as saucers, and for a moment I think she's going to run at the window and leap through to freedom. Instead, she shuffles across the room and sits down beside me, curling her feet beneath her. I see she's wearing Gabriel's clothes – she's swimming in an old tour t-shirt and a pair of drawstring sweatpants, but in an adorable way they suit her.

"I shouldn't have run," she says. "I just... I already knew about the rule when we went outside for lunch, but I didn't think anyone would care until I saw Cleo staring at me. She was even worse to me after you disappeared. I didn't want to give her a reason to—" George swallows. A spasm of pain hits her, and I'm ready to head back out to ram Cleo's head into a wall. "I'm sorry.

I thought you were tricking me. You and Cleo – just like in the old days. You'd pretend to be my friend so I went against the rule and then the two of you would do something horrible to me."

"I used to be a mean bitch, huh?" I place my hand over hers.

"The meanest."

I smile, and in that smile I pour all of my cruelty. Cleo will *burn* for this. "Let me say this once, and know that I mean what I say. You have nothing to fear from me. This mean bitch is on your side now."

The grin on George's face could light up the Emerald Beach NYE bonfire.

"Now that's taken care of, anyone for a drink?" Gabriel has a cocktail shaker in his hand. He still hasn't put a shirt on, but I'm not going to be the one to ask.

"I think Mackenzie just needs to lie down," says Eli.

"Guess again." I hold out my hand. "Make mine a double."

While the guys get snacks from the kitchen, Gabriel does a big show of tossing the shaker over his head and behind his back. He drops it on his second go and alcohol splooshes across the floor. Gabriel mutters something into an intercom, and a few minutes later a guy in a spotless white uniform arrives to clean up the spill.

I throw my arm around George's shoulder. She leans in and rests her cheek on my chest, and even though I've had the shittest possible day, something featherlight flutters inside me. Like maybe this is the start of something. Like maybe Stonehurst Prep will turn out just like those dumb teen movies.

"For you, m'lady." Gabriel holds out a drink for George. She reaches for it, then seems to think again. She pulls her phone off the table.

"I can't. I wish I could, but I have to get home." She gives me a final squeeze. "I hope you're feeling better."

"I am, thanks to you." I grin. "I'll see you at lunch. We're eating together, right?"

Her whole face lights up again, and for the first time in a long time, I feel like I might've actually done a *nice* thing. It was odd. Good odd, but still odd.

When I get out of the shower, wearing Gabriel's clothes that I plan never to take off, the guys have put on a Marvel movie. Noah and Eli sink down next to me, while Gabriel meets his concierge at the door and carries in even *more* food – pizza, fries, Chinese food, tubs of cherry-flavored ice cream.

By the time the first Stan Lee cameo plays, I'm already asleep. Just as my eyelids droop closed, I imagine I hear Eli whisper, "I swore to protect you once, and I failed. I'll never, ever let that happen again."

NOAH

Mackenzie's head droops on my shoulder, and in minutes she's asleep. Her breathing steadies, and occasionally she lets out these snorting noises that make my chest feel tight. With her hair freshly washed and fanned over her shoulders, and her face soft and free of tension, she looks... peaceful.

Beside me, Eli watches me allow my arch-nemesis to drool on my shoulder. His expression says exactly what he thinks about that. "What happened out there?"

My hands curl into fists as I tell them the whole story – how I went to visit Alec in the hospital, and how I let him talk me into being part of his revenge stunt. How we jumped Mackenzie as she strutted into cheerleading trials and put her in the trunk of Alec's Shelby Cobra.

"Alec said we were going to drive her into the desert and leave her for a couple of hours. Scare her a bit. But she was screaming – this horrible, inhuman scream. The longer we drove, the angrier he got, and by the time we pulled her out, he was ready to..." My fingers tighten around Mackenzie's arm at the memory. "He wanted all of us to have a go at her, starting with me."

A cold shiver runs down my spine as I recall that feral look in Alec's eyes as he leaned over Mackenzie. A feral hunger fueled by rage.

I couldn't watch any longer. I *snapped*.

Do I look like that? Am I so consumed by hate that I wear it as a second skin? It's been so long since I felt anything but rage that I don't remember who I am without it.

I saved Mackenzie from Alec today, but I also helped shove her in that trunk in the first place. It's my fault she was even out in the desert. Shame burns in my cheeks. *I hope you can't see me now, Felix. I really fucked up.*

"That's dark." Gabriel stares at his drink. I notice he hasn't taken a sip.

"I know. What the fuck was he thinking? The others were too chicken shit to say anything. They were just going to stand around like idiots while he *raped* her. I said no fucking way, and a couple of them backed me up, but then Alec went for her, and I snapped."

"You laid him out?" A grin tugs at the corner of Eli's mouth.

"I hurt him pretty bad. That doctor of his is going to have a time rebuilding his face. Again."

I can feel Felix in the room with us, sucking all the air away as he flaps his angel wings and shoots me a disapproving look.

I'm just so angry.

Mackenzie snorts, her head burrowing into my shoulder. My fist rests on her back. I watch – detached, with no control over my limbs – my fingers uncurl, becoming a flat palm that rubs reassuring circles on her back.

This is fucked up.

Eli folds his arms. "Alec and Cleo can't get away with this.

We have to do something. Tell the school what happened to Mackenzie and George. Call the police. It's *assault*."

Gabriel glances at me, and I know what he's thinking. If we report Alec, I'll go down with him. I'll kiss my college acceptance goodbye. Yet another thing Mackenzie Malloy has taken from me.

I don't care.

I'm not sure I see it that way any longer.

My fingers brush her warm skin, and I catch the faintest scent of my brother in the air.

"Reporting them won't do any good," Gabriel says. "Alec will just get his dad to pay off the school. The whole thing will be hushed up, and we'll never hear about it again. No, this is personal, between us and them. This is war, and I'll take the Ice Queen's shilling."

"Are you really going up against Alec over me?"

Mackenzie lifts her head. Her cheeks flush, and she runs her fingers through her hair, pushing the golden threads away from her face.

"It doesn't mean we like you," I growl, whipping my hand off her back.

"I like her just fine," Gabe says.

"Me too," Eli pipes up.

She's wearing Gabriel's aftershave as perfume. Against her skin, his scent takes on an intoxicating danger. I'm drunk with the need of her, the way I was at that party when she pressed her body against me. Hot skin on skin, her golden dress clinging to every curve. How good she felt in my arms, her body molding to mine...

No. I can't.

I tear myself from Mackenzie and cross to the windows. Beyond Gabriel's pool, waves crash against golden sand, almost the exact color of Mackenzie's hair. Even the view makes me think of her. I shove open the window and gulp in fresh air. *Get a grip, Noah.*

"This isn't happening." Mackenzie fixes us all with her glacial stare. "I handle my own problems. This is between Alec and Cleo and me."

"Alec got me to help him attempt to rape you," I say. "Even though things didn't go as far as they could, it's disgusting. I won't let that stand."

Mackenzie shakes her head. "I don't like this. I don't work with outsiders."

"I don't like beans, but Maria makes me eat 'em." Eli smiles. "This is happening, so get used to it."

"Before we do anything, we need to get a few things straight." I whirl around and fix on Mackenzie. I can't believe this is happening. I can't believe I'm on the side of a Malloy. *The* Malloy. But today broke everything. Or maybe I've been breaking apart ever since she started at Stonehurst, and giving her a slice of chocolate cherry cake in the desert after rescuing her is the first piece put together again. "Who were those guys you sent to terrorize us all?"

"Friends of my family." She flips her hair and shoots me that defiant Mackenzie stare.

"Do they work for hire?"

"They do, but it's probably not a path you want to go down, not if you want to graduate with honors and go on to your fancy colleges. Blood on your hands has a habit of sticking."

"Why do you say that like you don't have a future to worry about?" Eli asks.

She snorts. "Noah can tell you."

Two sets of accusing eyes swivel to me. I shrug. "She's flunking out."

"And that bastard refuses to tutor me." Mackenzie glares at

me. Climate change would be sorted if the UN employed Mackenzie to glare at the ice caps until they froze again.

"Wanker," Gabriel grins.

"That's right." She leans back on the sofa, arranging her hands behind her head. "He's a wanker."

This conversation is ridiculous. "So we're *actually* talking about how we're going to make Alec and Cleo pay."

"You boys seriously don't have to worry. I've got this. I will be brutal. The fact they went after George..." she tips her head. "I remember something George said to me in the bathroom. I think Alec might've done something to her before."

"Everyone's bullied George," I say. "She's weird. You and Cleo were her worst tormenters, if you recall."

A flicker of something that might've been regret passes through Mackenzie's cold eyes. *Or maybe she's just blinking away a piece of dust.* "That's ancient history. The new Mackenzie stands up for the little guys. That reminds me." She glares at me. "I need your phone."

"Why?"

"Because mine fell out of my pocket in the middle of the desert and I don't particularly want to go back to look for it." She whips the phone from my hand and starts tapping the screen. "Relax. I'm not downloading radical feminist tracts over your porn or anything. I need to see what's stored on my remote drive. And check in with my cat sitter."

"You... have a cat?"

"Duh. You know this. Eli told you and Alec about the secret entrance to my house and you broke in and tried to *disembowel* her."

What the fuck? "That's sick."

"Agreed." She jabs the screen with surprising force. "Why do you think I branded my initials into his forehead? You would've got the same treatment, but I know you were at school that day."

"If Alec did that, it was his own idea. He never said anything about breaking into your house or hurting a cat."

"And if he came in through the secret entrance, it's not because I told him," Eli adds. "Even these guys don't know about that."

"I'll have you know I'm an expert on entrances, secret and otherwise—"

Eli throws a cushion at Gabriel's head. "Ignore him. Fuck, Mackenzie, is your cat okay?"

"She's a fighter." Mackenzie tosses her head back. "I needed to send you all a message – I don't care what you do to me, but don't fuck with Queen Boudica."

"Your cat's name is Queen Boudica?" Eli grins.

I feel a smile tugging at the corner of my mouth, but I'm not yet ready for it to take over. Today has been... strange. Mackenzie Malloy isn't the thirteen-year-old-girl who gave me my first wet dream and ruined my life anymore. She has a *cat*. She's stronger than anyone I've ever met. And... she's bug-nuts crazy.

The worst thing is... I think I kind of like it.

MACKENZIE

fter I fall asleep in front of the movie for the third time, I wake up in Gabriel's arms as he carries me up to his room.

Before I realize I'm doing it, my body curls around Gabriel. I cling to his neck and breathe in that rich, pagan scent of his. The horror of the day fades into a distant nightmare as I bask in the beauty of him. The tips of his silken hair brush over my face, and it's the most amazing sensation – his music come to life inside me.

I want him.

The thought hits me like a fist to the chest. Gabriel lights up the darkest, most hidden parts of me. *I want him.* I don't give a fuck about Antony's plan or my own fragile mind. I don't care that I don't yet trust Gabriel or that two other guys who confuse me with their kindness are right beneath us. I don't care that I have no idea what the fuck I'm doing. Gabriel fucking Fallen sings the stars against my skin and *I want him.*

Mackenzie Malloy always gets what she wants.

Upstairs, he lays me on the bed and pulls the covers over me. I'm cocooned in his scent, in the cavern carved out by his body.

My fingers lace in his, and I pull him close. Our cheeks brush together, and the touch sends a fire thrumming through my veins.

"There is one thing I want to know." Gabriel's voice touches my ear, and I turn into a puddle of melted, bubbling Mackenzie hormones. "If Eli's a stalker and Noah's a dick, what did I do to deserve a visit from your friends?"

I manage to choke out a reply. "I didn't want you to feel left out."

Gabriel's laugh is a low rumble that reaches right to my toes. "Seriously, Mac. I'm intrigued."

"It was because of the party." The words are barely a whisper.

"Because I pushed you in the pool?"

I nod. But it's not the truth. I sent Antony after Gabriel because of what happened before the pool, because of the kiss. I want so much for the way Gabriel makes me feel to be real, but that kiss proved it's not. Gabriel is who he is – the perfect fantasy, the broken prince who sings the stars and the blood and the pain. But singing it isn't the same as living it. He'll never be real to me.

Maybe I don't care.

"Come to bed with me," I whisper.

Mischief flickers in Gabriel's eyes. He leans in, pressing his lips to my forehead. The kiss is starlight dancing beneath my skin.

"Not tonight," he whispers. "Not while you still have the ghost of another guy's violence behind your eyes."

"Then lie with me." I tug on his shirt, pulling him against me. Gabriel sighs and crawls under the blankets, wrapping his body around me. For the first time in so many years, I fall into a deep and dreamless sleep.

THE SCENT of bacon wakes me. Panic surges in my gut as my mind immediately flies to burning human flesh, to the smell of Alec's skin under my brand. I throw out my hands, reaching for Queen Boudica, desperate to hold her to my chest and feel her tiny heart beating.

My fingers grasp not fur but warm human flesh. *Someone's in my bedroom. Someone's broken into the house again. They're in my room—*

I thrust my hand beneath my pillow for my knife, but it's not there.

I scream.

My feet kick out, catching the intruder off-guard. He grunts as he rolls out of bed and slams into the floor. I fling myself over the side and lift my leg to stomp on his head and—

"Bloody hell, Mac. It's me."

Gabriel rolls on the ground, wincing as he clutches his knee. He wears only boxers and an utterly perplexed expression.

"Fuck." I sink back into the comforter as it all comes back to me. Alec in the desert. Noah rescuing me. George being beaten up. The guys looking after me, offering to get Alec for what he did. And Gabriel carrying me to bed and holding me while I slept.

I spooned with Gabriel Fallen.

And then I kicked him out of bed.

I groan, resting my head in my hands. Heat flares in my cheeks. As my gaze falls on my body, I realize I'm not wearing any clothes. At all.

I grab the corner of the comforter and yank it over my chest, glaring down at Gabriel. "Why am I naked?"

Gabriel chuckles. He tosses me a faded tour t-shirt, which I yank over my head. "Don't blame me. You must've got too hot or something about 3AM, because you threw off all your clothes. I tried to stop you, but you *bit* me."

"I did not."

Gabriel lifts his arm to show me a row of red welts on his bicep. Teeth marks. An even deeper blush of heat pools in my cheeks.

"It's been a long time since I—"

"—shared a bed with someone. I figured." Gabriel leans in close to flick a strand of hair from my face. His fingers brush my skin, leaving a pulse of heat behind. "You hog all the blankets, you crazy wench."

I poke my tongue out at him and pull on his t-shirt. It's so big and I'm so short that it's more like a dress. Gabriel shoves his feet into a pair of tight black jeans. I try not to stare at his perfect ass, but I have no self-control. He blows me a kiss as he heads downstairs.

I grab a belt from the rack in his walk-in closet and loop it twice around my waist, cinching in the shirt. I run Gabriel's brush through my tangled hair, and splash water on my face. My expression in the mirror is... weirdly calm. I do not look like a woman who survived an assault and fell asleep in her rock god's bed.

As I pad downstairs, a delicious smell wafts up to greet me. Gabriel kneels in front of his record player, cleaning a record and placing it on the turntable. Eli's in the kitchen, flipping pancakes in a skillet, an enormous pile of crispy bacon already stacked beside him. He has a frilly apron tied around his waist, and it looks completely ridiculous and also adorable in a way that makes my stomach tight. There's something about Eli that's so... earnest. He may be rich and popular, but I still see that guy who took me to Disneyland to cheer me up. That day got a whole five pages in my diary.

I just wish I had a memory of it. It sounded pretty special.

Of course, Eli loses points for the stalking. After reading my diary, that at least makes more sense. Now that I know Eli's not a serial killer, it's comforting in a fucked-up way to think he's watched over me even after all these years.

I cross the room and plop down on one of the stools at the breakfast bar. Eli turns around and smiles at me. When Eli smiles, his whole face lights up. It's so different from Gabriel's grin, which can't help but be full of mischief and lewd promise. Eli's smile is warm and safe and beautiful – I can't believe I thought he was annoying before.

"I hope you're hungry, because I made enough to feed an army." He dumps an enormous stack of pancakes onto a plate and pushes it over to me.

"I approve. I'm an entire Roman legion desperate for my *posca*." I reach for the maple syrup.

"What's *posca*?"

"It's vinegar from wine gone bad, mixed with water and herbs and shit. It was basically the Gatorade of the Roman Army, kind of like how pancakes with blueberries and maple syrup are the Gatorade of the Mackenzie Malloy army."

"Personally, I'll give the moldy wine a miss, although those Romans sound like they know how to party." Gabriel comes up behind me and rests his head on my shoulder so his cheek touches mine. My fork flies out of my hand and maple syrup dribbles over the edge of my plate as a rush of heat impales my coordination.

"You're really interested in all this Roman history stuff?"

I'm startled by the not-violence in Noah's voice. My once-bitter enemy slumps into the stool on the end of the breakfast bar, as far from me as he can possibly get. Those coal-black eyes study me, hard and intense. But I don't get that sense of danger from him, of rage rolling off his body like waves ready to sweep me away.

I shrug. "My father was into it – Caesar and Augustus and all the emperors. I read all the fancy-ass books in the study. I might not be able to pass a Calculus test, but I do know tons of super useful facts about Ancient Rome I'm sure will be applicable in everyday life."

Gabriel laughs as he helps himself to a pancake stack twice as high as mine. "What are we doing with our little stowaway?"

"Plotting Alec's downfall." Noah accepts a plate from Eli.

Eli looks me up and down, this worried frown on his face. "We should take you to a doctor, make sure you're okay."

"You should, but you're not going to." I jab a forkful of pancake in Eli's direction. "Not unless you want another visit from my family friends. I'm not having some stranger root around in my lady bits."

Noah grinds his teeth, and I notice he hasn't touched a bite. The air twangs with tension, like a bowstring pulled taut. Gabriel slouches over the end of the table, but even he looks uncomfortable.

"What?" I glare between the three faces. "How was I supposed to know you'd all turn into my knights in Armani armor?"

"I'm not hungry." Noah pushes his plate away and stalks off to the bathroom. A moment later, the door slams behind him.

Eli winces. "He just got a call from the hospital. His stepmom, Grace, is being discharged after the scare your 'friends' gave her."

"If you want me to feel sorry for doing that, it's not going to happen. Alec came to *my* house and hurt my cat."

Eli taps the table with his fingers. "I'm starting to wonder about that."

"What do you mean?"

"Did Alec really do it? He would've boasted about it if he had, posted photos on Facebook, nicked some of your panties."

"Gross."

"Exactly. That's Alec for you, and that's why it's odd that none of us heard a peep. And since I didn't tell him about the secret entrance—" Eli glares at Gabriel, silencing him before he can say something crass, "—how did he get in?"

"I haven't decided I believe you about the secret entrance," I glare at him. "I saw Alec run away – he vaulted the wall like a pro, and he was wearing his letterman jacket."

"Alec had his jacket stolen," Eli says.

I snort. "Oh, sure. I believe that. He can't wear it because it's covered in my cat's blood."

"Is it possible that Alec wasn't responsible for breaking into your house?"

"Who else could it—" I choke on my pancake.

I know exactly who it is.

Brutus.

Fuck.

Fuck.

Fuck, fuckedy, fucklestein.

I'm an idiot for not considering it before. I thought we had him under control, that there's no way he'd be able to connect the dots. But with my face in the news, he might've put everything together. He might've stolen Alec's jacket. He might've seen me use the secret entrance.

If he's figured out our plan, he might be back to finish what he started.

He might be here to bury my secrets for good.

MACKENZIE

Gabriel wants me to stay and hang out for the day, and as tempting as that is, I need to get home and call Antony and check on Queen Boudica. Eli offers to drop me at Malloy Manor, and against my better judgment, I accept.

"I'm sorry about Noah," Eli says as we pull out into traffic. "It's going to take him a while to stop seeing you as his brother's killer."

"I understand. I've lost people I loved, too. It's impossible to let that shit go."

"I don't know. You seem adept at letting shit go." Eli drapes his hand out the window. He's got the top up now, and my playlist on low volume. It's quiet enough to talk. I squirm in my seat, feeling the layer of sand grind into my ass through Gabriel's sweatpants. "You don't seem cut up about the fact you terrified Noah's stepmom or branded Alec's forehead in error."

"You don't seem cut up about your father being in prison," I shoot back.

"You of all people should know how I feel about it," Eli says. "Maybe I think he deserves it."

"Alec deserves what he got, even if he didn't hurt Queen Boudica. Call it revenge in advance. As for Noah, I *am* sorry about his stepmom, but I can't do anything about it now. He's got to learn to move the fuck on."

"And me?" Eli stares straight ahead, deliberately not meeting my eyes. It's almost more concerning than his usual intense focus. "You scared my cat. Does that make us even for my perceived slight?"

"You have a cat?"

"Yeah. A little black-and-white ball of energy named Gizmo. Maria found her living in the basement of her brother's apartment complex. It was the year after you disappeared, and I wasn't doing so hot. She thought caring for an animal might help me move on." Eli tries for a smile, but it doesn't quite reach his eyes. "It worked."

It didn't work, that much is obvious. Suddenly, more than anything in the world, I want to meet this Gizmo. "Tell her I'm sorry I scared her. I thought—"

Eli pulls up at a stoplight and whips his head around, focusing those ocean eyes on me. "I'm going crazy here, Mackenzie. What's happened to you? Where are your parents? If I didn't tell anyone about the maintenance shed, then who snuck into your house? The look on your face this morning... you looked terrified. I've never seen you look like that, ever. Not even when your dad—"

"It's nothing."

Eli punches the wheel. "It's not fucking *nothing*. You're in danger and you won't let me help. You disappeared on me all those years ago, and after the news about Noah's brother came out, I thought... I thought maybe you'd skipped the country so your dad could avoid some kind of blowback from Noah's family, but that's not what your eyes say. You're not afraid of Noah, so what is it?"

His chest heaves. A lock of golden hair falls over his eye. When he's upset like this, his Tennessee accent comes in full force, and it's fucking hot as hell. I watch him peel back those layers of rigid perfection to reveal the broken man beneath. Noah may have lost his brother, but Eli's been in mourning for four years, and the pain of losing me still burns as bright as the day I left him without a goodbye.

I want nothing more than to take his pain away, but I can't. It doesn't belong to me. Eli's heart is reserved for another Mackenzie, a Mackenzie trapped in time.

I take a deep breath.

I do a selfish thing. Or a selfless thing, depending on how you look at it. I throw up a barrier to protect my heart and his.

"I have an agreement with Gabriel, and I'm making the same one with you," I say. "I'm not talking about my family or what happened four years ago. All you need to know is that my parents aren't coming back. I'm the ghost of Malloy Manor, and it's imperative I graduate Stonehurst Prep this year, with my sanity and my head intact. Actually, the former is optional."

"And you don't remember anything about your life before." Eli swipes at that uncooperative lock of hair. "Dissociative amnesia, right? I've been researching it. It's when your mind rejects memories and feeling and events that surround trauma—"

"Yes, amnesia. Exactly. So even if I wanted to talk about it, which I don't, I wouldn't have anything to say."

Eli sighs. "Fine. I agree. On one condition."

"I don't do conditions."

"Not even for an old friend?" Eli tries for one of his warm smiles, but it doesn't quite reach his eyes. "I promise not to ask, but you have to promise not to lie to me. I can't take it, not after losing you once already. I only want to protect you, because even after all this time you're still everything to me. If you lie... I'll break. I'll fucking *come apart*."

Oh, super.

"Deal. No lies. Just evasive not-answers." Eli turns into Harrington Road. "Take me along the back road."

"Why not the front gates?" Tension hunches Eli's shoulders.

I glare at him. "That counts as asking."

Eli throws up his hands. "Why won't you tell us anything?"

"Jesus." I grab the wheel before the car spins out of control. "You're too pretty and I'm too amazing to die in a car crash, okay?"

Eli takes the wheel again, drumming his fingers against the leather. "The other two I get. Gabe is Gabe and Noah hated your guts until yesterday. But we've been friends since we were five years old, Mackenzie. We've been through hell together, and I've always proven myself to you. Why can't you talk to me?"

I fix him with my Ice Queen glare. It's all I have to hold Eli's gaze; that's how intense his eyes are right now. "Did it ever occur to you that *maybe* I'm trying to protect *your* ass for a change?"

"Or maybe you're just trying to protect yourself." Eli's gaze drops to the locket at my throat. He swallows and tears his eyes away. "Even though he's not here, your father's still coming between us."

He pulls over in front of the woods at the rear of my house, out of view of the other mansions on the hill. I give him one final glare as I slide out, but he pulls away before I can get the final word in. The Porsche roars around the corner and out of sight. I remain fixed in place, still watching the road, part of me expecting him to come back. My chest heaves. Finally, I pull myself together and duck into the trees, letting myself in through the maintenance door.

"Meow." Queen Boudica leaps from hood to hood across the rows of ghost cars. She skids to a stop just as I reach the top of the metal stairs, and lets out a howl of anguish.

"I know, I know. I'm sorry I left you for so long." I scoop her into my arms. She settles into her scarf position, her whole body rumbling with pleasure at my return.

"She'll tell you a story of woe, but I swear I fed her according to your detailed instructions." A shadow emerges from beside the garage door. My heart clenches before he steps into the light and I recognize Tiberius. I'm not used to seeing people inside the house. It's unsettling, but I'm glad he's been here. "And we played at least three rounds of hide and seek."

The idea of this hulking cage fighter crouching behind the sofa while my tiny, scrappy kitten stalks him fills me with mirth. "Thanks for cat-sitting, Tiberius."

"My pleasure. Anything for Antony's family. Antony dragged me out of the gutter, turned me into a fighter, gave me a family. Dude's like a father to me." Tiberius claps me on the shoulder, and I nearly go flying. "Don't worry, your secrets are safe with me, *Mackenzie*."

I nod. I don't like trusting this guy. But if Antony says he's solid, then I trust Antony.

Tiberius opens his jacket to show me the holster and large knife strapped against his tight body. "Antony said you wouldn't want anyone else in the house, but we've got men watching the perimeter 24/7. No one's coming near this place without us knowing about it."

I nod. "You saw the guy who dropped me off in the Porsche?"

"Sure did. He giving you trouble?" Tiberius grins, cracking his knuckles. "Name your torture, and it shall be done."

"No. He's safe. If you see him around, don't shoot him full of bullets." I pause. "Or the other two, either. I'll send Antony photographs."

Tiberius grins that maniacal grin of his. "As you wish. If you change your mind..."

As soon as I hear the maintenance door click shut behind him, I take Queen Boudica to my room and snuggle down in bed with her. She falls asleep instantly, her tiny face pushed up against my cheek. I call Antony to tell him about Brutus, then I pick up my diary and read it from cover to cover again, my fingers tracing the hearts doodled around Noah's name.

The girl who wrote this diary was so taken with Noah's dangerous eyes, she didn't see the golden boy right in front of her. Now, that same girl had three impossible boys who tugged her in all directions, and all she wanted to do was save them all. But saving them meant pushing them away, and just the thought of it made my heart ache.

If Brutus is after me, this can only end in blood. I had to make sure it's his blood and no one else's.

I have more to lose than ever.

But Mackenzie Malloy doesn't go down without a fight.

I look forward to school on Monday with a mix of trepidation and excitement. On Sunday, Tiberius calls to tell me a package has arrived for me. I go to the front gate to collect it from him and find a brand new iPhone inside, with a note from Eli and his, Gabriel's, and Noah's numbers already programmed in.

Eli and Gabriel blow up my phone all weekend. Eli sends videos of his cat, Gizmo – a black-and-white tuxedo mix who loves sleeping in boxes – and Gabriel sends me links to bands and albums he loves. I make a playlist of Gabriel's recommendations and listen to it while trying not to swoon.

A couple of times I find my finger poised over Noah's name, the insane itch to message him twinging under my skin. I don't succumb.

On Monday, Eli picks me up at the rear of the property. When we pull into the student parking lot, I notice Alec leaning against the columns in front of Stonehurst, sans jacket, a handful of his jock friends and cheerleaders surrounding him in a tight circle. The gaggle of bears and vipers who usually sit on the periphery of the group is nowhere to be seen, and other students seem to be taking a wide berth to avoid them. Alec's face is stormy as hell.

He's lonely up there on his pedestal.

Eli notices me watching. "We spent the weekend putting the word out. Alec LeMarque is canceled at Stonehurst Prep. No one except a few loyal fuckheads will go near him now."

My hands curl into fists, and I miss the satisfying weight of my knife against my leg. I lost it in the desert, along with my phone and the last thread of my humanity. "I'm still going to claw his eyes out."

Eli's smile warms me from the inside out. "I'd like to see that."

Walking to my locker with Eli is a new experience. It takes us three times as long because he keeps stopping to talk to people. Unlike Gabriel and Noah who breeze past anyone they deem beneath them, Eli always has time to comment on a teammate's performance or wish the Theatresports team good luck for their upcoming competition.

Who knew popular boys can be so damn nice?

Who knew basic human decency is so fucking *hot*?

By the time we reach our lockers, I'm ready to jump Eli's bones, consequences be damned. Then Noah leans against my locker door, and I'm momentarily stricken by the contrast. Whereas Eli is all Southern charm and fashion-magazine good-looks, Noah's the bad boy with the fuck-you attitude and haunting eyes. Those coal-orbs fix me with a devastating glare. "5PM, library. Don't be late."

"What's this?" I raise a perfectly-sculpted eyebrow.

"Your tutoring session." Noah gives me one final, penetrating glare, then storms off.

I glare at Eli, who bursts out laughing. "Don't look at me. I didn't make him tutor you. Grumpypuss must've decided for himself you're worth the effort."

Intriguing.

Eli walks me to homeroom, where Gabriel waits to escort me on his arm like I'm the queen. He does this between all my morning classes, keeping up an easy conversation in an attempt to distract me from the eye-daggers Cleo's throwing at my back. *I could get used to this.*

Cleo I can handle, but when we step into third-period English and Alec LeMarque glares at me from a seat in the second row, my body recoils against Gabriel. It's this visceral sense of *wrongness*, like space bends around Alec's body, and he not a person so much as a portal into a dark void where a cosmic god devours souls.

Okay, that might just be my imagination recalling this reverse harem book, *Kings of Miskatonic Prep,* that I read last night, but still. Alec's assault left a mark on my psyche that all my bravado and vengeance cannot heal.

My mind flicks back to George, and I wonder again if this is something she feels, if the hurt Alec has done to her runs deeper than just bullying. It's enough to make me wring his neck right there. Gabriel senses my body stiffening and leads me to a desk as far from Alec as it's possible to get.

I don't hear a word of the lesson.

One of the guys remains at my side during every class. In History, we're supposed to be working on our essays about the impact of colonialism on indigenous cultures, but Eli studies me instead, no doubt searching my face for signs that this fresh trauma is making my amnesia worse.

By the time lunch rolls around, I'm sweating from the stress of seeing Alec everywhere. I tense up in the halls, certain he'll be waiting around the next corner to leap out and attack me.

On the way to lunch, we pass George with her pockets stuffed with food, heading to the bathroom. "Hey, George," Eli waves. "Over here."

Every face in the hallway turns to watch the exchange. Eli Hart, king of the school, talking to weirdo freak George? No one knows what to make of it. Gabriel saunters up behind us, and he flashes George his cheekiest, friendliest smile.

George's face goes red as a beet, but she falls in step beside me. I throw my arm around her shoulders, marveling at how tiny she is – I'm short as fuck and she's a good two inches shorter than me, and her unusual hair and nose piercings only make her look even smaller and more pixie-like.

Eli leads us through the dining hall, his jaw set with determination. When we arrive at the Royal table, it's already occupied with three of the jocks, the same three guys who were standing with Alec on the front steps. Just seeing their faces, remembering the way their features twisted like horror movie monsters as they came at me in the desert, made me want to run. But I held my ground. *Mackenzie Malloy isn't afraid of her attackers.*

Mackenzie Malloy will fuck you all up.

Everyone falls silent. Gabriel takes a seat right in the middle and pulls me down next to him. George looks like she's going to bolt, or vomit, or possibly both, but I pat the seat next to me and she sits gingerly on the edge.

Everyone's staring at us. All conversation has stopped. I glare at the guy sitting opposite me, whose name is Darren. I dare him to speak, but he just frowns at his lunch.

Gabriel's the one who breaks the silence. He points to the patch from a punk band on George's satchel. "I love these guys. You have good taste."

George glances down, as if seeing her bag for the first time. She bites her lip. "Yeah, I—I guess I listen to a lot of punk."

They start an intense conversation, throwing obscure bands and song titles back and forth. Everyone around us takes this as a cue to that conversation is allowed to begin again, that an uneasy truce has been reached at the royal table—

"What the fuck?"

It's not Darren who rasps those words, but someone behind me. Someone who drives a shard of ice through my chest.

My whole body clenches. I don't have to turn around to recognize the voice. I'll remember it forever, the way it hissed in my ear as an unwanted cock brushed against my thigh.

Alec.

The urge to run consumes me. I'm tough, sure, but this guy tried to rape me and he's standing *right behind me,* close enough that I can smell him. I grip the edge of the table and force my shoulders to relax.

We could have reported you, Alec. We let you believe you've gotten away with this, that the worst I can do to you is over.

You are wrong.

Gabriel and Eli stand up, flanking either side of me. Eli folds his arms, and I'm aware suddenly of just how toned and fucking sexy his forearms are. He's not quite as ripped as Noah, but all that running left him in fine physical fitness. Between Eli and pretty-actor-boy Alec, I have no doubt who will win if Eli decides to bring fists into play.

That's not Eli's style, though. "This isn't your table anymore, LeMarque."

Alec steps toward him, his lips curled back into a snarl. "My boys were here first. You don't own this table, Hart. It's a free fucking country. So why don't you take your psycho-bitch-ghost-slut and move along. Unless she's dragged you back to me because she's so desperate for my cock—"

Eli moves so fast I don't see it. One moment he's standing beside me, his shoulder tense, his usually-kind eyes filled with loathing. The next moment, Alec's on the floor, his nose bleeding. Eli winces as he shakes out his wrist.

"I'll get you for this," Alec huffs, clutching his nose as he smears blood on the floor.

"Eli, *fuck*." I scan the dining hall. Hundreds of faces are trained on us. I notice Ms. Drysdale moving across the cafeteria toward us. She won't be able to see much over the heads of the students crowding around, but if anyone says a thing to her, Eli will get in trouble. I stand up to try and salvage the situation, but my rage takes hold of me. I lean over Alec and kick him squarely between the legs.

Alec wheezes like a shitty car struggling up a hill. His hands fly off his face to protect his legs. The dressing flops off his forehead, revealing the healing scar of my initials.

MM. Property of Mackenzie Malloy.

He's marked for death, and everyone here knows it. A couple of brave students lean over and snap pictures.

"Jesus. Look at you. You're pathetic. Just get out of here, Alec."

It's Noah. He holds his tray under one arm, all casual-like. His other hand smooths dark strands of hair from his aristocratic face. His eyes burn with the full depth of his hatred, but this time it's not directed at me.

Alec rolls to his knees and crawls to the outside door. His three friends hurry to vacate our table and scurry after him. A few students clap, but one glare from Noah shuts them up. Ms. Drysdale is nearly on us. Gabriel tosses his bookbag on the floor, covering up the bloodstain.

Noah sits down opposite me, his head bent over his food. Ms. Drysdale appears at his side a moment later. "What's going on over here?" she demands.

"Nothing, ma'am," Gabriel flashes her that impish grin of his. "I was demonstrating a dance move from my latest music video, and I got a little carried away and accidentally kicked Alec LeMarque. He's fine, he's just gone outside for some air."

Ms. Drysdale looks to the French doors. She sees Alec heaving himself onto a bench, barking orders at his friends while blood dries on his face. She must see the MM branded into his forehead. I brace myself for trouble.

Instead, a smile tugs the corner of Ms. Drysdale's mouth. She turns to me, and in an almost imperceptible movement, she winks. She fucking *winks*.

I'm too floored to say anything. Ms. Drysdale turns back to Gabriel. "Very well, Mr. Fallen. But you shouldn't be horsing around like that in the dining hall. Someone could be seriously hurt."

Gabriel hangs his head, feigning regret. "I'm sorry, ma'am."

She turns to Noah. "Mr. Marlowe, I'm glad to have caught you. Mackenzie informs me you refused to tutor her. That's in violation of the school's tutoring policy, and I'll have to speak to the principal about revoking your status as—"

Noah shakes his head. "That was a misunderstanding, ma'am. Mac and I have a tutoring session this afternoon."

I nod. "It's true."

"Ah. Very good then." She lets that smile play ever so faintly across her lips. "Carry on, students."

As she walks away, I sink into my seat between George and Gabriel and plow into my food. Noah takes a seat across from us, shooting me a glare lacking in his usual fire. I flip him the finger and stick my tongue out, but inside my stomach's doing backflips.

He called me Mac.

WHEN THE BELL rings after Political Science, I fly out the door to beat Noah to the library. He must know some kind of apparating spell because he's already there when I dash in, seated at the same table as last time, a stack of books beside him.

It's weird to be around him at school after everything that's happened. Stonehurst Prep feels like a different world to the desert or hanging at Gabriel's condo. I fell asleep on Noah's shoulder and it felt nice, and right. But staring across the table at this aristocrat with his perfectly starched collar and his eyes of burning embers, I wonder if I imagined the whole thing.

"Why did you change your mind about tutoring me?" I ask as I plop down across from him. "I thought I was hopeless."

Noah ignores my question. Instead, he opens a page in our mathematics textbook. "Explain to me how to solve this equation."

"I can't."

"Why not?"

"Because it's all gibberish. Didn't Eli tell you? I have amnesia. I don't remember this shit. You might as well ask me to translate Egyptian hieroglyphics."

"You know all about ancient history," he points out. "You were telling us all about *posca*."

"That's because..." I sigh. I can't explain. I don't have to explain. "Fine. It's like... Just help me understand what I'm looking at."

Noah tugs on his school tie. He's always so *orderly* – Gabriel dresses as though he peels his uniform off the bottom of a pile of groupies every morning (at least partially true), but Noah's always perfectly buttoned and pressed. It's sexy as fuck, actually, how much control he exerts over himself and everything in his life.

He's a good teacher, too. He writes out each stage of the problem and uses real-world examples so I can grasp what exactly it is I'm trying to work out. He's strict – he doesn't let me mouth off. Of course, that only makes me do it more. He gets so flustered around me. I don't fit neatly into the box he assigned for me in his head, and he doesn't know yet if he still hates me or... I remember the hardness of him pressing against me at the party. He was flustered then, that's for sure.

I like having this effect on him.

At the end of our hour, Noah hands a page of problems back to me, with only two wrong answers. "I think you might actually have a shot of passing the next quiz."

I dare a grin. "They'll think I cheated."

"Probably. A word of advice – if you're going to cheat, don't copy Gabriel's work. He's almost as behind as you are." Noah stands up and shrugs his bag over his shoulder. He doesn't look me in the eye as he turns away. "See you tomorrow, Mac."

ANTONY GETS BACK to me with the news that he 'sent a few guys around' to sort out the Brutus situation. He doesn't elaborate on the details, but I don't need to ask. "The weird thing is, when we got past the guards, he wasn't inside," Antony says. "His head-quarters have been completely cleared out. We've put out the word, and he's nowhere to be seen in Emerald Beach. He must've been tipped off I was coming for him, so he skipped town to save his pretty ass. He's probably in Mexico by now. You've got nothing to worry about from him."

Even so, Antony keeps the guard on my house. I feel a weight lifted from my shoulders – for now, Queen Boudica and I are safe. I'd be happier if I had Brutus' head on a plate next to Alec's, but that might come in good time.

After Antony's good news, the rest of the week flies by – I eat lunch with the guys at the royals table while Alec stares dagger eyes into my back from a lonely corner of the dining hall. I walk the halls with Gabriel or Eli's arm around my shoulders, basking in their warmth and popularity. Noah and I throw barbs at each other while he tutors me. We toss around ideas for getting our vengeance on Alec and Cleo. I send videos of Queen Boudica chasing a fuzzy mouse to Eli and receive strings of hilarious Roman History memes from George.

I dare to believe that maybe the rest of the year could go like this – a normal teenage existence, with normal friends and normal hormones and normal revenge plots and not the gaping hole of loneliness that's been threatening to devour me.

I should have known better.

The next Thursday night, I don't go to tutoring with Noah. Instead, I pull on the world's tiniest red skirt and head to my first cheerleading practice.

That's right, I, Mackenzie Malloy – the Ice Queen witch bitch ghost slut extraordinaire – am officially a base for the Stonehurst Prep cheer squad. When Mrs. Anderson heard from Ms. Drysdale about the 'family bereavement' that prevented me from completing my previous audition, she allowed me to do a make-up. Her verdict: my 'pep' could definitely use some work (it's hard to look smiley with Cleo staring daggers at you from the bleachers) but my tumbling skills and strength would be an asset for the team.

After class on Thursday, I head outside for some fresh air before practice starts. Gabriel's smoking weed under the bleachers. I jump down beside him and whip the joint from his hands, leaning my head against his shoulder as my head fills with lovely THC clouds.

Eli and Noah are on the field, running drills with the rest of the track team. Eli's clearly the star of the team – he's out in front during all the sprints. When they practice their starts, he explodes from the ground like he's about to fly off to the moon. Something happens to him when he runs – in his face, it's like he's finally going fast enough that he can run away from his life.

But Noah... he's a mess. He's strong, and fit, and his ass looks damn fine in those tight shorts, but he's no track star. He lags behind the others in the sprints, and during the drills you can tell he doesn't know what to do with his body. I read the frustration on his face and the tension in his shoulders as he comes in last again.

Gabe notices me watching Noah. "He knows he's bollocks. But he won't quit. Noah thinks everything in life is like passing exams. You just have to learn the answers and you're set."

"But why is he on the track team if he sucks at it?" Noah is such a perfectionist over-achiever, it doesn't make sense.

Gabriel gives me that look. "Because of his brother. Are we still on for tonight?"

That's right. I read in the news articles that Noah's brother Felix had been a track star headed to the Olympic team. I want to ask Gabriel more about it, but it will only bring up questions in his mind about why I don't remember the court case and Malloy International's role in Felix's death, and I don't want to poke that bear if I don't have to. So I nod.

"Dinner and cherry cheesecake at your place, followed by a hot tub under the stars? How can I forget?" I swallow hard. My stomach flips with nerves at the thought of the 'not-date' Gabriel has planned for us tonight. Not least of all because it'll just be the two of us. No Eli. No Noah. And that's thrilling and terrifying and a little... disappointing. And I don't understand why.

Since hanging out with the guys, I've decided I'm done with virginity. It's impossible to be around so much male hotness and not think about sex 24/7. A vibrator under the covers while Queen Boudica purrs in my ear just isn't cutting it any longer. Antony's right – if I'm going for the normal high school experience, I need to have normal, high school sex. And who better to do it with then flirty, beautiful, no-strings-attached Gabriel?

Who better to take me to the stars than the one who sings them?

It doesn't matter that Eli's ocean-eyes haunt my dreams, or I can't stop thinking of how powerful I felt with Noah's hard cock rubbing against me at the party. It's not as if I can have all three of them. I mean, there's normal high school sex and then there's... reverse harem. And that may be fun in books, but it doesn't happen in real life.

Does it?

I'M HAPPILY BUZZED from Gabe's weed and my head's filled with hot tub thoughts when I head into the gym for cheerleading practice. I'm the last one to arrive – the other girls are scattered across the floor, gossiping as they do their stretches and limber up. All conversation dies when I enter – a sure sign I'm probably the main topic.

Cleo flashes me her too-white smile, and I know I'm in trouble.

"Melrose, hi," she purrs, bouncing over to me. Her sleek black hair is pulled back into a severe ponytail, giving her this panther-like expression. Her snakes coil on either side of me, girls surrounding me in a tight circle of ponytails and bitch-face. "We're *so happy* to have you on the team."

Daphne's leg brushes my gym bag. They're standing so close their designer perfumes all mingle together into the scent of bullshit.

"What's going on here? Girls, on the mat for warm-ups."

Mrs. Anderson blows her whistle, and the snakes move away. Cleo sets me with one final chilling smile that sets my teeth on edge. I toss my bag down near Cleo's and line up for drills. As I circle the gym at a jog, I notice Principal Foster and two police officers standing at the entrance to the gym, deep in conversation with Mrs. Anderson.

This can't be good.

We start on stretches. I'm warming up my hamstrings when Principal Foster comes over. "Miss Malloy, you need to come with me."

"Can I ask why?"

Her lips purse. "We're administering a random drug test."

Hands on hips, haughty expression in place, I size up the principal. *Mackenzie Malloy doesn't stand for this treatment.* "Excuse me?"

"You heard me. It's standard practice for athletes competing at the college level. As the cheerleading team will represent our school at the state competition next month, this applies to you, and you agreed to it when you signed the Stonehurst charter. If you could step this way, it won't take long."

I think of the weed I smoked earlier. I narrow my eyes at Principal Foster. Behind her shoulder, Cleo cannot hide her smirk. "Why am I the only one being tested?"

"As I said, this is a random drug test, and you've been—"

"It doesn't feel very random to me. Why don't you test Cleo? You don't get cheekbones like hers without a steady diet of heroin."

"Miss Malloy, if you refuse to take the test, I have to drop you from the team—"

"I'm not refusing. I just don't believe I should be the only one taking it." Mrs. Anderson reaches for my bag, but I yank it out of reach. "Watch it. I've got private stuff in here."

"Ms. Malloy—"

"Oh, Principal Foster." Cleo beams at me as she hands her bag over. "If it will make Mackenzie feel more comfortable, I'm happy to submit to a random search and test."

Principal Foster glowers at me as she hands Cleo's bag to the officer, who paws through it. She frowns as she draws out a small bag of white powder. "Ms. St. James, can you explain this?"

Cleo's face goes white. "That's not mine."

"Then explain how it came to be in your possession."

"I—" Cleo's eyes land on my smirking face. Her mouth twists into an ugly scowl. "She must've planted it to frame me."

Principal Foster tsked. "Ms. St. James, I'm disappointed. The whole reason we were called down here today was to address *your* concerns about drug use on the team. Since Ms. Malloy had no knowledge of our random test, she cannot be responsible for slipping drugs into your possession. This is not the behavior of a senior role model. You'd better come with me."

"But, it's not mine," Cleo yells. "It's Mackenzie's. It was in her bag and—"

As Cleo is marched off the field, I wave cheerfully. The remaining cheerleaders glare at me. They were all in on it. Bitches. Well, they learned something tonight – don't try to plant drugs on Mackenzie Malloy. I caught onto what they were doing as soon as Daphne brushed up against me, and I slipped the baggie into Cleo's pouch before I joined them on the field.

Gabriel's waiting for me after practice. One look at my face and he shakes his head sadly.

"We're not having hot tub shenanigans tonight, are we?"

I lean into his shoulder as I whip out my phone and text Eli and Noah. "Cleo just tried to plant drugs on me."

Gabriel lets out a string of beautifully poetic British profanity. My phone beeps. It's Eli. He says he'll swing around to school and pick us up. (Gabriel usually leaves his car behind because his place is walking distance from school.)

"We need to get together to strategize," I say. "We want to teach Alec and Cleo that they can't do whatever they want to people without consequences. The thing about that is that people like them *can*. They'll always have Daddy's money to bail them out. Cleo's parents are probably in Principal Foster's office right now, writing a check for a new tennis court to make this go away."

"I believe it." Gabriel lifts an eyebrow. "I take it you have a plan?"

"I thought hurting Alec's face would wound him, but he's got enough money to just keep repairing it. I have a feeling the desert isn't the first time he's tried to take without permission, and I don't want a woman to ever feel afraid of him again. We need to take away the one thing he values over everything – his fame – so people aren't afraid of him anymore. That's how we destroy and take away his power." I rub my hands together. "This is going to be *fun*."

"You're ready for this?" Gabriel nudges me, his grey eyes sparkling with mischief.

It's Thursday night, and the three of us are in the parking lot of the Emerald Beach country club, facing rows of fancy-ass sports cars and giant, gleaming SUVs. Since Gabe paid off the security guard to abandon his post for an hour, the lot is empty apart from us and a few goths smoking weed in the bushes. Everyone else is inside watching the regional tennis match. As I stand here, Alec LeMarque is running and sweating in tiny white shorts, with not a clue what will await him when he returns to his car.

I stare down at Alec's car – a rare candy-apple red 1967 Shelby Mustang GT500 in mint condition. He clearly loves the car, because even though I saw it only days ago covered in sand out in the desert and I *know* my nails scratched paint off the hood, it gleams like new.

I suck in a breath. "It's criminal what we're about to do to such a beautiful vehicle."

"It's criminal what Alec tried to do to you," Noah growls.

"Yes, but it's not *her* fault." I rest my hand on the hood. Big mistake. My mind flashes back to the desert, to Alec holding me against the burning metal, leering down at me, his fingers tugging my panties—

I jerk my hand back.

"You chickening out, Mac?" Gabriel reaches for me, but I jerk away.

"Not on your life." I stride forward, screwdriver in hand. I tug off my sweater and wrap it around my fist, then punch out the back window. Glass shatters on the seat. I reach inside and unlock the driver's side door.

Gabriel climbs into the passenger seat, watching as I unscrew the casing on the steering column and tug out the ignition wires. "How do you know how to steal a car?"

"Remember our agreement – you don't ask. I don't tell." I strip the insulation from the battery wires and twist them together.

"But that's about your disappearance, not about car-jacking—"

"Gabriel, shut your beautiful mouth so I can concentrate."

In a few minutes I have the engine purring. Noah comes around to the driver's side and motions for me to get out. I shake my head. "I'm driving."

He looks like he wants to argue, but he obeys. Eli uses my sweater to sweep the glass off the seat, then he and Noah slide in, their legs tangling together in the tiny space. I gun the engine and speed out of the parking lot. We have a specific destination in mind, but I turn onto the highway, picking up speed as I dart between cars.

I'm driving a Shelby Mustang.

This is fucking *wild*.

I toss my phone to Gabriel. "Take my picture."

Gabriel leans back and snaps a few shots. I grin. "Text it to Antony. He's in my contacts. He's going to be *pissed* at me."

"Who's Antony?" Gabriel asks. I shake my head at him and plant my foot hard against the floor.

I take the off-ramp and tear up Santa Casilda Drive, taking the corners as fast as I damn well please. I laugh as the adrenaline surges in my veins, and Gabriel looks at me like I'm mad and he can't decide if he's terrified or turned on by it.

I could drive around in this car all night, but we have a job to do. Reluctantly, I turn around and head back toward the city, toward Stonehurst Prep.

We pull up into the school parking lot. There's no one around, either. Noah paid off all the school security guards to make themselves scarce for the night. Eli and Noah go to the bushes where we hid the tools we need, and lay them out on the ground in front of the car.

I pick up a wrench and grin at my conspirators. "Let's get to work."

BY THE TIME I get home and crawl into bed, it's nearly 3AM. Queen Boudica lifts her head from the pillow and shoots me a 'what-time-do-you-call-this' look. I cradle her against my chest and fall asleep listening to her steady purr. It reminds me of the purr of the Mustang's engine.

When my phone alarm rings, I throw it against the wall. But five minutes later I drag myself awake. No way do I want to miss school today.

I pull on my uniform, cake on makeup to hide the dark circles around my eyes, and pour myself a thermos full of coffee. I walk down to the corner where Eli's waiting for me in the Porsche. He looks as shit as I feel.

"You brought coffee?" He holds out his hand.

"Get your own." I sip from the thermos as we cruise around Harrington Hills toward Stonehurst.

Eli stops at a drive-thru and grabs a ridiculous coffee with whipped cream and caramel. It smells a hundred times better than mine. He slurps it happily as we drive into school.

Dick.

George, Gabriel, and Noah are waiting beside Eli's parking spot. Noah has his hands in his pockets. He looks a little less put-together than usual, his dark hair rumpled, his shirt collar askew. The dark circles under his eyes only make him look more dangerous.

Beside him, Gabriel bounces on the balls of his feet, his shirt open to reveal his butterfly tattoo swirling around his regal neck. George looks between us, confusion written across her features. *I hope she likes our surprise.*

"We waited for you." Gabriel throws open my door and tugs me out. "Hurry that sweet arse up, would you, Mac?"

Gabriel links arms with me and George, dragging us toward the entrance. All around us, voices swirl with laughter, with shock and surprise, as the word of what we did spreads through the student body.

We pass under the colonnade into the main courtyard. It's so crowded with students craning for a look that it's impossible to see a thing. Noah glares around us until people step aside and let us through.

"Mackenzie, is this some kind of—" George's eyes widen, and her hand flies to her mouth as she lets out a whoop. "Is that... Alec's car?"

"It sure is," I beam.

Alec LeMarque kneels on the cobbles, his head in his hands, while students toss spitballs at him and snap photographs of his shame. In front of him, in the middle of the quad, is his beloved car, taken to pieces and perfectly remade again – only now, there's a statue of Leda and a swan growing right through the middle of it, so the swan appears to be driving with its beak.

In her hands, Leda holds a picture. It's a photograph taken by accident on my phone as it was flung into the sand, and then saved automatically to my cloud account. It shows Alec, his face carved in cruelty, as he leans over a girl held against the hood of a car. You can't see her face, but she's clearly not enjoying herself.

Beneath the picture are the words, "Alec LeMarque hurts women. So we fucked up his shit."

I hit reply on the video again, slowing down the speed to watch Alec's face as a student captures his humiliation on their camera phone. Nothing ruins a self-centered famewhore like Alec better than a public scandal.

The images are plastered all over social media, and just as I suspected, stories have started to come out about his treatment of female co-stars and producers. There are rumors the police will open an investigation. Two major film projects dropped him from their cast, his agent fired him, and many say they'll never work with Alec LeMarque again. Principal Foster sent around an emergency announcement declaring he's been expelled from school and offering counseling services to anyone victimized by him. Even his own father has taken to Twitter to denounce his son and publicly cut him off.

All this hours after we walked into school. The Stonehurst student body sensed Alec's blood in the water, and they tore him to shreds.

Thanks to us, Alec LeMarque is done in Emerald Beach.

"Wow, Mac. You know how to bring a man down," Gabriel whistles as he pulls up a particularly damning article on the large-screen for us all to see. "Remind me never to get on your bad side."

We're back in Gabriel's apartment, which seems to be 'neutral territory' for the guys. I'm not bringing them to Malloy Manor, and Eli and Noah never offer up their houses for reasons I'm sure have to do with Eli's father being in jail and Noah's family having their beef with the Malloys.

I'm high on the sheer audacity of what we did. Who knows how many women we might've saved from Alec? Every loop of the video sends a thrill down my spine. My veins flush with heat, and I'm itching to do something... *momentous* to mark my triumph.

George arrives from her shift at the vintage store, and she dumps an armload of clothing and shoes on my lap. "These look about your size," she tells me. "I know you've probably got a whole wing of your house filled with clothes, but I wanted to do something to say thank you for your public service."

"You didn't have to... but these are fucking beautiful." I pull out a red halter top and high-waisted shorts set with rows of silver buttons. I hold them against myself. George digs out a pair of red stilettos with rhinestone straps that match perfectly. I got to the bathroom, toss my uniform on the floor, and pull on the outfit. Everything fits perfectly, including the shoes. George is a miracle. I fish around in my bag for a red lipstick and apply it in the mirror with an expert hand. Those YouTube makeup vloggers know their shit – I'm an expert at applying my armor now. I blot the lipstick and strut out into the room.

Eli makes a choking sound, spitting his drink down the front of his shirt. Noah's eyes narrow before he looks away. Gabriel wolf-whistles.

"Fuck, Mac. I thought you were hot in that school uniform, but your ass is *unreal* in those shorts." Gabriel holds his hands over his heart. I whack him with a pillow.

"Ow, yeah, hurt me, baby," Gabriel grins as I whack him again. "I'll do anything you want, as long as you're wearing that outfit."

I toss the pillow down on the sofa and glare at them all, hands on hips. I'm running this show. "Let's go out. We should celebrate properly, with ridiculous cocktails and too-loud music."

"Not me." Eli glances at his watch, then glares at Noah. "*Someone's* making me do an early morning training session tomorrow, and I'm currently running on two-hours sleep."

Noah shakes his head. "I told Grace I'd be home early tonight."

He turns away so I can't see his face. I know he cares a lot about his stepmother Grace, but I wonder if he's declining for another reason.

George looks from Gabriel to me. I suspect she feels the tension crackling in the air between us, because she quickly says, "I have to be home tonight, too, but I'd love to do something this weekend."

"It's a date," I grin. "I'll text you."

Her whole face lights up. She leans forward and wraps her arms around me, squeezing me surprisingly hard for such a tiny human. "Thank you, Mackenzie. You don't know what this means to me."

I can guess, but it's George's story to tell. I hug her back. George – my friend. I never had one of those before, and now that I do, I'm not going to let her forget it.

"That just leaves us two for a night of debauchery." Gabriel grabs my hand and hauls me to my feet. He fixes me with that devilish grin of his, and a bolt of fire hits me right between the legs. "Allow me to escort you on a night you'll never forget. I know a place filled with wonders to impress even the Ice Queen herself."

NOAH

I walk to my car in a daze. Every muscle aches, begging me to turn back around and join Gabe and Mackenzie for their 'night of debauchery,' to drive off this guilt and rage and hope with pounding music and the sweet oblivion of alcohol.

But what will that achieve? I know where Gabriel will take her – the only place worthy of Mackenzie fucking Malloy. I can't sit in that magical grotto drinking absinthe with Mackenzie looking tight as fuck in those shorts and heels of hers and not think about... and not consider...

The more I hang around her, the more the hatred I'd held onto all these years weighs like a noose around my neck, dragging me down. But as soon as I contemplate casting it aside – like in the desert when we were eating our cakes – Felix's face flashes in front of me, staring up at me from an open casket, and I remember. I *remember*.

Every stirring inside me feels like a betrayal of his memory.

I hurry to the car, my veins on fire. My fingers grip the wheel like it's the only thing holding me upright. My body aches as it recalls the way she felt at the party – wet, naked flesh pressed against me.

I need to get home.

I need to remember.

The drive is a blur. I don't see the other cars on the road, only faces zooming past me at high speed. Felix with his glassy eyes peering from his coffin, Howard Malloy and my dad facing off across the courtroom, my mom's serene expression as she floats in our pool, Gabriel with his come-to-bed smile, Mackenzie with her golden halo of hair, looking every bit as fearsome as she had four years ago... And then the two of them, lips locked under the floating lights of the Midnight Grotto.

Why shouldn't Mackenzie fuck Gabriel? He's every girl's wet dream. And it's not as if you can have her. No matter how much you might...

I hit the brakes as I nearly drive past my house. *Fuck.* I back up and stab the button for the garage door. I park up next to my brother's car. The white cover flaps in the breeze swooping in under the garage door. I launch myself at the car.

I tear at the cover, my nails scraping on the paint beneath, my fingers tight with rage, with a wanting that will never go away.

I wish everything was different.

I wish he never died.

I wish she could be mine.

But wishing is for losers, and nothing will ever be the way I want it.

I fling the cover aside, revealing the gleaming beast beneath. The car my brother deserved. The car he dreamed of. I pick up a brick from a stack the groundskeeper left in the corner and throw it through the windscreen.

Glass shatters everywhere, scattering across the concrete and ruining the leather seats. It's going to be a bitch to clean up, but I don't even care. My shoulders heave. My heart stutters in my chest.

Something inside me is tearing open. I'm falling over the edge, and on the other side is only darkness and Mackenzie's golden hair. I tear from the garage and fly through the house. My boots slam on cold tiles. Everything about this place is cold and dead to me now.

I run my hand over a table in the hallway, sending Felix's track trophies flying. They scatter across the tiles – metal surfaces scratching and denting, glass dedications shattering into pieces.

"Noah?" Grace leans over the balcony, her face pinched with concern. I can't bear to look at her. I storm down the hall, heading for the reception room where Dad's voice booms. I hear a glass smash and someone swear.

I come up short, hesitating on the threshold. Dad's not alone. He's not raging into the void. He stands in front of the fireplace, in the shadow of my brother's portrait. He faces off against a wide set man with broad shoulders practically bursting the seams of his pinstriped suit.

As I study the man's face, another memory flashes in my mind. Dad had given his evidence at trial, sharing the toxicology report showing how Felix had died, and how the Malloys were responsible. It was the smoking gun that should have sent Howard Malloy to jail for his crime, but the judge dismissed it. We had the verdict – not guilty. Howard Malloy killed my brother and got away with it.

Mom withdrew into herself, and Dad... Dad had a heavyset man in a pinstripe suit over for dinner. They talked all night in the reception room, and I wasn't allowed anywhere near them.

The next week, Mackenzie and her parents disappeared.

My breath hitches. I press myself against the wall, listening hard. Dad gave no indication he was aware of my presence. He keeps on berating the man.

"You fucked everything up last time, Brentwood. Now you'll be able to put it right."

"I'm not doing it," the man snaps back, his voice rising with every word. "I don't care what you do to me. I'm not going near that house again, and I won't send one of my boys, neither."

"You're being ridiculous. This is a seventeen-year-old girl we're talking about. How can she possibly—"

"You can't know what I saw." The man – Brentwood – rasps his words, his voice tight with terror. "You find someone else, Mr. Marlowe. That's no sweet-sixteen beauty queen you're facing off against. She's a cold-blooded killer."

MACKENZIE

Gabriel has the Uber driver drop us off at the docks. Not the cool, hip docks on the south end of the boardwalk with all the restaurants and clubs, but the creepy, abandoned docks with the rotting boards and gross fish smell and spiders.

"Where are we going?" My foot slips on the wet boards. I grab hold of Gabriel before I go flying. "I said I wanted to *party*, not get stoned in a smelly fish graveyard."

"You'll see." Gabriel leads me down a set of dingy steps. Waves lap at the pier on either side of us. I can see a weird light glowing beneath the water.

Goosebumps rise on my arms. *This is just the kind of spot a serial killer would take me before he cuts out my heart and turns my tits into a pompom hat.*

Gabriel gives three short raps on an enormous steel door. A small hatch slides open, and I can just make out a pair of glitter-soaked eyes beyond. Gabriel leans close and whispers, "Mermaid." The door swings open, revealing a narrow, steep set of stairs heading down. The woman is nowhere to be seen.

A prickle of excitement mixed with fear rattles in my chest.

We clamber down the steps, down, down, down into the darkness, feeling our way, bumping into each other in our blindness. There's an oppressiveness to this place. The walls feel heavy, the air damp. We must be under the waterline, although it's impossible to tell as there's no light, no indication of depth.

Light pricks the gloom, and from somewhere in this strange space, a relentless thrum, like a heartbeat, trembles through the walls. My feet touch a floor that sways gently. *Maybe I'm already drunk. Maybe I'm drunk on Gabriel Fallen.*

Gabriel leads me down another narrow hallway. The thrumming grows louder. He pushes aside a curtain, and I gasp.

This is impossible.

I stand in a room half the size of a football field, lit by hundreds of glowing lanterns that seem to float between the booths and tables, moving of their own accord. A girl in a glittering bird costume performs acrobatic feats from a crescent-moon-shaped swing in the center of the room. There's not a smooth surface in the place – columns twist up into the blackness, supporting a ceiling so high I cannot see it. The walls are gnarled with rock formations and coral growth, revealing wide openings of glass that look out into the water beyond.

It's like I've stepped into some magical alternative universe.

Gabriel leads me to a bar shaped like a conch shell and hands me the cocktail list. I'm too giddy with the joy of this place to decide what to have, so I tell the bartender to make us something fruity and delicious.

The bartender hands us our drinks. They're in glasses encrusted with glittering jewels and hundreds of tiny shells, and on top is a delicate sculpture of a mermaid tail made from sugar diving into the emerald alcohol. It's almost too perfect to drink, but I take a sip anyway. It tastes like blueberry sherbet.

We take an empty booth in the corner, sipping our drinks and watching the dancer. When she finishes her act, the bobbing lanterns float up to the ceiling, and three musicians emerge from the murky depths of the room and carry instruments onto a narrow stage – some kind of stringed thing, drums, a weird double-barreled flute. The music isn't like other club music – it's ethereal, hypnotic, with a beat that matches my heart. As if in a trance, every patron of the club moves toward the dance floor.

"Feel like shaking that shaggable arse?" Gabriel grins. I let him take my hand. He holds it aloft, his fingers just grazing my skin, and I feel like a queen.

Tonight, I'm his queen.

The music pounds through me, and I'm not in Emerald Beach any longer. I'm a mermaid in an underwater palace with a prince on my arm. Gabriel leads me to the center of the floor. We grind against each other, our bodies moving as one while others twist and undulate around us. Gabriel's hands are all over me – sliding in my hair, skimming my hips, cupping my chin, brushing the edge of my breast until I can't stand it anymore. He moves like the music he writes – breathless and beautiful, singing the stars against my skin.

"This night doesn't have to end," Gabriel's eyes burn into mine. "There are rooms upstairs."

My heart stutters. I know what he's asking.

Gabriel's playboy ways are notorious, but he doesn't know I'm a virgin. Well, maybe he can guess. I've been living alone since I was thirteen – not exactly the prime environment to get my freak on. And as hard as I've tried to hold Gabriel at arms' length – for his safety, for mine – I came to this club with him tonight with the hum of anticipation building between my legs.

All I want is to exist in this magical place a little longer. I want to lie in the arms of a beautiful boy whose words and music touch my soul, and believe that I deserve a fleeting moment of happiness. I want to tear down the shield wall I carry to protect myself, and embrace my enemy.

Embrace the darkness that lives in my heart.

Embrace the boy who sings of blood and rain.

I smile, and that smile reaches all the way to my toes, all the way to the edges of my soul. "You're on."

ELI

I manage to spend three hours in bed, staring at the ceiling with Gizmo jabbing my eyeballs, before I can't take it any longer.

What the fuck am I doing?

Why did I let them go on their own?

Why did I lie to myself?

I did what I always do – I hung back and let my actions speak for me. I *let* Gabriel seduce her with his fucking Gabriel-ness, and waited and hoped that she'd see us both for who we truly are.

I lost her.

Again.

No. Not this time.

I throw off the covers and creep back downstairs, hoping Maria's already asleep. I back the Porsche out of the garage and drive to the docks. I know Gabriel will take her to Midnight Grotto.

I don't have a membership, because I usually come with Gabriel. The lady behind the secret door recognizes me (and she definitely recognizes the stack of Ben Franklins I wave in her face), and ushers me inside. The main room is dark, the booths filled with shadowy figures drinking drinks shimmering with dry ice, while a woman dances on the bar with an enormous boa constrictor wrapped around her neck.

I push through the crowd, searching absinthe eyes and fae faces. Finally, I spot them.

Gabriel and Mackenzie.

He holds her hand and leads her up the spiral staircase to the bedrooms. In her hand, I catch the glitter of a silver key.

The world stops.

Gabriel and Mackenzie.

He's one of my closest friends, and right now I'd happily see him garroted.

I sink to the floor.

I can't breathe.

Am I breathing?

Pain arcs through my chest.

I'm too late.

She's made her choice.

It isn't me.

MACKENZIE

A woman hands us a giant silver key, like something from a fantasy film. I hold it up to the light, watching the silver twinkle under the lanterns. Gabriel leads me by the hand, up a winding staircase and down a narrow hallway filled with crooked doorways. From behind the doorways, all kinds of lurid sounds fill my ears, heating my veins until my blood boils with lust.

At the end of the hall, we continue our climb on a narrow metal staircase. A school of fish swims past the window as we wind and wind our way upward. At the top of the stairs, there's only one door. Gabriel steps aside so I can thrust the key into the lock.

I push the door open and step into an oddly-shaped room, enclosed in the same eldritch architecture as the club downstairs, with those eerily beautiful lanterns bobbing across the ceiling. The bed sits in an alcove of glass thrust out over the water, which is several feet below – it appears as though we're floating. Or flying, for the night sky stretches above us – a blanket of midnight tinged with blood and sprinkled with Gabriel's magic. I kneel on the edge of the bed and peer down at the water lapping below. Pleasure boats circle around the docks, and in the distance, the lights of a superyacht add their own magic to the skyline.

"How did we get this high?" I ask.

"Were you so distracted by my remarkable personage you didn't notice all those stairs we climbed?" Gabriel leans down beside me, his hand falling oh-so-casually on my thigh. My skin burns beneath his fingers, and I press my lips together to keep from moaning, from begging.

"Who even says *remarkable personage*?" I hit back at him, but it's without my usual fire. Now that I'm here, the buzz of the club and the hypnotic dancing has worn off a bit. I'm alone in a room with Gabriel Fallen – expert fornicator. My celebrity crush, in flesh and blood with his haunting grey eyes focused entirely on me. My nerves kick in.

In response, Gabe tips my chin toward him, brushing his lips against mine so softly, so sweetly, I might've convinced myself I dreamed it. But my dreams never light up my body like Fourth of July fireworks, nor do they involve soft fingers tangled in my hair or a hard chest pressed against mine...

Don't stop. Please, don't stop.

Fuck. I should probably...

"Gabe..." It takes all my self-control to fist a handful of his shirt, to hold him as I lean back, giving me an inch of breathing space.

"Let me guess, you've never done this before?" Gabe cocks his eyebrow.

"You got a fetish about taking delicate virgin flowers?" I growl. "And you'd better give me the right answer, or I'm kneeing you in the balls."

"No fetish, I'm just..." Gabriel kisses the tip of my nose. "It would be an honor, Mac. But are you sure you want it to be me? What about Eli?"

I shake my head. Eli... if I chose him, it would *mean* something. Eli couldn't have sex with someone without giving away a piece of himself, and I'm already broken enough as it is without carrying someone else's pain around with me. It would open a window into things I'm not ready to say, not when there are still so many secrets.

Not when I promised him I wouldn't lie.

Eli would be wonderful as a boyfriend, but I've already hurt him so deeply he'll never heal. I may be the Ice Queen, but I'm not cold enough for that game.

But Gabriel... he doesn't bring emotions to us – there's no weight of a history only one of us recalls crushing us together. Gabe can make me *feel* without giving away a piece of himself. He does it night after night on stage, and judging by the pure sex that spills from his mouth every time he sings, he'll be damn good at it.

"Everything's messed up," I murmur, stroking his arm, tracing the lines of the snake tattoo encircling his wrist. His skin feels so good. "But I don't care. Right now, tonight, I want you. I want you to make me feel *something*. Just, you know... don't expect one of your sex-crazed groupies."

"How about this? We've got this room all night. We can go back downstairs if you want, or we can stay up here, and kiss, and touch..." Gabriel circles his thumb on my bare shoulder, playing with the edge of the strap. "And if you want to take things further, we can. Either way, we'll have a fun night."

A fun night. Part of me needs that, desperately, and part of me wants to be so much more to Gabriel. But the way he has my body purring like a kitten with just his thumb, I'm not saying no.

"Will this cause problems with the others?"

"Only if we let it." And then he's kissing me, slow and reassuring, and it feels so good, I don't ever want him to stop.

Gabriel kisses like he sings, throwing his whole self into it.

He reaches inside me and drags up my demons from their lockbox and dances with them under the stars. It's in the dark places and the fae shadows that Gabriel Fallen rules with his crown of thorns. I groan as his lips part mine, so slow, so assuring. Our tongues touch, and I get my first taste of starlight, and I know I'll never, ever have my fill.

I wind my arms around his neck and pull him closer, my body aching for more, more, more, as if I can somehow crawl inside his skin and wear that sexy ass of his. Which sounds totally crazy and serial killer-ish, but I've got Gabriel Fallen's tongue in my mouth – coherent metaphors ain't gonna happen.

His tongue-stud is this whole other sensation, and I can't resist playing with it, holding it between my teeth and tugging on it lightly. Now it's Gabriel's turn to moan, his grip on me tightening, his body tense with need.

Gabriel breaks the kiss to trail his lips along my jaw. He nibbles on my earlobe, his fingertips stroking a tune along my neck. Who knew having someone touching your neck is so fucking hot? Gabriel presses his lips to the hollow of my throat. The coolness of his piercings hits the heat of my skin, and I'm a trembling mess. The urge to beg him for more, for something I don't yet know, dances on my lips, but I resist. Even when she's horny as fuck, Mackenzie Malloy doesn't beg.

"Let me make you feel good." Sometimes the shit Gabriel says is so cheesy, but with that British accent purring in my ear, I'm not going to complain. A tiny moan escapes my lips, and it's all the signal Gabriel needs.

His fingers twine in my hair as he pulls me back to him, our lips meeting with a rush of fire. He lays me back against the sheets. His weight on mine feels so fucking perfect. I stare up into a blood-stained sky shot with glittering stars.

Gabriel's hands are everywhere – touching my cheeks, cupping my chin, in my hair, skimming my hips the way he did back on the dance floor, leaving us both panting. My stomach aches with a hunger that isn't for food, and I raise my hips to grind against him, my body desperate for more, more, more.

Gabriel chuckles darkly as he slides a hand underneath my red top, pushing the fabric over my skin. I raise my arms above my head as he drags it over my head.

"Fuck, Mac." Gabriel shoves my bra up, not even bothering to undo it. "If I'd known you were hiding *these,* I'd have had you sooner."

His mouth circles my nipple, and I gasp. It's wet and hot and intense and magical, especially when his piercing rubs against the sensitive bud. Gabriel cups my other breast, rolling the nipple in his fingers as his stormy eyes watch me, drinking in my reaction.

It feels fucking *amazing.*

So amazing in fact, I'm not even aware that Gabriel's pulled off my shorts until he trails kisses across my stomach, his fingers teasing the edges of my lace panties. He pulls down one edge of the lace and stops, his face tipping toward me, his eyes wide and that cocky grin frozen on his perfect lips. The barbell jerks up and down.

"What are you waiting for, Fallen?" I growl. "A written invitation?"

Gabriel tears the flimsy material away and dives between my legs. His tongue finds my clit, and he flicks his stud across it until I'm a writhing, blubbering mess. My hands claw at his shoulders as I come undone. He slips a finger inside me and moans against me. The heat that rises inside me could burn the world. Gabe strokes his finger inside me while he makes circles around my clit, that stud doing magical things as he gets faster and faster. The stars swim in my eyes and I'm gone, I'm fucking gone.

I've made myself come plenty of times. I lived completely

alone for four years. If I didn't have a vibrator, I'd have gone full psychopath by now. But it's a completely different thing to come by your own hand in an empty room in an empty house while your cat bats impatiently at your face so you'll get out of bed and feed her, and to tremble with pleasure in the arms of the world's hottest rockstar while the heavens dance around you.

Gabriel pulls me against him, holding my body to his chest, his fingers stroking my face. He picks up my limp hand and examines my fingers. "Looks like you ruined your manicure digging your nails into my back."

"Don't look so fucking smug about it," I manage to choke out. "I'm going to *marry* your tongue stud."

Gabriel tsks. "Marriage? Without sampling all the goods? Mac, I'm disappointed in you."

He rolls me over so that I'm cradled in his arms, my back against his broad chest. At first, I'm confused by this position – in every teen movie, your first time is supposed to be missionary style, gazing wide-eyed at each other for an awkward condom sequence before your mother walks in.

Only now, I'm looking at water and sky, and I feel as though I'm floating. Or maybe that's the head full of orgasm endorphins or the fact Gabriel's hands still trail over my skin, leaving paths that scorch so hot they'd show up under infrared.

Gabriel tugs off his shirt and kicks his jeans and boxers off the end of the bed, then his arms circle me again. Tattooed hands play with my nipples, and his barbell scrapes across the skin on the back of my neck. "Touch me, beautiful."

I reach down between my legs and grasp him. The first time I've ever held a cock in my hands. I'm shocked by the size of him. I run my fingers down his shaft, feeling the ridge of the tip and the veins standing out from his skin. How the fuck does this fit inside me?

I touch metal. I feel along the length of a curved bar

protruding from the tip and out the bottom of the head, with a ball on each end. Gabriel's teeth stutter against my skin as I give the piercing a little tug.

I've heard rumors in the press about Gabriel's cock piercing, but I've been a little distracted with *all the fucking rest of him* to recall it until now.

That thing is going inside me? How's this going to work?

"What do you think?" Gabriel whispers.

"I think you're a crazy motherfucker," I whispered back. "Why would you do that to yourself?"

"Just you wait and see," he purrs in my ear. "Put me out of my misery, Mac. Open those sexy long legs for me."

I obey, dropping my grip on him to lift my knee. Gabriel's body fits perfectly against mine. The tip of his cock brushes against my opening. I'm wet and waiting, and I want so badly to rock my hips back and let him inside. I hear a package tear, and I'm grateful I can't see what he's doing and that he doesn't need my help because I got all my sex ed from *Game of Thrones*.

"You sure?" Gabriel's lips find that spot on my collarbone. His cock brushes me again, and I feel how wet I am, how desperate.

"Just fucking do it already." I'm ready to scream at him.

Gabriel pushes the tip of his cock inside me, and I *do* scream. A little. It hurts, but the good kind of hurt. The kind of hurt that makes you feel alive. He pushes deeper and I'm so full of him, full of Gabriel fucking Fallen, and he's rolling his hips and driving deeper and fuck fuck fuck it feels so goddamn good.

I bend my head back to stare at my dark prince, his eyes hooded with an approaching storm, his silhouette ringed with a bleeding sky. I wonder if this is who he is backstage, night after night, for a hundred different girls. Or right now, in this room inside the stars, I'm a part of Gabriel Fallen he never gives to anyone else. A part that's just for me.

Gabriel moves inside me, and if I died right now I'd kick the devil's ass for taking me away from this because no way is hell as dark and delicious as Gabe's cock inside me. His piercing is this hard nub rubbing and moving, and I wish so bad that I could feel it naked against my skin.

Tattooed arms cross my chest, holding me close, rolling my nipples. A hand snakes down between my legs, and Gabriel presses a finger against my clit. It's too much, too new; there's so much of him everywhere. I fall over the edge again. I'm swimming in a blue abyss. Stars swirl around me, but I don't know if they're the ones outside the window or inside my head.

Gabriel's teeth scrape my neck as he rocks inside me. I tilt my head back and accept his mouth to mine, tugging at his tongue stud until he's unraveling at the edges, too. His body tightens around me, and his hips thrust harder. I slam mine back to meet him, and he keeps one finger hammering against my clit. I come again in a shower of sparks as Gabriel curls around me, his breath hitching as his own release takes him.

Gabriel sorts himself out, then rolls me over so his arms are around me but we're face-to-face, our bodies radiating heat, our noses touching. The bleeding sky dances in his eyes as he talks to me in that low, melodious voice of his. There's an intensity to him right now I've never seen before.

"What do you see?" I ask before I can stop myself. "When you look at me, what do you see?"

"Dylan," he replies, pulling me into a smoldering kiss. I struggle against him for a moment, but he's too much for me, and I sink into him, allowing him to pull me under his spell. But even as I give myself over to the song of Gabriel's body, his answer drums against my skull.

What does he mean, I remind him of Dylan? We've just had sex and he sees his dead best-friend? That's dark as fuck.

I love it.

MACKENZIE

The night blurs into one long, intense fuckfest. I come so many times from Gabe's lips and cock that I lose feeling in my legs. Piercings are magical and everyone should have them.

We fall asleep just as the sun sets fire to the horizon, tangled together in the sheets, our skin reeking of each other. My dreams are filled with Gabriel's heady scent and his tattoos dancing across my skin.

I wake to a delicious smell. Gabe's at the door, talking to someone in the hall. He comes in, wearing only his jeans and carrying a tray piled with steaming food.

'Mmmm, breakfast." I rake my fingers down his chest, over those glorious tattoos. Gabriel laughs as he sets the tray down to pull me against him. I wiggle his tongue stud with my tongue, and he scrapes his teeth along my collarbone and our food is cold before we get to it.

Gabriel hands me a napkin as I tuck into my pancakes. They're not as good as Eli's, but still delicious. "So... our concierge says she saw Eli come into the club last night."

"We didn't see him?" I cock an eyebrow.

"I think we were... otherwise occupied."

Ah. So Eli knows about us, then. I push my plate away. Suddenly, I'm not hungry. I scramble across the floor to find my clothes and pull my phone from my jacket. No messages from Eli or Noah. Nothing. Weird. Usually, Eli messages me several times a night with pictures of his cat.

"You okay? You look a little freaked out." Gabriel leans across and swipes a syrup-drenched pancake from my plate. "You're not having regrets?"

"That's it exactly. I deeply regret not jumping your bones the first day at Stonehurst." I hold up the phone. "I'm just thinking about Eli. Why would he come here when he said he needed to sleep?"

Gabriel snorts. "You may be a blonde, Mac, but playing dumb doesn't suit you."

"That's fair." I stare at the screen, my finger poised over the call button. With a growl, I toss the phone on the bed. *Fuck Eli. And fuck his adorable kitty.* He doesn't get to make me feel guilty about the best night of my life.

Gabriel makes off with my second pancake. "So... you want to do something today? We could drive down the coast? I know this great private beach where we could skinny dip."

"Tempting, but I think I need to go home." Now my mind's on Eli, I can't stop thinking about him. I didn't want him to find out like this, but that ship has sailed so now I need damage control because Eli Hart is smart enough to unravel my stolen life. Too much is at stake, and even though Antony's assured me about Brutus, I can't risk Eli doing something stupid that will destroy our whole plan. I need to talk to him.

It's weird, because even though I know it's pointless and I owe him nothing, I want to try to explain.

Gabe pays for a cab to take me back to Malloy Manor. Even

though I'm desperate to crawl into bed, I hold Queen Boudica in my arms to steady my nerves and call Eli.

He doesn't answer.

He ignores twenty-two other calls from me over the weekend, and an entire stream of nonsensical texts I frantically type out at 3AM Saturday night go unanswered. By Sunday lunchtime he's either turned his phone off or it's gone on strike, because it sends me straight to voicemail. I even call Noah, but he won't answer, either.

I left my uniform at Gabriel's from Friday night, so I take a cab there before school on Monday so I can change, and we can walk in together. The first thing I notice as we enter the central courtyard is that Alec's car is gone from the fountain, and so is he. For the first time, I walk down the corridor and I don't feel his snake eyes slithering over my body. I overhear two students talking about his father sending him to military school, and I burst into genuine laughter. Alec's asshole will be ragged after a week as the army slut.

The second thing I notice is that Eli and Noah aren't here, either. I ask Chad, and he says neither of them was at track practice in the morning. My stomach twists. I know why Eli isn't at school, but Noah?

What's up with that?

MACKENZIE

abriel wants to hang out after cheerleading practice, but I tell him I have too much studying to do. It's not a lie. What I *want* to do is find Eli and see if he's okay, but I have an essay due for Ms. Drysdale's class that I've put off to the absolute last minute and I need to pass this time.

So I walk home alone as the sun streaks pink flames across the sky, relishing the chance to be with my own thoughts for a while. I nod to Tiberius in his car on the corner, and check behind me for anyone watching before I duck into the woods to approach the maintenance shed. Queen Boudica meets me at the top of the stairs, her tiny body rumbling with pleasure at my return. It's nice to be wanted.

I take Queen Boudica through to my bedroom and drop a handful of cat treats on the rug while I flick through my playlist. The latest Octavia's Ruin album blasts through the speakers, filling my head and my heart with Gabriel's bewitching voice.

I'm pulling off my Stonehurst uniform when I get this itching feeling crawling along my skin, like I'm being watched.

Eli's here.

I guess we're having that talk now.

I retreat into the bathroom, pull on a pair of designer jeans and a pink racer-back tank. I peer out my window, which is on the same side of the house as the ballroom, overlooking the pool. I can't see him anywhere. Then I notice a light at the front gate.

Hmmmm.

I walk through the house to a dusty sitting room at the front I never use and peer out the window. Sure enough, someone's out there with a flashlight.

Fuck. Why isn't Tiberius all over this?

Fear twists in my gut as the figure shimmies up the gate like he's a fucking chimpanzee after the best bananas in the jungle. Joke's on him because I don't have bananas, but I do have a brand new knife from Antony. I withdraw it from my pocket and slink into the shadows at the edge of the window, watching the intruder as he vaults over the wall and lands on top of an impressive cactus. He curses as he shakes his leg, which is now stuck with hundreds of spines.

I start as I recognize him.

Not Eli.

Noah.

He limps up to the window and knocks on the glass, then jabs his thumb in the direction of the front door. My mind flicks back to the police officer who came to the door all those weeks ago and started this whole nightmare. I glare at Noah through the glass. *Why's he come here like this?*

I take my time getting to the front door. I don't want him to think I'm desperate to know why he didn't answer my call or wasn't at school today or why he's shown up, *here*, on enemy territory.

As I crack the door, Noah's already halfway back down the driveway, a trail of cactus spines scattered in his wake. He turns and runs back, pressing his face in the narrow gap.

"Hello."

"Just open the damn door so we can talk like normal people," he growls.

"We are not normal people, Noah. I'm not in the habit of opening this door to anyone, most especially people who hate me."

"I want to not hate you." He searches my face with those intense eyes of his. It's as though in those dark depths is a museum of locked rooms and dark spells – all Noah's past hurts and present rage painted bright across his soul, but he's got the lights off so all I can see are the edges. "Tell me something that makes me not hate you."

I raise an eyebrow. "So this is the wrong time to show you my 'Hitler is my Homeboy' T-shirt."

The corner of Noah's mouth tugs up. It's not quite a smile, but it's the start of one.

It looks good on him.

Damn good.

"I came to talk about Eli. And... other stuff. But mostly Eli. He saw you guys at the club on Friday." Noah's shoulders rise and fall. "You and Gabe. Heading upstairs to the bedrooms."

I nod.

"He's not taking it well."

"Does he want me to kiss it better?"

"This isn't funny." Noah's eyes flare with fire. "I've just come from his place. He's... I haven't seen him this bad since you left. Don't you see? This is you deserting him all over again. I know you're a stone-cold bitch with ice for a heart, but I thought you at least cared about Eli—"

"I *do* care." I glare at Noah. "Eli doesn't have a right to be pissed at me. He has no *claim* over me. If you want the truth, Noah Marlowe, I slept with Gabriel and it was *brilliant*. But I'm not his girlfriend." I open my hands. "The truth is I don't know what the fuck I'm doing."

Noah's jaw is so tight I'm worried it might snap. "Why him?"

"Why not him?" I shoot back. "And while we're on the topic, *why you?*"

"What the fuck do you mean?" he growls.

"I know why this matters to Eli. He thinks we have a connection because we were friends when we were kids, but so what? A lot has happened since then. I'm not the same person, and he needs to stop believing I am. I'll only end up hurting him worse, and I don't want to do that to him. What I want to know is why it matters to *you.*"

"I'm here for Eli."

I fold my arms and fix him with my Ice Queen glare. "As Gabriel would say, *bollocks.*"

Noah turns away. I sense a hundred unanswered questions rolling through his head. Finally, he decides on one. "Eli says you don't remember what happened four years ago. He says you've got some specific type of amnesia. Is that true?"

I buckle under the severity of his gaze. My hand flies to the locket at my throat. Right now I really, *really* don't want to lie to Noah. "I remember some things. I know your brother died because my father gave him experimental supplements that caused his heart to fail. But I don't know what I did specifically to make you hate me, beyond the fact that I wear the surname Malloy. I know that doesn't excuse your pain, but that's the truth. I don't fucking remember."

Noah looks back at me then. The anguish in his eyes is so raw, so primal, it draws me toward him. The two of us are magnets drawn together by wrath. "My brother never would have taken those pills if it weren't for you."

I unlock the door and hold it open, not wide enough that he feels as though it's an invitation, but enough that the two of us breathe the same air. I sense the tension coiling around him, wrapping his body in a cocoon of hostility that's supposed to repel me but draws me like a Valley Girl to a designer shoe sale.

"I don't know if you ever met him – he was four years older than us. Top of his class every year, star athlete with a shot at the Olympic team, but he wasn't full of himself. He was the nicest fucking guy you could ever hope to meet, so much nicer than I could—" Noah stops himself. His Adam's apple bobs as he swallows once, twice. "One day at school, Eli was out sick and you sat with me at lunch. You told me that your father was looking for athletes to trial a new performance-enhancing drug. All-natural, developed from an ancient remedy, won't show up on a drug test. You set up a meeting with our families. You—"

A sound explodes between us, like the pop of a Champagne bottle being opened, only louder. Chips of concrete blast off the side of the house and rain down on me and Noah.

I don't have time to form a question. Noah's body slams into mine, pushing me to the ground as a rain of bullets hits the house behind my head.

MACKENZIE

$\mathcal{M}$y back slams against the tiles. Noah kicks the front door shut. The security lock clicks in place, and the pop of the bullets reduces to a dull thwack as they hit the bulletproof door.

That's right. My house has a bulletproof front door, bitches.

"What the fuck was that?" Noah breathes hard, his chest heaving against mine.

But I can't focus, because Noah fucking Marlowe is on top of me, and I can feel every part of him press against every part of me. And I flash back to the party when our bodies mashed together and I squeezed him and that fucking beautiful *moan* he made—

"Gunshots," I answer when I find my voice. "They're gunshots."

"I know *that*. I mean, why the fuck is some maniac shooting at your house?"

I have no idea. Well, I have some idea. If I'm right, it's very, very bad. But I'm not ready to look at this situation intellectually while bullets still riddle my front door.

I grab Noah's hand and drag him to his feet, then take off down the hall.

"Mackenzie, we have to—"

Queen Boudica saunters out of the kitchen, licking her lips. "Mew?" she asks. I fling her into my arms and toss her over my shoulder. She howls with outrage and scrambles for freedom, but no way am I letting her run around with an active shooter outside.

"Mackenzie, what are—"

"Shut the fuck up," I growl. I drag Noah into the study and yank the first volume of *The Decline and Fall of the Roman Empire* in a sharp downward motion. A bookcase swings outward, revealing a steel-lined room about the size of an elevator shaft. I leap inside. Noah stands there, mouth open. I fist his shirt and yank him in after me.

I slam my hand into the control panel, and the door swings shut, the locks engaging with an electronic hiss.

"Mew!" Queen Boudica cries.

"Where the fuck are we?"

"Panic room," I gasp. Is it just me, or is it hard to breathe in here?

It's probably something to do with having my chest pressed up against Noah. Queen Boudica squirms against my grip, her claws raking across my shoulder. I relax my hold so she can step onto the top of the control unit. She curls up there, whipping her tail across my face as if to inform me she's pissed off.

"Is this room secure?" Noah asks. His breath's a little raspy, too. I chalk that up to the fact he just about had his ass made into Swiss cheese.

"It's invisible from the outside. You'd have to know it was here in order to locate it. So unless the shooter is some old close family friend my father let in on his little secret, we should be safe."

"I don't know what's safe right now," Noah growls. "Someone shot at us, and now I'm locked in here with *you*."

I nod, then realize that's pointless to do in the dark. I feel along the panel for the button that turns the internal light on. The first try, I get a sprinkler. Queen Boudica yowls with fury. I quickly turn that off again. On the second try I pop up the footage from the CCTV cameras. On the third try I manage to get a low red LED strip to light up, illuminating the corners of the room and giving me a faint outline of Noah's features.

"We can't have the lights on." He reaches up to turn it off.

"Relax. They can't see it from outside. The walls are so thick, we won't even show up if they do an infrared scan of the building. At least, that's what the manual said." *I think.* After I read all the books in the library, I moved on to the panic room manual. (Hey, *you* try being stuck in a mansion for four years with only a cat for company). I got halfway through the weighty tome when Queen Boudica let a rat loose in the ballroom and I used the manual to crush it. I wasn't going to pick it up again once I'd covered it in rat innards.

But Noah doesn't need to know that.

"Impressive." Noah gazes around, his hands fiddling with something in his trouser region. I hear a clattering noise. "Shit. I dropped my phone."

"Serves you right for playing with yourself during our time of crisis." I focus on the CCTV cameras, flicking through the different views. I can see the damage to the front door and stone pillars from the bullets, but no sign of a shooter near the gate or at the perimeter.

Noah does this weird penguin hobble, but his shoulders are too broad for him to bend down. "Can you pick it up? We need it to try and call for help."

"Oh sure," I roll my eyes, even though he probably can't see. "With you in here taking up all the valuable real estate. I'll just wrench my arms out of my sockets to save your precious phone."

"You should be able to manage it. You were always freakishly flexible in gym."

"There's flexible and then there's defying the laws of physics. Besides," I slam my palm into an invisible panel on the wall. A dial pad and receiver slide out. "We don't need your phone. This is a secret line. No one can tap it."

"Impressive." There's a dark edge to Noah's voice I don't like. "Howard Malloy thinks of everything."

I grab the phone on the wall and punch in a number. "Antony? I need your ass over here, now."

"At your Barbie Dreamhouse? Why? Someone giving you trouble again?"

"Close. What happened to Tiberius? Someone shot Barbie's Dreamhouse to hell, and I need you to take care of it. "

Even in the low light, I can see Noah's eyebrows shoot way up.

"I'll find out," Antony growls, and the fury in his voice is terrifying. "I'm on my way. Stay where you are."

I burst out laughing. It's a joke we have – he can see from his phone's ID that I'm calling from the panic room. I'm not going anywhere.

I hang up the phone. Noah cups his hand on my shoulder, his fingers digging into my collarbone. It hurts. Maybe the situation has my head all fucked up, because I don't want him to stop. "What do you mean, *take care of it?*"

"It's better you don't know. Antony will call when he's assessed the situation. He's the only person who has this number."

"And who is this Antony? He's the guy you had Gabe text in Alec's car. You don't seem the type to trust a boyfriend, especially one you're sleeping around on."

"Fuck you, Noah. He's my..." I search for the right word to describe him. 'Bodyguard' doesn't cut it, and 'enforcer' is just going raise questions with Noah I'm not answering. Finally, I settle on something that approaches the truth. "...cousin."

"Your cousin who's somehow going to sort out a fucking shooter? What is he, a mob boss?"

I smile. *Time to change the subject.* "Did you know my father didn't even tell me about this panic room?" Yet another secret they kept from me. "If this guy came to the house while Daddy was away on business, I'd have been fucked."

There's a dark tone in Noah's voice. "Knowing what I do about your old man, I can't say I'm surprised."

"I found this one day when I was searching for something new to read. I pulled that book off the shelf and this door swung open. I pushed all the buttons and figured it all out." I kick the steel cabinet behind me. "There are guns in here, but I don't know how to use them."

Another lie.

"Who knew your weird obsession with Ancient Rome would save our asses." Noah's words strain against the darkness. "Can I use your magical phone to make a call? I was supposed to meet Eli. I was already late, but I thought I'd try to talk to you first. I thought if I could get answers I could tell him... something to cheer him up. Joke's on me."

A panicked thought hits me. "Do you think he'd try to come here? What if he was outside when they started shooting—"

Noah shakes his head. Strands of his hair flick against my skin, leaving lines of fire like the welts of a whip. "He's somewhere safe. There's a place Eli and I go when we need... peace or some shit. We've been using it since... well, since you left. Our families don't know about it. That's where he is now."

I hand him the receiver. "Call him. But I don't want him anywhere near the house until Antony's cleared the place."

Noah takes the phone. He cups his hand over the receiver. "Eli? I'm me... I'm not going to be able to make it back. Yeah, I'm with her right now, but it's..."

As he relates what happened, I hear Eli swearing on the other end. I lean my back against the cool steel and try to calm my pattering heart. Noah sucks all the air out of this metal cupboard.

He said he came to talk about Eli, and something else. So what's the other thing?

Noah hangs up the phone. "Eli and Gabriel are coming. They'll hang back until we give them the okay. Gabriel's bringing pizza because apparently that's what you need after you've just been shot at. What do we do now?"

I wipe a bead of sweat from my cheek. *How did it get so hot in here?* "We wait. Antony will call."

"I don't suppose your dad put a gaming console in here?" Noah runs his fingers along the walls. "A movie screen, a magnetic chess board, *anything?*"

"You want to play magnetic chess with me?" My chest feels tight, and I'm not sure if it has anything to do with the confined space.

"You haven't made any other suggestions," Noah fires back.

"How about you tell me the other reason you came to talk to me? The *real* reason?"

Noah leans forward, his nose touching mine. His inky, shadowed scent folds around me. All our rage and hatred fills the space, and there is no room to breathe anything except Noah fucking Marlowe.

"I know your secret, Mackenzie Malloy. I know you killed—"

I don't let him finish the sentence. I do the only thing I can think of to do. I launch myself at him, pressing my lips to his. I expect him to push me away, but the darkness calls to him too because he rises up to meet me, his mouth slashing against mine with cruel, delicious need.

Noah plants his hands on either side of my face, trapping me against the cool steel as he grinds his cock into me. I grab him roughly, pull him closer, try to climb inside his skin.

Who am I? Last night I lost my virginity to his friend, and now here I am kissing Noah Marlowe like I'm daring him to break me.

Noah tosses off my top and paws at my breast. This isn't Gabriel's careful, languid pace. We're wild, frenzied. Noah twists my nipple so hard it sends a shockwave through my body, straight to my clit. I throw my head back and moan. Thank fuck the gunman stalking the house can't hear us through the steel walls.

He unzips his jeans and mine. I step out of them and wrap my legs around him, pulling him close, lining him up to plunge inside me. A brief thought enters my head that I don't have a condom, but then Noah's cock is inside me and I *can't* think.

Noah grunts as he takes my weight, his hands resting under my ass as he grinds against me, driving me into the wall with his hatred. He crushes his mouth to mine, and he drives inside me like he can fuck the pain from his soul. It's so different from Gabriel and so, so fucking good.

He's grinding against my clit, and my orgasm builds inside me like a well about to spill over. Noah's teeth glide over my shoulder, and I hate the way he's undoing me. He's the only one who could have figured out my secret – the only one with a darkness as deep as my own.

I want to undo him.

I want to see perfect Noah Marlowe come apart at the seams.

I want a puddle of Noah goo on the floor of this panic room.

I press my finger to his lips, letting him suck on it, letting him roll it around on his tongue. Then I withdraw it.

"What the fuck do you think you're doing?" Noah growls against my ear as I reach behind him.

"This." I smile against his lips as I shove my finger into his ass.

Noah's body clenches at the intrusion, but he's close, too close to be angry. As I work my finger deeper inside him, he practically impales me through with the force of his thrusts. I work my finger in and out, in and out. The splendid twist of his face as he falls over the edge carries me over too.

We explode together – a fury of rage and darkness unleashed on the world. When I surface, Noah's still pressed against me, his forehead slick with sweat as it rests against mine.

"Fuck," he mutters, over and over again. "Fuck. Fuck...*Fuck.*"

"Mew."

I laugh as two yellow eyes peer at us through the darkness, wider than I've ever seen them. "I think we traumatized Queen Boudica."

"I bet she didn't know her mama's a deviant bitch. I'm going to get you for that." Noah fights for my grip, wrapping his fingers around my wrist to trap my hand above my head. He attacks my mouth again, and I'm ready for it, ready to do battle with his man until he succumbs to me.

Noah yanks my waist, flipping me around like I weigh nothing. I splay my fingers against the wall, and he reaches between my legs to curl his fingers inside me, pumping me and rubbing circles on my clit until my legs turn to jelly. He grinds against me, and he's already hard again. "I bet your dad never intended his panic room to be used like this," he growls in my ear as he pumps me faster, and I'm so close, *so fucking close.* "You're not his perfect little girl anymore."

"You like that, don't you?" I growl back at him, knowing if I make him angry he'll go even harder. "You like fucking Howard Malloy's daughter fast and dirty in his house. You like that I—"

Brrrrrrring.

Fuck!

Noah slams his fist into the wall. His back crashes against the panic room door as he flings himself away from me. My whole body trembles like someone just threw a bucket of ice water over me.

What the fuck am I doing?

Brrrrrrring.

I pick up the receiver and jam it to my ear.

"I hope I'm not interrupting anything, Claws." It's Antony, and he's got that smirk in his voice like he knows exactly what I've been up to.

I suck in a breath, trying to force my heart rate back to normal. Beside me, Queen Boudica swipes at Noah's bare ass as he tries to bend his huge frame to pull on his pants. "Quit being a smartass and tell me what you've got."

"Nothing, I'm sorry. The bastard got clean away."

"Did you see who it was? Who are they working for? Did Alec send them?" I close my eyes. "Is it Brutus?"

"I can't say. I'm going to follow up with my networks, see if anyone's claiming this, but I'm stumped. I took care of Brutus, and I'm not sure this is your Pretty Boy's work. Putting out a hit? That's a bit extreme."

"It's got to be Brutus." My blood runs cold. I don't have to ask. The world I ran from, they've found me again.

Antony clicks his tongue. "Calm down, Claws. Honestly, this doesn't seem like Ole Brutey Boy, either. This was messy. If you're going to gun down someone on their front steps, you don't spray bullets all over the place. This isn't a professional hit with a sniper rifle – this guy's a cowboy who can't shoot for shit. It could be someone trying to get in good with Brutus by taking you out. Let me find out. In the meantime, we'll step up security. We'll keep you safe."

Aware Noah's listening to every word, I don't ask questions, even though I have a million swirling around. "He's gone now?"

"Long gone. And I've found Tiberius. He's out cold, but he'll be okay. How they snuck up on him I can't figure. Oh, and your two loverboys arrived. We're all out front if you wanna let us in."

I set the phone back in its cradle. Noah stares at me with those dagger eyes, the ones that slice right through me.

"You wanna explain what the fuck's going on?" he growls.

"Nope." I flick open a panel on the wall and slam my palm onto a button. With a wheeze, the door springs open. Noah topples out and lands on his back on the rug. Queen Boudica bounds out and pounces on his chest.

I tug on my clothes and leave Noah pinned by the cuteness to unlock the front door. There's no broken glass and only a couple of chipped tiles. Daddy's security measures get an A+ from me.

I never knew why a house needed to be bulletproof until this morning.

I fling open the front door. Antony stands there with Tiberius, who's locked Eli in a chokehold. Gabriel stands off to the side, smoking a joint with a stack of pizzas in his hands.

"Help me, you bastard," Eli snaps at Gabriel.

"Why? Watching you struggle is so much more amusing." Gabriel opens the top box and pulls out a french fry. "I wish I brought popcorn."

"You can let Eli go," I say. "I told you, he's on the safe list."

Antony shook his head. "He's the one who's been watching you through your windows. Sounds like crazed shooter behavior to me."

"It wasn't him."

"You know that for a fact?" Antony must've noticed the look on my face because he nods to Tiberius, who drops Eli.

Eli glances between us. "Mackenzie, what's going on? What happened to you?"

"Why's your shirt on inside out?" Gabriel adds.

I look down. *Fuck.* "Some psycho shot at us. Noah and Queen Boudica and I hid in the panic room. We're all fine."

"Panic room? Like in the Sandra Bullock film?" Gabriel looks interested. "I want to see, especially if it's a magical panic room that makes your clothes fall off."

Eli looks so wounded I want to throttle Gabe. Instead, I hide my flaming cheeks as I throw the door open. "You'd better come in, and make it snappy. If the shooter's still out there, I don't want him getting all trigger happy again."

The four of them traipse into the foyer just as Noah comes around the corner with Queen Boudica wrapped around his neck, purring away.

"Hey, Marlowe. Your fly's undone." Gabriel's mouth is all mischief as he slaps Noah on the back. I wonder how fucking clueless it's possible to be, but when Gabriel turns back to me I see the fear in his eyes.

Eli falls in step beside me. His gaze flickers all around, taking in the gilded modern art, the weird furniture, the clear plastic chairs mixed with the bedazzled lampshades. Or maybe he's trying to avoid my gaze. "This place..." he breathes. "It looks exactly as I remember it."

"Not exactly." I fling open the door to the ballroom.

Eli makes a choking sound. I gotta admit, looking at it like this, as if I was one of them seeing it for the first time, it's a *lot*.

The ballroom is *my* place. It's the only room in the house I've ever tried to make *mine*. And it's so large that it's accommodated a number of my interests over the years. In one corner is an absolute *mountain* of history books I ordered online, because academic publishers apparently have never heard of ebooks. I've stacked them into a sort of fort and placed a mountain of blankets inside for Queen Boudica. The marble floorboards have a maze of painted lines from when I drew my own basketball court. I've used old furniture and dragged up gear from the basement gym to create my own workout space, and I spent six months testing all the sofas in the house before dragging the comfiest in here. I've got a wine fridge and drinks cart, an arts-and-crafts corner, a big-screen TV, a knife-tossing range (and several porcelain dolls with their eyes stabbed out), a cat jungle-gym that reaches the tip of the vaulted ceiling and—

"Is that a... a skate ramp?" Noah chokes out.

"I went through a skating phase." I flop down on the sofa. It used to live in one of the upstairs drawing rooms. Antony and I used it as a sled to slide down the stairs, and then relocated it here. It sags a bit in the center as Noah sits down. "I'm afraid I have no staff, so if you want a drink you need to get it yourself."

"I'm gonna need one." Gabriel hugs the drinks cart. Eli perches gingerly on the edge of the book fort while Gabe shakes and pours. He hands around six fancy-looking cocktails. Eli rests his feet on the cover of a book on Greek vase painting and stares at it like it will eat his soul. Queen Boudica bounds over to him and nudges his hand. Eli strokes her, and the tension in his shoulders eases a fraction.

"Well, well, well." Antony's ice-blue eyes dart from Gabe, to Noah, to Eli. Nothing escapes him. "The rockstar, the arch-nemesis, the stalker."

"Arch-nemesis?" Noah tugs on his collar. He won't look at me. Or Eli, for that matter.

"Pleasure to make your acquaintance." Gabriel downs his drink in one gulp and reaches for Eli's while holding his other hand out for Antony to shake. "And you are?"

"I'm Claws' cousin, Antony. And this is Tiberius."

"You're the guy who was in my house." Eli leaps up, his hands clenched in fists. "Who the fuck do you think you are?"

Tiberius cracks his knuckles as he advances on Eli. His face twists into a maniacal smile. "You want to see how many chicks you'll pull with your nose sticking out your ass, pretty boy?"

"I wouldn't fight him if I were you," Antony says. "Sit your ass down, Stalker Boy. You should've learned by now what happens if you keep Claws waiting."

"Claws?" Gabriel nods at me. "Nice nickname, better than Mac. It suits you, *Claws*."

"It's just a dumb name from when we were kids," I mutter. I know what's coming. The big questions. The questions that will destroy everything.

I glance at Antony, trying to convey through eye movement and grimacing that we have to rescue this situation somehow. The guys cannot find out the truth. But Antony sits beside his prizefighter on the ramp, swinging his feet and smoothing the lapels of his fancy suit like he hasn't a care in the world. I can't read him, and I can't count on him to come to my rescue here. I'm the one who bought the guys into this mess. I let them get close.

"You're Mackenzie's cousin? From the Long Island Malloys?" Eli glares at Antony. "I don't remember Mackenzie ever mentioning you."

"I'm from the Malloys up your ass," Antony shoots back. Gabriel sniggers. Eli's drink has disappeared.

Eli turns to me. The raw hurt in his eyes fucking *burns*. I swallow as my chest constricts. There's even less air in this ballroom than when I was trapped in that tiny panic room. "Mackenzie, can you explain what's going on here?"

"Eli, I know you're pissed, but shut up a second." Noah grips his glass so hard his knuckles turn white. He runs his fingers through his hair but forgets he's holding the glass, and ends up tossing sticky alcohol across the rug. "Can't you see Mackenzie's upset? Someone *shot* at us."

Gabriel grabs his friend's shoulder and shakes him. "Who are you and what have you done with Noah Marlowe?"

"What I've done is bring this whole fucking mess down on our heads," Noah says.

What?

I open my mouth to protest, but Antony's eyes flick to me. I snap my jaw shut.

"What the fuck, man?" Eli yells. The Southern twang creeps into his voice. That's not good.

Noah's fingers rake through his hair, again and again, until the bit at the back he soaked in alcohol stuck out like a reverse unicorn horn. "The pieces didn't fit together until now, but... it's what I came to talk to Mackenzie about. When I got home on Friday night, my dad was in his receiving room, having a conversation with Brentwood."

"Who's Brentwood?" I ask. Antony leans forward, interested. He knows that name, which can't be a good thing.

From the way Eli's face has gone all pale and weird, I suspect he knows this Brentwood, too.

"Let's just say he's known to do a few favors for the richer families in Emerald Beach." Noah shuffles his feet. "The kind of favors where certain people disappear and Brentwood adds another wing to his mansion."

"He's an assassin?" *What the fuck?* Why is Noah's father, *Senator* Marlowe, talking to an *assassin?*

Okay, that's fucked.

I guess I'm not the only one with secrets in this room.

Noah nods. "Look, my father and Brentwood have some legitimate business dealings, so I never thought much of their acquaintance before, but... the last time that guy came to *our house* was shortly after we lost our case against the Malloys, and then Mackenzie and her family disappeared. Yesterday he was there again, and today someone shot at Mackenzie."

"Bloody hell." Gabriel's given up all presence of mixing drinks. He takes a swig straight from a vodka bottle, cradling it in his arms like a baby. A storm of conflict brews in his eyes, and I see a glimpse of that strange moment in the Midnight Grotto, when he said I remind him of his dead drummer. A glimpse of the true depth of his fractured soul.

I wish I could feel like Gabriel feels, but someone has to sing the blood and the rain for those of us who live in the ice palaces. I'm the Ice Queen now, all the warmth Noah had stoked inside me frozen into hard, bitter truth.

Antony looks unconvinced. "Did you overhear any of their conversation? I find it hard to believe someone with as much to lose as Senator Marlowe would want to get his hands dirty going after a seventeen-year-old girl."

Noah nods again. "My father said Brentwood had fucked something up, and he has a chance to put it right. Brentwood seemed... angry. But also scared. He said, "I'm not going near that house again. That's no sweet-sixteen beauty queen you're facing off against. She's a cold-blooded killer.""

"That's what he said?" Antony sneers. "He never said Mackenzie's name explicitly?"

"No, but—"

"And you believe if this Brentwood – the most highly trained expert in his field in all of Emerald Beach – refused a job from your father, his only remaining option would be to hire a shooter so incompetent he let off several rounds at relatively close range and managed to miss you both?"

"I don't know what I fucking believe, except that bullets sailed past my skull today and I need to know if my father's behind it. There's only one way to know for sure." Noah meets my gaze, and the fire in his coal-eyes isn't hate this time, but *need*. "Mackenzie, you have to tell us what happened four years ago."

ELI

*N*oah's words hang in the air, like icicles formed under the porch railing at our family hunting cabin. I feel them now – the cold biting my flesh, a thousand needles piercing my heart.

Cold-blooded killer.

Killer.

Killer.

Mackenzie's cheeks burn with color. I can't decide if she looks furious or terrified. Maybe a little of both. She exchanges a look with that guy – her cousin, I can't remember his name (since when did Mackenzie *ever* have cousins?) – but I can't infer anything from it other than he knows whatever secret she's hiding and he doesn't think she should give it up.

Killer.

Killer.

Killer.

Mackenzie turns to me, and her eyes are pure ice and malice. The change in her is quick and so profound I gasp out loud. It's like a magician snapped his fingers, and I'm looking at Mackenzie's face – the same heart-shaped face and perfect nose I fell in love with as a kid – but behind her frosty eyes is a completely different person.

"I told you my one condition," she says, her words calm, measured. And all the more chilling because they no longer sounded like Mackenzie's words. "I won't dig into your secrets, and you wouldn't ask about mine. If you don't trust me, there's nothing else to say. Get out of this house. All of you. I never want to see you again."

I open my mouth to protest, but Mackenzie spins on her heel and storms off.

"You heard the lady." Antony stands, reaching into the inside of his jacket. I see an outline of something beneath the fabric. A gun? The huge guy cracks his knuckles again.

"Fuck this, and fuck you," I spit.

"Eli, wait." Noah reaches for me. He smells like her, and I hate him, I hate him more than I ever thought it possible to hate, more than Gabriel because he at least never pretended to give a shit about my happiness. I duck under Noah's grip. If that fucker touches me right now I'll flatten him.

I fly out the ballroom door, darting a look left and right. She's disappeared into one of the endless rooms. I'll never find her without a map and a summoning spell.

I have to try. I need to know.

Killer.

I pick left. I've barely gone three steps when—

CRUNCH. My foot lands on something, and I feel it snap under my heel. I bend down to examine the twinkling pieces of metal I've ground into the Persian rug.

Mackenzie's locket.

The one she wears under her shirt. The one she never takes off.

I let the pieces fall across my palm. The chain has snapped in two places, and there's an ugly crack across the front of the locket. I notice it's not gold, but gold-plated. Odd that Mackenzie Malloy would wear something so cheaply made. An inscription on the back reads, 'To our daughter.'

As I close my fingers, the cracked piece breaks away and the locket falls open, revealing two faded photographs cut to fit inside.

I stare at the pictures.

Wait.

What?

MACKENZIE

Istand in the study, facing the wall of books. Tomes on ancient history, military achievements, economic theory, and traditional medicines of the world glare down at me, the spines rigid with silent accusation. I grip the edge of the desk and suck in a breath, fighting to bring air to my frozen lungs.

The door to the panic room hangs open. I rub my thighs together – they ache from being wrapped around Noah. But it's nothing compared to the ache in my chest.

I have to send them away. It's the only thing I can think to do. They were supposed to be a bit of fun for me – a chance to live out the teen movie fantasy life that was stolen from me the night I woke up in my own grave. But I can't have them like this. I can't keep them. They're not mine to keep.

I'm a fucking *idiot*. I let myself get attached to all of them – beautiful, broken Gabriel, kind, intense Eli, even sulky, bitter Noah – and that's put *everything* in danger. Not just our plan, but their *lives*. If what Noah says is true, if his dad hired this Brentwood guy to take out—

"Mackenzie."

I whirl around. Eli stands in the doorway, his back rigid, an unreadable expression on his usually warm face. He holds out his hand in a fist, palm facing up.

"Your locket fell off. That's what happens when you wear cheap chains like this – they snap when you least want them to."

Shit. *Shit.*

"Eli—"

Eli opens his hand. My locket tumbles from his fingers and bounces on the rug. The pieces fall apart, revealing the photographs of my parents I keep inside.

Of my *real* parents.

Eli turns to me, and I read my betrayal in his features.

He told me that he can't handle being lied to, not after losing me the first time. I knew that, and I've done it all the same.

"Eli, I can explain."

But I can't. Not in a way that he'd understand. And so I do what I always do around these guys, I go silent. I hide behind the mask I created.

Except Eli has just ripped my mask away and stomped on it. The locket is broken, the life I stole on display for all to see. I can't put the pieces of my lie back together again. And I didn't want to.

"That's not Howard and Ainsley Malloy in these photographs. You're not Mackenzie Malloy." Eli's face hardens to stone. "Who the fuck *are* you?"

TO BE CONTINUED

Three spoiled princes who own my heart of ice.

Keeping them secret is the only way to save them.

By my betrayal will drive them into my enemy's hands.
Find out what happens next in book 2,
My Secret Heart.

I should have kept my mouth shut.
I should have let them win.
Now the kings of the school are out for my blood,
... and they're not the only ones.

Need more dark, gothic, and delicious reverse harem bully romance in your life?

HP Lovecraft meets *Cruel Intentions* in the paranormal reverse harem bully romance readers are calling, "The greatest mindfuck of 2019". Warning: Not for the faint of heart – this story of three broken bad boys and the girl who stood her ground contains dark themes, crazed cultists, books bound in human skin, high-school drama, swoon-worthy sex, and potential triggers. Grab book 1, *Shunned*, in KU now.

Turn the page for a sizzling excerpt

FROM THE AUTHOR

I wrote this book during the apocalypse.

All over the world, countries locked down to halt the spread of COVID-19. In my tiny country of New Zealand, our Government committed to preserving the lives of our citizens by instituting a tough lockdown that, at the time of writing, has meant the virus is all-but-eliminated from our shores.

And that's a huge, amazing achievement, but it comes at a cost. And I know that we've been incredibly lucky here in Middle Earth and many other countries are dealing with a much higher cost – in terms of loss of life, loss of jobs, loss of the systems we thought kept us safe. In the middle of this, I wrote a story about a girl with a secret life and a darkness inside her that both terrifies and liberates her.

Mackenzie came to me in a dream. She is... not like any other heroine I've ever written. Even though I've sworn up-and-down that I'd never write contemporary romance (imagine, romance *without* vampires? What even *is* that?) she wouldn't shut up until I told her story.

I wrote her for *you*. Because it's scary out there, and I know when I'm scared I so often find myself in the pages of a book.

Sometimes I even borrow a little strength and a little audacity from the characters I love. I think we all need as much of those as we can get right now.

I'm in awe of the incredible health workers and other essential staff who've kept the world running and done their best in an impossible situation. If you're one of them, there are no words I can say to thank you enough for your contribution.

I'm just a teller of stories. I can't save lives or keep food on tables or make sure businesses stay afloat. But if I can give you a new world and a new life and a strange mystery to lose yourself in for a few hours, then that's some small way I can help you survive this wild and crazy world.

Writing *My Stolen Life* has been a joy and a pleasure, but as always, it takes a village to bring a book to life. I'd like to thank my cantankerous drummer husband, for reading this manuscript and giving me so many ideas to make it better. And for being my lighthouse. And for making me so many bacon butties and keeping the house stocked with chocolate during lockdown.

To Kit, Bri, Elaina, Katya, Emma, Jamie, Kim, Mila, and Jenna, for all the writerly encouragement and advice. To Meg and Eveis for the epically helpful editing job, and to CJ for the stunning covers. To Sam and Iris, for the daily Facebook shenanigans that help keep me sane while I spend my days stuck at home covered in cats.

To you, the reader, for going on this journey with me, even though it's led to some dark places. Warning: if you thought book 1 was tough, book 2 is a whopper.

If you're enjoying *Stonehurst Prep* and want to read more from me, check out my dark reverse harem bully romance series, *Kings of Miskatonic Prep*. HP Lovecraft meets *Cruel Intentions* in this dark paranormal reverse harem bully romance that's definitely not for the faint of heart. Hazel is the most badass FMC I've ever written, and I think you'll love meeting her.

You should also check out my new reverse harem academy series, *Manderley Academy*. Book 1 is *Ghosted* and it's a classic gothic tale of ghosts and betrayal, creepy old houses and three beautifully haunted guys with dark secrets. Plus, a kickass curvy heroine. You will LOVE it – you'll find a short preview on the next page.

I've also got two other reverse harem series. The Nevermore Bookshop Mysteries is what you'd get if you crossed Agatha Christie with Black Books and added a harem of famous literary men. It's my most popular series to date, and it's a lot more light-hearted and fun (despite all the murder). Start book 1, *A Dead and Stormy Night*.

If you want to hang out and talk about all things Broken Muse, my readers are sharing their theories and discussing the book over in my Facebook group, Books That Bite – facebook.com/groups/steffanieholmes. Come join the fun. And for updates and a free book of cut scenes and bonus stories, you can join my newsletter here – steffanieholmes.com/newsletter.

I'm so happy you enjoyed this story! I'd love it if you wanted to leave a review on Amazon or Goodreads. It will help other readers to find their next read.

Thank you, thank you! I love you heaps! Until next time.
Steff

Sorry 'bout that.

The problem is, someone else knows too.
Someone dangerous.
Someone who's already buried me once.
This time, they're determined to finish the job.

Three broken princes stand between me and my doom:
The fallen king with his thirst for vengeance.
The rock god who sings of blood and stars.
The sweet one who's drowning in hate.

Three spoiled princes who own my heart of ice.

Keeping them secret is the only way to save them.
By my betrayal will drive them into my enemy's hands.

Alea iacta est.
Let the die be cast.
Welcome to Stonehurst f**king Prep.

Get it now
books2read.com/mysecretheart

EXCERPT: KINGS OF MISKATONIC PREP, BOOK 1
READ THE FIRST CHAPTER OF SHUNNED

Who the hell builds a school on top of an inaccessible cliff?

Whoever built Derleth Academy, my new school. I answered my own question as the car's wheel skidded over the rough gravel on the way up the steep peninsula. A scream escaped my lips as the car lurched toward the edge of the cliff, one wheel spinning completely free.

Muttering under his breath, the driver for the school slammed the car into reverse and backed us onto the road before slamming on the gas again. We continued our wary climb along the narrow gravel path.

Surely the Academy can't be completely *cut-off.* The school had to bring up food and supplies. Parents must visit on the weekends. My driver was certainly giving it his all, tearing around the corners like he was on a Formula 1 racetrack and not a goat path hugging the side of a mountain. I gritted my teeth and gripped the back of the seat as rocks rolled from beneath the wheels and clattered over the sheer drop into the raging waters below. One wrong move, and we'd tumble down a two-hundred-foot cliff and be dashed against the cliffs so hard and fast that boats would mistake our remains for rock paintings.

Not the way I ever imagined I'd go.

We passed into thick vegetation, the cliff and ocean on one side giving way to looming trees that blocked out the grey sky. I let out the breath I'd been holding. Branches scraped the sides of the car, and my phone beeped with protest as we moved out of cell range. *No contact with the outside world*, the school brochure read. *At Derleth Academy, we foster a competitive academic program requiring the full attention of our students. Distracting technology or personal items will not be tolerated.*

In other words, I couldn't call for help. It was the opening sequence to every horror film, ever.

Not that I had anyone to call. Not anymore.

"Almost there," the driver said, swinging the car around a hairpin corner and launching my stomach into my throat. It was the most words he'd spoken to me the entire trip. "You can see the school through the trees."

I squinted into the forest, trying to make out some kind of building that might pass as a school. But I couldn't see a thing. We rounded another corner and—

Well, that's terrifying.

We rolled between two towering stone pillars obscured by creeping vines, past an ornate sign that read DERLETH ACADEMY. A wide, pristine concrete drive flanked by an avenue of towering trees and wide, manicured lawns led up to an imposing stone building, stretching in all directions with narrow arched windows, spiky towers, and a row of leering gargoyles along the roof.

What is this place? It looked more like Dracula's castle than a prestigious preparatory school.

I couldn't believe the wealthiest people in the country sent their children up that winding road to get educated. *Who's the headmistress, Morticia Addams?* But according to the brochure, that was exactly what they did. In droves. Derleth Academy had a waiting list a mile long, and you couldn't even pay to get in. You had to be *invited*.

Somehow, I, Hazel Waite – an overachieving orphan from the wrong side of Philly – ended up on their radar.

I flashed back to the day two weeks ago, when a banging on the door of my dingy apartment dragged me from a deep slumber. A woman with coiffed hair and a designer suit that cost more than a car staggered backward in surprise when I glared at her through the chain wearing only my pajamas and what must have been a terrifying scowl. Well, *she* wasn't the one being dragged from a pleasant Jason Momoa sex dream during the four-hour reprieve between night shift at the diner and cleaning rooms at a retirement home.

"Are you Hazel Waite?" she asked, her brown eyes wide and curious.

"No. Piss off." I glowered, slamming the door in her face. She was probably from CPS, trying to force me into foster care. Fuck that. I only had seven more months to survive before I turned eighteen. No way was I going to spend it in the hell that had killed Dante.

The woman didn't go away. She sat out on the road in her sports car and waited me out. I had to leave for work or I'd lose my job, and it wasn't easy to find work when you were underage and using an obviously fake ID. As soon as I left the house, she ambushed me.

"I'm not here to hand you over to the authorities," she said hurriedly, shoving a thick envelope into your hands. "I'm a scholarship administrator from Derleth Academy in Arkham, Massachusetts. Your current school put you forward for one of our four senior scholarship positions – a fully funded year at a first-class prep school, where our students go on to attend the top colleges in the world. I know the first quarter has already started, but it's taken me this long to track you down. You've only missed a week so far."

I stared at the envelope in my hands, at the red, black and gold school crest – a crooked five-pointed star inside a shield with some kind of Latin phrase beneath it. *This has got to be a joke.*

"I know what you're thinking," the woman said. "It's not a joke or a trick. I promise you that it's not. If you come to Derleth, we will assume guardianship duties until you turn eighteen. You'll be housed, clothed, and have all your schoolbooks and other needs met, as well as receiving a first-class education. You're a promising student, Hazel, and I know you've been dealt a cruel lot in life. This could be where you turn everything around. Don't answer me now. Read over the paperwork, and I'll return tomorrow for your decision."

And now, just ten days after I signed my soul over to this school in exchange for paid tuition, room, and board, I stared up at the imposing facade and wondered if I'd made a terrible mistake.

Sure, my life was miserable. I was drowning in grief, and even working two jobs I could barely pull in enough money to survive. College was out of the question, because I couldn't finish high school without going into foster care. But at least all that was familiar territory. That was the world I'd grown up in – the world of pain and struggle and loss. Derleth Academy was the exact opposite. Every element of this building screamed wealth and privilege and *you don't belong here.*

The driver pulled to a stop on the wide circular drive beside a towering stone fountain. A black woman in a drab grey smock darted out of the shadows of the porch and approached the car. I held my hand out to her. "Hello, I'm Hazel Waite—"

The woman ducked her head, avoiding me. She popped

open the trunk, hauled out my heavy suitcase and bookbag, and hurried off to the house with them before I could offer to help.

Weird much? I swiped a dreadlock off my face. My friend Dante's foster sister had done them for me last year, back when things were perfect and the most I had to worry about was whether my mom would ground me for getting dreadlocks.

An awful feeling twisted in my gut. I wished Mom was here, hating my loss, right now. But she was gone, gone, gone, and so was Dante, and it was just me and this terrifying school and no other options.

Three figures descended the grand stone steps toward me: A woman with translucent skin and a flowing black dress, flanked on either side by two students wearing the Derleth uniform. Fallen leaves skittered away from the woman's hem, and she moved with such poise that she appeared to float over the steps. With her severe features and a gauzy black ribbon pinned in her hair, she looked more like she was attending a funeral. Behind her, the two students – a guy and a girl – glared at me, distrust emanating from their every pore.

The woman stopped on the second-to-last step, peering down her nose at me as if I were a bug that wasn't even worth squashing. "You'll have to do something about that hair. We enforce a strict dress code in my school, Ms. Waite. I'll not have you flouting it on your very first day."

This must be the principal, Hermia West. My Morticia Addams guess wasn't far off. This woman looked like she drank the blood of students to sustain her beauty. The way her grey eyes stabbed right through me sent a cold shiver through my body.

There was nothing in the student handbook about dreadlocks. Although, of course, I'd only skim-read the thing on the bus from Philly. The handbook was boring. And *long*. "I'm sorry, Ms. West. I didn't know—"

"Ignorance is no excuse. That's 3 demerit points for you. And you're to refer to me as Headmistress."

Beside her, the boy sniggered. I turned my gaze to look at him, and my heart nearly stopped. *Wow, he's beautiful.* I had no idea boys that hot existed outside of magazines and Hollywood movies. He stood practically the same height as Ms. West, his broad shoulders accentuated by the tailored cut of his red-trimmed blazer. Prefect and merit badges decorated both lapels. Dark brown curls caught the grey light filtering through the clouds, throwing back beautiful shades of russet and silver. His clean-shaven face and high, majestic cheekbones appeared angelic, but his ice-blue eyes were cold and cruel.

The girl moved closer to him, touching his arm and shooting me a possessive glare, like a cat in heat. She had the appearance of a cat, too – slanted green eyes accentuated with heavy makeup, pointed chin, and the lithe body and long legs of a panther. Beautiful but deadly.

"This is Trey Bloomberg and Courtney Haynes," Headmistress West said. "I've appointed them as your student guides. They will show you the dorm, library, and dining hall, go over your schedule and classrooms, and ensure you understand *all* our rules. You will dine with the student body in two hours' time, and tomorrow you begin classes. I've had a copy of your schedule and the school handbook placed in your room. Memorize them, for failure to comply will result in further demerits. Here's your dorm room key."

In my pocket, my phone gave another defiant chirp. *Great.* I'd practically worn down the battery looking for a signal on the death road.

Headmistress West descended the last step to drop an ancient-looking metal key into my hand. Her pointy black boots lined up with my scuffed Docs. She loomed over me, her disapproval seeping into my bones. "You have a phone in your pocket." It wasn't a question.

"Yes."

Behind her, the boy smirked. I felt naked, exposed. My legs itched to make a run for the woods. Headmistress West held out her hand, unfurling long fingers topped with red-painted nails, the tips pointed like talons. "Hand it over. We don't allow outside technology on campus."

Instinctively, my hand flew to my pocket. "I won't use it to call or text. It doesn't work here, anyway, so what's the—"

"Ms. Waite, failure to obey a teacher's command is an automatic loss of 10 points. You seem most anxious to find out what punishments await the students at the bottom of the class list."

A lump rose in my throat. My phone contained photographs – snaps of my mom smiling demurely or brushing her hair in the mirror before she went out to work at the strip club. Of Dante and I hanging out around the neighborhood, smoking on the rusted playground beside his house, tagging the concrete wall behind the boxing gym on the corner. Every other one of my possessions had been destroyed in the fire. Those photographs were practically all I had left of them.

Trey and Courtney covered their mouths with their hands, barely disguising their laughter. Courtney leaned over and whispered something to Trey. They both cracked up. Despite myself, my cheeks flushed. *Better get used to this.*

Headmistress West, of course, ignored them. She wasn't backing down on this phone thing. My fingers closed around it, the comfortable weight of it in my hand reminding me that it was one of the last connections to my old life.

What does it matter? They're gone. Looking at their photos won't bring them back. But this school could be the only chance I have at a real future.

My hand trembling, I dropped my phone into her talons. As

soon as it left my hand, I itched to get it back. Headmistress West slipped the phone into a fold of her dress, where it disappeared from sight.

"Follow me." The headmistress swirled on her heel and floated up the stairs. Numb, I fell in step behind her. Trey came up beside me. His arm brushed mine, and a jolt of warmth rocketed through my body. I dared a look up at his face. As we moved into the shadow of the porch, the colors in his hair changed, becoming a deep brown and blood red. A curl flopped over his eye, and I noticed flecks of silver on the edges of those arresting blue irises. My fingers itched to reach up and swipe that curl off his face, to touch his smooth skin, feel his cheek move beneath my fingers, to cut myself on his cheekbones. A familiar longing pooled in my stomach, an ache that I'd never been able to sate before, and now never would.

I'd never seen a boy that *perfect*.

Trey's fingers brushed me again. My breath froze in my mouth as his hand lingered on my elbow. To anyone looking at us from a distance, it would appear as though he was helping me, steadying me up the steep steps. The touch on my skin was white-hot, lighting up parts of my body that hadn't felt anything since Dante... since before the fire. *How can this boy with such cruel eyes have this effect on me?*

When he caught me looking, Trey's perfect lips curled back into a sneer. His fingers tightened on my arm, squeezing my skin. Tighter, tighter, until he was cutting off circulation. I yelped in protest.

"You don't belong here," he murmured, his perfect lips forming hateful words. "You should leave now."

He said it so casually, like he was chatting about the weather, and that self-satisfied smirk never left his face. My stomach twisted, the air driving from my lungs as though he'd punched me.

"No thanks," I said brightly, pretending that I misunderstood him. "I'm good."

"We don't want you, and we're used to getting what we want. We're going to eat you alive, new meat." Trey flashed me a smile that was all teeth and violence. The venom in his eyes frightened me. *This is not a guy to mess with.*

Too bad he seemed to already have it out for me, and I hadn't even got inside the school yet. My plan to keep my head down and stay invisible fizzled before my eyes. Already I could see how the school year was going to play out. *We don't want you here.* Trey spoke for the entire student body. He was a King in this school. It was written in his smile, dripping from the menace in his words.

I'd pissed him off. Just by existing. Just by setting foot on the hallowed grounds of his kingdom. *Well, fuck you, Trey Bloomberg.* I could handle a year of insults and loneliness if I got my diploma at the end of it. My life was already hell on earth – if Trey Bloomberg thought he could break me, he'd have to try a lot harder.

I wrenched my arm away from us. "Don't touch me." Behind us, Courtney giggled.

"Yeah, Trey. You should know not to handle garbage. She's a gutter-trash whore who's probably fucked so many guys that your dick wouldn't even touch the sides."

The comment stung. I thought of my sweet mother, all candy smiles and sticky skin as she stripped off her sweat-soaked lace g-string and six-inch heels after her shift and pulled on the cloud-pink pajamas I found for her in a thrift store. A hard lump rose in my throat. I shoved the image aside. *Not now.*

Wait until you get to your room, until you're alone, then you can break down.

"I guess we're not going to be braiding each other's hair," I muttered to Courtney.

"I wouldn't touch that rat's nest on your head if someone hid a *Faberge* egg inside," Courtney sneered. "I bet it's got real eggs in it, though. Insect eggs, laid by the gross things crawling around in there."

Instinctively, my hand flew up to my face, to touch the dreadlock that always fell over my eye, to tuck it behind my ear – a gesture that Dante would so often do when he noticed my loss in my eyes, which was all the time because I liked them unruly. Ever since the fire, I'd been touching my own hair more and more, seeking the comfort of the familiar weight of a hand moving the dreadlocks. But it wasn't the same. It would never be the same.

Courtney wrinkled her face in disgust, while Trey continued to smirk at me. The force of his loathing sank my stomach to my knees. He didn't even know me, but it didn't matter.

At the top of the stairs, the headmistress turned and frowned at me. "Don't dawdle," she snapped. "The school doesn't bite."

"She's wrong," Trey whispered. "Are you ready to find out just how bad we bite?"

The lump of hard, bitterness burned at the back of my throat. They were right. I didn't belong here. I was the poor gutter-trash girl from the wrong side of the tracks, and they were *royalty*. They were the monarchs. *They're going to make my life miserable, and there's nothing I can do.*

Read Shunned now

The fire took everything.
My parents. My best friend. My life.

Now I have a second chance.
I only have to endure one year at this prestigious academy for rich snobs.
One year of being the charity case no one wanted.
One year of taunts and insults and bullying. Then I'm free.

But I didn't count on Trey, Ayaz, and Quinn.
Arrogant, privileged, dangerous.
Drop-dead gorgeous.
They want me gone.
They want me to suffer.
They're determined to make my nightmares real.

Tough luck, bully boys – I won't hide away.
I'm not afraid.
But maybe... *I should be.*

HP Lovecraft meets *Cruel Intentions* in book 1 of this dark paranormal reverse harem bully romance. Warning: Not for the faint of heart – this story of three broken bad boys and the girl who stood her ground contains dark themes, crazed cultists, books bound in human skin, high-school drama, swoon-worthy sex, and potential triggers.

START READING NOW
books2read.com/shunned

WELCOME TO MANDERLEY ACADEMY

From the author of *Shunned*, the Amazon top-20 bestselling bully romance readers are calling, "The greatest mindf**k of 2019," comes this chilling new dark paranormal reverse harem romance.

Ivan, Titus, Dorien.
These Bad Boys of Baroque may play like angels,
but they're determined to make my life hell.

When my mom got sick, my dreams of a career in music imploded. That is, until Madame Usher wafts into my life like a ghost from the past, offering me the chance to study at the exclusive Manderley Academy – a music school for the most gifted and wealthy.

It's an offer I can't refuse – free room and board at the gothic mansion where elite students immerse themselves in mastering their art. But there's a catch, and it's a big one.

I'm her slave.

I clean the rooms. I polish the piano keys. I serve her and the three pretentious a-hole guys who rule this school.

I must endure their bullying in silence. Even when they destroy my things, sabotage my performances, and try their best to drive me from Manderley.

Rich. Arrogant. Cruel.
They won't have the poor little charity case ruining their fun.
They've heard me play.
They know I'm a serious contender for the prestigious Manderley Prize.

These broken muses aren't used to losing, especially to the help.

But they're not the only ones haunting me.

Something twisted and evil shrouds Manderley Academy. Maybe my bullies are the least of my problems. Maybe Dorien, Ivan, and Titus aren't the ones behind the strange noises in the walls, the warnings scrawled on my mirror, and the gruesome murders on the school grounds.

Maybe…maybe Manderley's ghosts are real.

A dark mystery unfolds around musician Faye de Winter in book one of this gripping gothic college reverse harem bully romance by USA Today best-selling author Steffanie Holmes. Warning: This tale of three spoiled rich boys with unsettling secrets and the girl who refuses to put up with their shit contains dark themes, a creepy house, a smoldering second-chance romance, college angst, cruel bullies and swoon-worthy sex.

READ NOW
books2read.com/manderley1

AGATHA CHRISTIE MEET BLACK BOOKS

What do you get when you cross a cursed bookshop, three hot fictional men, and a punk rock heroine nursing a broken heart?

After being fired from her fashion internship in New York City, Mina Wilde decides it's time to reevaluate her life. She returns to the quaint English village where she grew up to take a job at the local bookshop, hoping that being surrounded by great literature will help her heal from a devastating blow.

But Mina soon discovers her life is stranger than fiction – a mysterious curse on the bookshop brings fictional characters to life in lust-worthy bodies. Mina finds herself babysitting Poe's raven, making hot dogs for Heathcliff, and getting IT help from James Moriarty, all while trying not to fall for the three broken men who should only exist within her imagination.

When Mina's ex-best friend shows up dead with a knife in her back, she's the chief suspect. She'll have to solve the murder if she wants to clear her name. Will her fictional boyfriends be able to keep her out of prison?

The Nevermore Bookshop Mysteries are what you get when all your book boyfriends come to life. Join a brooding antihero, a master criminal, a cheeky raven, and a heroine with a big heart (and an even bigger book collection) in this brand new steamy reverse harem paranormal mystery series by *USA Today* best-selling author Steffanie Holmes.

READ NOW:

books2read.com/adeadandstormynight

ABOUT THE AUTHOR

Steffanie Holmes is the *USA Today* bestselling author of the paranormal, gothic, dark, and fantastical. Her books feature clever, witty heroines, wild shifters, cunning witches and alpha males who *always* get what they want.

Legally-blind since birth, Steffanie received the 2017 Attitude Award for Artistic Achievement. She was also a finalist for a 2018 Women of Influence award.

Steff is the creator of Rage Against the Manuscript – *www.rageagainstthemanuscript.com* – a resource of free content, book, and courses to help writers tell their story, find their readers, and build a badass writing career.

Steffanie lives in New Zealand with her husband, a horde of cantankerous cats, and their medieval sword collection.

Steffanie Holmes newsletter

Grab a free copy *Cabinet of Curiosities* – a Steffanie Holmes compendium of short stories and bonus scenes – when you sign up for updates with the Steffanie Holmes newsletter (www.steffanieholmes.com/newsletter).

Come hang with Steffanie
www.steffanieholmes.com
hello@steffanieholmes.com